The Haunting of Paynes Hollow

Also by Kelley Armstrong

Rip Through Time
A Rip Through Time Disturbing the Dead
The Poisoner's Ring Death at a Highland Wedding

Haven's Rock
Cold as Hell
The Boy Who Cried Bear
Murder at Haven's Rock

Rockton
The Deepest of Secrets Watcher in the Woods
A Stranger in Town This Fallen Prey
Alone in the Wild A Darkness Absolute
City of the Lost

Cainsville
Rituals Deceptions
Betrayals Visions
Omens

Age of Legends
Forest of Ruin
Empire of Night
Sea of Shadows

The Blackwell Pages (co-written with Melissa Marr)
Thor's Serpents
Odin's Ravens
Loki's Wolves

Otherworld
Thirteen Living with the Dead Industrial Magic
Spell Bound Personal Demon Dime Store Magic
Waking the Witch No Humans Involved Stolen
Frostbitten Broken Bitten
Haunted

Darkest Powers & Darkness Rising
The Rising The Reckoning
The Calling The Awakening
The Gathering The Summoning

Nadia Stafford
Wild Justice
Made to Be Broken
Exit Strategy

Standalone novels
I'll Be Waiting Aftermath
Known to the Victim The Life She Had
Hemlock Island The Masked Truth
Wherever She Goes Missing
Every Step She Takes

The Haunting of Paynes Hollow

Kelley Armstrong

ST. MARTIN'S PRESS
NEW YORK

This is a work of fiction. All of the characters, organizations, and events portrayed in this novel are either products of the author's imagination or are used fictitiously.

First published in the United States by St. Martin's Press, an imprint of St. Martin's Publishing Group

THE HAUNTING OF PAYNES HOLLOW. Copyright © 2025 by KLA Fricke Inc. All rights reserved. Printed in the United States of America. For information, address St. Martin's Publishing Group, 120 Broadway, New York, NY 10271.

ISBN 978-1-250-36056-4

The publisher of this book does not authorize the use or reproduction of any part of this book in any manner for the purpose of training artificial intelligence technologies or systems. The publisher of this book expressly reserves this book from the Text and Data Mining exception in accordance with Article 4(3) of the European Union Digital Single Market Directive 2019/790.

The Haunting of Paynes Hollow

One

The morning of my grandfather's funeral, I open the last email he sent me, the one that's been sitting in my inbox for six weeks. Sitting there unread, and even now, I don't feel the slightest twinge of guilt about that.

I pop it open, read and—

Fuck.

The text is innocuous enough.

> Dear Samantha,
> I think you need to see this.
> Douglas Payne (your grandfather)

Who the hell signs an email to their twenty-six-year-old granddaughter that way? The same guy who insisted on calling me Samantha when from birth I was Sam, named after a character in a book my mother loved. As for the "your grandfather" part, that was just him being passive-aggressive, because he's a jerk.

Was a jerk.

Damn it.

I sit up in bed and roll my shoulders, as if I can slough off the prickle of guilt. "Douglas Payne (your grandfather)" never deserved my guilt. Never deserved my respect. Never even deserved my love. He'd wanted the respect, and he'd sure as hell wanted the guilt, but the love was immaterial. He did not give it, and he did not expect to receive it. As for the respect, he forfeited that when he cut my mother off without a cent after my father's death.

My father's *suicide*, which is how Dad chose to deal with the fact that I'd caught him burying Austin Vandergriff.

I instinctively stanch the surge of rage. Then I pause, letting it wash away the irritating wisps of that misplaced guilt.

I cross my legs and pat the bed for my cat, Lucille. Then I remember Lucille is gone, put down last week because I couldn't afford to treat her cancer. Grief washes over me, only to lift guilt back to the surface. The guilt of grieving over a cat but not my grandfather.

Well, one had been there for me, and one had not.

I wipe away tears and go to delete the email, only to remember why I'd cursed. Not because of the message, but because of the podcast link below.

My finger hovers over that link. Hey, maybe it'll be so bad that I'll have an excuse to skip the funeral.

I can't do that. I'm going for my aunt. I owe Gail that and more. So much more.

I click the link, and as soon as I see the episode title, I exhale in a long hiss.

Paynes Hollow: The Bermuda Triangle of Upstate New York?

"The Bermuda Triangle isn't a thing," I mutter. "It had a normal amount of accidents for a high-traffic zone."

I know that's not the point, but I still seethe. At least the title tells me this will be nonsense. Thankfully, there's a transcript, so I don't need to listen to the episode.

> Paynes Hollow is swathed in shadow when I visit. Massive maples and oaks cast the world into shade and shadow, the only sound the distant roar of Lake Ontario. It's an empty

place, desolate and overgrown, the wind howling through the trees, wisps of fog settling over the land. The kind of place where you feel as if you've stepped back in time, and the Headless Horseman will ride out at any moment.

I snort. "Wrong part of the state, dumbass."

"Sleepy Hollow" was set in Tarrytown, just north of Yonkers, over a hundred miles from Paynes Hollow. While my grandfather *did* claim that Washington Irving wrote his story after a visit to Paynes Hollow, that was just more of his bullshit.

Also, it'd be weird to have the wind howling *while* it's foggy, and the idea that Paynes Hollow is a desolate wasteland is ridiculous. I remember forests and beaches and a picture-perfect summer getaway spot, bustling with visitors.

I keep reading.

> It's not the Headless Horseman that resides in Paynes Hollow, though. It's the Grim Reaper himself, riding across the land and slicing down the unwary. Yet the dead here don't fall to the ground. They disappear.
>
> For two hundred years, people have vanished around Paynes Hollow. Hikers. Boaters. Campers. Even local residents. Gone without a trace.
>
> Until Harris Payne murdered a thirteen-year-old boy and was caught red-handed—literally—by his own daughter.
>
> That's how the story goes.
>
> But is it the truth?
>
> I don't doubt young Samantha Payne saw something that day, but I believe, in that shadowy place, where nothing is what it seems, what she really witnessed wasn't her father, but the Grim Reaper of Paynes Hollow.

My shaking finger jabs the X to close the tab and keeps jabbing long after it's gone.

* * *

I know what I saw. I wish to God I could say otherwise, but I can't.

I take a deep breath. This is why my grandfather exiled Mom and me from his life. Because he believed there was another explanation. Our father wasn't the monster. We were, for thinking Dad could do that.

The last time I saw my grandfather, I'd been sixteen. He'd invited me to visit, and Mom wanted to seize the olive branch. I'd endured a week of my grandfather trying to convince me that I was wrong about Dad, until I broke down, shouting at him, my voice raw.

"Do you think I *want* to believe he did that? Do you think I wouldn't give *everything* to be wrong? I loved my father. I *adored* my father. If I had any chance of getting him back—even just getting back the good memories—don't you think I'd jump on it?"

I sit on the bed, fists clenched. When my phone buzzes, I almost pitch it aside, as if it's my grandfather reaching out from the beyond. Then I see the text.

> Gail: Pick you up in an hour? Grab a fortifying breakfast before the service?

The thought of breakfast sets my stomach roiling.

> Gail: And by "fortifying" I mean so leisurely that, whoops, looks like we'll barely make it to the service on time

I have to smile at that.

> Sam: Sounds good. See you in an hour.

Gail zips into the funeral-home lot and snags the last spot reserved for family. We jump out, and we're moving fast when a couple catches up. They look familiar, but I can't place them in any context related to my grandfather.

The man is in his fifties, rawboned and angular with silvering blond hair and a tanned face. He reminds me of a cowboy, and that nudges a memory, as if I've thought it before.

His wife is about the same age, with close-cropped curls, smooth dark skin, and wide-set brown eyes that radiate kindness.

I've thought that before, too.

"You probably don't remember us," the woman says, extending a hand and a tentative smile. "Liz Smits. This is my husband, Craig."

"Oh!" I shake her hand. "Mrs. Smits. Sheriff Smits. From Paynes Hollow. Of course."

"I was hoping to see your mother again," Mrs. Smits says. "It's been far too long."

"Uh, yes. She . . . isn't well." I swallow. "Dementia. She's in a home."

She blinks. "Already? I know she has early-onset dementia but . . . ."

An awkward silence, broken as a young woman hurries up, her heels clicking. "Found it." She passes the older woman a pack of tissues. Then she looks at me. "Sam?"

When I hesitate, she thrusts out her hand. "Josie Smits. I was that tagalong brat always following you and the other summer kids."

"Josie. Right. Of course."

I do remember Josie, not as a brat but as an adorable little girl who'd done her damnedest to keep up with the big kids. It just takes a moment to reconcile that little girl with the woman in front of me, tall and willowy, light brown skin, her short hair styled in a gorgeous twist-out.

I quickly introduce Gail, who shakes hands and murmurs, "We really do need to get inside, Sam."

"Right. Yes. We're already running late."

"Then let's move," Josie says, and we head inside together.

The service lasts forever. Or that's how it seems when I spend the whole time trying to keep a straight face as person after person says what a wonderful man my grandfather had been. I'd wondered whether my father's existence would be glossed over. But Dad is there, especially in stories, where he comes to life as I remember him, and that's when I do cry.

Do I notice people glancing my way, leaning in and whispering? Of course I do, because while my grandfather liked to forget what Dad did, no one else has. I will forever be Samantha Payne, the girl who caught her dad burying his victim.

Tragic figure worthy of pity?

Or a monster with savage blood running through her veins?

One can be both.

The service finally ends, and then it's on to the cemetery for the burial. Gail manages to commandeer a separate town car, avoiding her brother and his family. At the graveside, we stand apart, and I retreat into my cocoon, where no one can see me, no one can judge me.

Sweat trickles down my face in the humid August sun. After the burial, my cousin, Caleb, plants himself in my escape route. His parents—Uncle Mark and Aunt Ellen—stand behind him.

I glance over my shoulder, but other mourners are talking to Gail, and she doesn't notice the ambush.

"Couldn't stay away, could you?" Caleb says. "You smelled money and swooped in."

"No, I came to say goodbye," I say evenly.

Caleb snorts. "You hated him. You blamed him for what your dad did, and you took it out on an old man who loved you, in spite of everything."

In spite of the fact you were responsible for what happened. That's what he means.

Dad's the one who killed Austin, but I'm responsible for Dad's death because I "tattled" to my mother, who was equally responsible because she took me straight to the police. To Sheriff Smits.

What's that old saying?

A wife and daughter will help you move, but a proper *wife and daughter will help you move a body.*

"I'm sorry you think that," I say, as placidly as I can, and I take my petty pleasure in seeing Caleb's eyes burn with frustrated rage. "Now, if you'll excuse me—"

"You have a reading of the will to get to?" he sneers.

I look him in the eyes. "No, I have a mother to visit."

"What? You're not coming to the reading?"

I arch a brow. "You just accused me of being here for the money, and now you're offended that I'm not staying for the will?"

Caleb seems almost apoplectic now, his pasty face dangerously red. "You selfish little *bitch*."

"Caleb!" Aunt Ellen says, but her eyes gleam, secretly pleased.

"Wait a second," I say. "So if I skip the reading, *that* makes me selfish?"

"Gail," Uncle Mark says as my aunt hurries over. "We discussed this. You promised she'd be there."

I slowly turn to Gail as Aunt Ellen says, "She needs to be there, Gail. The will can't be read otherwise."

"Oh for fuck's sake." I mutter the words under my breath, but Aunt Ellen still gasps, as if I shouted it at a funeral.

"I'm sorry," Gail whispers to me. "I was going to tell you." Then to the others, "I believe people want to express their condolences, and having us standing here whisper-hissing at each other does not look good."

I clamp my mouth shut, and after a moment, the others back up and let us through.

Congrats, Gramps. You win. Again.

What a surprise.

Two

An hour later, I'm dragging my ass into that reading of the will. Gail and I have already argued over this. If my grandfather left me anything, she wants me to take it for my mother, whose care is about to bankrupt me. I've said it's a moot point because if he left me anything, it's a teacup and a KISS MY ASS donkey sticker.

Now Gail hovers beside me, her whole body practically vibrating with apology. I force an "It's okay" smile. She doesn't buy it. Her round face is drawn and pale, her blue eyes shadowed to gray. She's run her hands through her short dark hair enough that it's sticking up, and when I motion for her to pat it down, she's too upset to bother.

Get it over with. Take the teacup and the sticker, say "thank you very much," and walk out with my head high.

For Gail's sake, I won't delay the reading. She needs and deserves whatever she gets. She's a social worker, which I always think of as more a vocation than an occupation. It sure as hell doesn't fill her bank account. I just need to be sure she doesn't try to give any of her inheritance to me.

To Gail, I pretend money's just "a bit tight." The truth is that I've bookmarked a dozen websites on bankruptcy, and I'd file if I weren't terrified of how it would affect my mother's care.

Mom is in an awesome facility, and I will do whatever it takes to keep her there. Initially that meant giving up on med school, lying to everyone and saying that my years of volunteering suggested medicine wasn't the job for me.

I'd landed a decent job in Chicago and zoomed from lab tech to researcher. Then the bank informed me that the med-school money was gone, and the doctors told me that Mom was declining fast. She needed me home to advocate for her. So I returned to Syracuse, where the only job I could get was an entry-level lab tech at half my former pay.

Then, six months ago . . .

"We hate to lose you, Sam, but we were told to cut in order of seniority, and you're our newest hire."

So now I'm running data from home, making minimum wage, every penny I'd saved in Chicago already gone to my mother's bills.

Could I use money from my grandfather's will? Yes, but it would kill me to take it.

And it would kill my mother if I didn't.

"I hope you get everything," I whisper to Gail as we enter the room.

"If I do, half of it goes to you."

She catches my expression, sighs and shakes her head.

What if she *did* get everything? My uncle has his own money—plenty of it. Maybe my grandfather finally did the right thing and left it all to Gail, and I could agree to accept a sliver. Just enough to banish the specter of financial ruin.

"Miss Payne," a voice says, and I look up to see an elderly woman in a perfect pantsuit. "Isabella Jimenez, your grandfather's lawyer. I'm so glad you're here."

I nod mutely.

"If you and Gail will take a seat." She waves at a table. "We can begin."

So, I get a teacup. Not even joking. Okay, that had been an educated guess. My grandmother had collected teacups, and she always said that she'd leave me my favorite: a Wedgwood decorated with rabbits.

Sadly, the ancient KISS MY ASS donkey sticker that adorned the basement beer fridge isn't mentioned.

There's a seemingly endless list of bequeathments. My grandfather's long-suffering housekeeper gets a few things, though far less than she deserves. Even the boy who cut the lawn receives the lawn tractor, and I can't help but wonder if this was why my grandfather insisted I be here.

Imagine what you could have gotten, Samantha, if you'd just sucked it up and pandered to me like everyone else.

When my phone vibrates with a text, I check it under the table. It's a nurse from Mom's care home.

> **Vickie: Your mom is having an excellent day, and she's asking for you. Can I tell her you're on your way?**

That isn't a guilt-nudge. Vickie knows she only needs to say the words "good day" and I'll fly out the door. For an excellent day, I might not even remember to put on shoes.

Gail sees the text.

"Go," she whispers.

Ms. Jimenez clears her throat.

Gail straightens. "Sam needs to leave. Her part is done—"

"Her grandfather required that she stay until the end."

"It's her mother," Gail says.

"If it's an emergency, we can postpone this and reconvene tomorrow."

"How much longer?" I say.

She flips through her pages. "Ten minutes?"

I nod, even as I simmer. The lawyer moves on to the disposition of property, and if some desperate corner of my soul hoped for a scrap, it is disappointed. The house—probably worth a couple of million—will be divided into thirds, one going to my uncle, one to Gail, and one to Caleb. That's another reason why I'm here. If my cousin was entitled to a share, I would have been, too.

Gail reaches to squeeze my hand, her look promising me half of hers. I won't take it. I can't. She's thirty-six, recently divorced, and considering in vitro fertilization for the baby she's always wanted. I won't steal that dream from her.

I still smile back. What matters is that the will is almost done. Mom's last "excellent" day, where I truly had my mother back, was two months ago.

My foot starts tapping. Gail gently touches my knee, and I grimace an apology.

"And now we come to what I suspect you've all been waiting for."

The end? Yep, definitely waiting for that.

"The dispensation of the Paynes Hollow property."

I go still. Shit. I'd forgotten about that. Willfully forgotten.

As the founding family, my ancestors had taken the best land and passed it down intact from oldest son to oldest son. My grandfather owned over three hundred acres of prime land stretching along the coast of Lake Ontario.

I haven't set foot on that land in fourteen years.

"I am supposed to share this." The lawyer lifts a piece of paper and adjusts her reading glasses. "During Mr. Payne's recent illness, he received an offer from a development firm."

My gut clenches as I envision my childhood summer paradise destroyed for high-end condos. Only it's not a paradise anymore, and it's certainly not mine.

"Mr. Payne wished for me to read the offer, which is valid for his heirs."

I check my watch. Then I tuck my phone under the table to text Vickie.

"That offer is . . ." Ms. Jimenez pauses. "Ten million dollars."

Aunt Ellen squeaks. Caleb fist-pumps, as if we're at a damn sports game.

Gail has gone pale.

Ten million dollars?

That's a joke. It must be.

No, actually, it makes sense. Three hundred acres. Forget condos, that could be a full-on subdivision. A hundred lakefront lots and more within a short walk of the water.

Ten million is not outrageous at all.

"It's divided the same as the house property, right?" Uncle Mark says. "Three ways. Me, Gail, and Caleb?"

I grin at Gail. I'm thrilled for her, but I also must admit to the rising hope in my heart. Even after taxes, she'd have two million. A sliver of that would solve all my problems, and she'd barely notice the loss.

"Split three ways, right?" Uncle Mark repeats. "No, wait, it goes to the oldest son. Which means me. Or Caleb."

My heart stops. Is this why I'm here? To see that ten million go to Caleb, who'll blow it on luxury cars and five-figure bar tabs while my mother moves into some squalid care facility?

"The property goes to a single beneficiary," Ms. Jimenez says. "As you said, tradition is that it goes to the eldest male."

Caleb chortles and fist-pumps again. At worst, it'll go to his dad, who will give him whatever he wants.

Here, have a million bucks for your birthday, son.

My hands clench on my lap. It's okay. I will walk out of here no worse than I entered.

"In this case," Ms. Jimenez continues, "it would have gone to Harris."

Caleb snickers, and every muscle in me tenses. If he says anything about my dad—

Ms. Jimenez says, "Since Harris predeceased him, tradition needed to be changed."

"It passes to me," Caleb whispers. "Oldest male—"

"The property—in its entirety—goes to Harris's daughter, Samantha."

My head whips up. Ms. Jimenez looks at me and smiles, a kind smile that tells me I didn't hear wrong.

To me? Did I misjudge my grandfather, tangled in my anger and grief?

"There is one stipulation," Ms. Jimenez says. "In light of the break with tradition."

My heart stops, and I stare at her, seeing apology in her eyes.

"It's a simple one, though, Sam. And once you fulfill it, the land is yours."

"Wh-what do I need to do?" I manage.

"Go back," she says. "You need to spend a month at your family cottage. In Paynes Hollow."

Three

When Gail drops me off at the care home, I'm still shaking. She says something as I go, but my swirling rage and impotence drowns it out.

I love my aunt. Adore her. But right now, as she tries to tell me it won't be that bad, that she'll come to Paynes Hollow with me, all I can feel is the scorch of betrayal.

I'm being unfair. I know that. Gail asked the lawyer every question she could think of to get me out of this devil's bargain. What if I refuse? Does the property go to Gail and her brother? She could gift me her share that way.

No, if I refuse, it goes to distant relatives, and I can't even tell myself maybe *they* need the money—they run a Fortune 500 company.

The only person I want to see right now is my mother. I want to see that light in her eyes that tells me she's my mother again.

After Dad died, Mom and I muddled through, growing closer in our grief and confusion. But then I hit my teen years, and when I lashed out, my wonderfully calm mom was so implacable it only enraged me more, like punching a brick wall.

Gail would blame my trauma, but I blame me. At the time, though, I blamed Mom—blamed her for marrying Dad, for not seeing what he was. All breathtakingly unfair, but at fifteen, I was a seething black hole of repressed rage and hormones and grief, and I aimed it all at my poor mother, to the point where I'd moved in with Gail.

I can't give my mom back what should have been our last few good years together, but I can make damn sure she gets the best care now, whatever the cost.

Even if the cost is going back to Paynes Hollow?

I stride through the care-facility doors, inhale the smell of fresh-baked cinnamon buns, and my pulse slows. Then I see Vickie, looking up from her paperwork to shake her head, and my insides shrivel. It's all I can do to cross those last few feet to her.

"I'm too late," I whisper.

"I'm sorry, honey."

"It was my grandfather's funeral. I couldn't get away."

She reaches over to pat my hands. "I know. And it was such a brief episode that you might not have made it even if you came right away. But it was so good to see, and I think we're going to get a lot more of those."

"With the new medication," I say.

Her warm smile falters. The new—and very expensive—medication. "It might not be that. Your mother is such a strong woman. I've seen this happen, where they rally on their own, and if anyone can do that, it's your mom."

It's a kind lie, but still a lie. If Mom is improving, it's the trial medication. Vickie was responsible for advocating to get Mom on that trial, but it's ending, and if she stays on it, there will be a price. A steep one.

A price for better medication. A price for this place, modern and yet cozy, like a Norwegian spa specializing in hygge living, as warm and comforting as a hug.

I didn't put my mother here. Given the choice, I'd have cared for her myself, which would have been a disaster to rival the *Titanic*, and at the end, we'd both have gone down with the ship.

Driven by guilt and love, I'd have surrendered any dreams of my own to care for my mother, who would have fought me every step of the way—with love when she was lucid and fury when she was not.

My mother's legendary calm slips as her memory does. She has rages, as if when her mind relaxes, her own suppressed anger at Dad finally rushes out.

Mom put herself here, without telling me, and as always, she did the right thing. She found this place, and it is exactly right for her.

"Is it okay to see her?" I ask tentatively.

Vickie smiles. "I believe so. Her episodes have been rarer, too."

I know that. I'm here daily, and I'm as involved as I'm allowed to be. She *has* been getting better.

Because of the medicine I soon won't be able to afford.

In a home that I soon won't be able to afford.

Unless . . .

I clamp down on the thought. I'd spend a month in that hellhole, only to discover that I'd failed to fulfill some minor stipulation and I'd lose the property.

My grandfather had been careful to close off every loophole, but I'm sure he introduced a few. Just to torment me. A final act of spite, punishing me for the sin of turning in my murderous father.

The lawyer's words ring in my head as she'd read from the note my grandfather left. Not a private note. One that he ordered to be read aloud to all.

> I understand that Samantha was a child when she thought she saw her father do that terrible thing. I understand that she truly believes she saw it, and that he could have done such a thing to another human being, much less a child. But she is wrong. I may not have been able to make her see that in life, but I can do it now, after my death. She will return to Paynes Hollow, and she will spend a month there, and she will remember the truth. She will finally remember the truth.

Fresh rage whips through me. There is no doubt of what I saw. My father never tried to deny it. He ended his life *because* of what I saw. He left a goddamn suicide note, begging my forgiveness, ranting about inner demons.

He never denied what I saw or my interpretation of it.

Vickie leads me into the sunroom, my favorite spot in the home. It's empty, as it usually is. You'd think that if loved ones cared enough to pay for this home, they'd be here as often as they could, but that's my naiveté talking. Paying for an expensive long-term-care facility only means you have money, and sometimes, having money means you can plunk Grandpa in a place like this and wash your hands of him, content in the knowledge you've done your duty.

I take a seat by the window overlooking the Seneca River.

"Gail," a voice says, and my heart cracks a little as I rise to face the woman entering the room. She's petite and beautiful, with hair just beginning to gray, her face unlined. She looks thirty-five, not fifty-five, a cruel trick, as if some higher power made up for her mind's rapid degeneration by letting her body stay young.

"Mom," I say. "It's me. Sam."

She stops short. Then she smiles. "Ah, you and Sam are playing a joke on me." She wags a finger. "My daughter would never dress like that. If you want to do this properly, you need to show up in jeans and hiking boots."

I look down at my funeral garb. She's right, of course. This dress is far more Gail than me. Yet Mom makes the mistake no matter what I wear. I look too much like my aunt, and Mom still expects me to be a teenager.

I don't keep trying to correct her. I know the drill. One or two attempts is fine, but more will upset her.

As her mind wanders, my trick for communicating is to imagine if the situation were reversed, and Mom kept insisting it was a different year or she was a different person. I would find it funny at first, but eventually I'd get angry.

"Do I smell cinnamon rolls?" I ask.

Mom sighs as she sits across from me. "They're as bad as your brother, always bringing me treats."

I tense. By Gail's "brother," she means my dad, who always brought us both treats, and Mom always teasingly scolded him until I offered to eat hers, too.

"It's a lovely day," I say. "Maybe we could go for a walk along the river?"

"Oh, I don't think that's safe," Mom says. "You never know what's in the water." She folds her hands in her lap. "Those cinnamon buns smell like they're almost done."

I smile. "Sure, we'll wait for your cinnamon bun, Mo—Veronica."

She leans forward, as if someone might be listening. "Have you seen Sam lately? I know she's busy, but she never comes to see me anymore."

"I was here yester—" Deep breath, even as my hands shake. "She'll be here soon."

Mom's hands twist in her lap. "I think she's still angry with me."

My eyes fill. "No. She's not angry with you. If she ever was, she didn't mean it."

Mom nods, gaze down.

"Really. Sam loves you so much. She'll be here tomorrow. I'm sure of it."

"I hope so," Mom says, in a tiny voice that breaks me in two.

An hour later, I'm hurrying out of the building, trying not to cry, when someone hails me. I turn to see the administrator bearing down.

"Ms. Payne," he says, panting slightly as he catches up. "We need to discuss your account."

I raise a hand. "I know. I'm behind on the latest payment—"

"You are two payments behind. It is the sixteenth. August's payment was due yesterday."

"I'll have July's payment on Friday."

"And August?"

"I . . . I'm speaking to my mother's insurance company next week. They promised to cover part of her stay, and they're dragging their heels."

"I understand, but you need to pursue that separately. We have bills to pay, too, Ms. Payne. If you cannot catch up by next week, you will need to make other arrangements for your mother."

I open my mouth, but he's already striding back into the building.

I stand there, staring at the door as it closes behind him. I'm not sure whether I want to scream or cry. Both. At once. I want to rage against the world that did this to my mother. That put her through that hell with my dad and then took away her mind.

Ten million dollars, a voice whispers in my head.

I swallow hard.

I keep saying I'd do anything for my mother. I gave up on med school for her. I left a good job for her. I moved back to Syracuse for her. I let my cat die for her.

Maybe I should be raging at the world that keeps demanding more sacrifices from me, but every time I feel that, I think of my mother, and *her* sacrifices, what she endured and keeps enduring.

I say I would do anything, but I won't spend a month at Paynes Hollow? I'm not being asked to sacrifice a limb. It's a month in a cottage on a private beach, for fuck's sake.

The world that keeps demanding more has finally offered something in return. Compensation beyond my wildest imaginings. Enough money that I could write a single check to cover Mom's stay for the rest of her life. Enough money to keep her on that trial and buy every medication she needs. Enough to get her the best help—private nurses, dedicated caretakers, anything she might need as she deteriorates.

I could give her that. I just need to have the guts to do it.

As I walk to the bus stop, I call Gail.

"Hey," she says, her voice tentative.

"I need to be sure," I say.

"Sure about . . . ?"

"That it's real. That if I spend a month there, I'll get the money for Mom. That there's no way this is a trick, no loopholes I can stumble through. I don't need ten million dollars. But I have to be sure that I will get *enough.*"

"Of course." Her voice firms, and I can imagine her straightening. "Let me call Ms. Jimenez. I'll tell her we want to talk. I won't let you go through this if there's any chance your grandfather is playing games. And I won't let you go through it alone."

Four

Three days later, Gail and I are on our way to Paynes Hollow, and while we've stopped arguing, we're now in a chilly stalemate.

I don't want her here, and I say that in the most loving way. It makes zero sense for her to come along. My job can be done remotely; hers can't. Spending a month in Paynes Hollow means she's going to juggle video sessions with twice-weekly two-hour drives to Syracuse, which is ridiculous. Then there's Carlos, the guy she was kinda-sorta seeing, who decided Gail spending a month with me meant she wasn't committed to moving forward, so he ended the relationship. There's also her apartment, which the landlord wouldn't let her short-term-rent to a visiting colleague, meaning she won't even catch a break there.

"I just inherited one-third of a multimillion-dollar estate, Sam," she said when I argued. "I don't need to sublet my apartment. And if Carlos balked at me being gone for a month on a family emergency, he's not the guy I'm looking for."

Maybe, but she's still putting her life on hold to babysit me. Which is uncomfortably close to when I'd moved in with her, oblivious to the fact that I must have seriously cramped her post-college lifestyle.

I haven't been to Paynes Hollow in fourteen years, but neither has Gail. Dad had been a teenager when Gail was born, and he'd been the one who took her to movies and concerts and came to her dance recitals and school plays. Her father certainly didn't.

I'm very aware of the sacrifice she's making for me, but it feels as if I'm still messing up, expecting everyone else to fix my problems. Like a toddler who insists she can make her own breakfast, but the adults need to hover, knowing she can't handle it on her own.

If Gail is adamant about coming along, I want us to pretend it's a vacation. Pretend I'm not terrified of going back to Paynes Hollow. Pretend our lives weren't shattered on that shore.

Hey, Gramps! Thanks for the month-long holiday on the lake! Oh, and thanks for the cool ten mil I'll get for staying there. Joke's on you.

But I'm not getting the fantasy. I'm getting this: driving in stony silence along the I-90, as if we're heading to another funeral.

"Maybe you could invite Carlos up for the weekend," I say. "Grandpa forgot to close that loophole. We could fill all three cottages and have a month-long beach party."

"If Carlos wanted to see me, he could have suggested that. He did not."

"Maybe you're upset because he didn't suggest coming to visit, and he's upset because you didn't invite him."

She shakes her head and adjusts her sunglasses. "You're seeing something there that wasn't there, Sam. I know you want me to be happy. But I am." She smiles over. "Happy to be spending the summer with a very dear friend, who happens to be my niece. How lucky is that?"

I sigh and look out the window.

Gail says, "If you'd like to discuss romance, we could talk about the state of your love life."

I snort.

"Yep," she says. "You haven't dated since you got back from Chicago. You're too busy with your mom, and I get that. So no dating talk. I also won't mention you getting another cat."

I tense, and she sighs, her voice dropping as she says, "That won't happen again, Sam. The next time you get a pet, you'll be able to afford any cost. Also, as I have pointed out many times, even the vet said there was only a twenty percent chance that chemo would have helped

Lucille. I couldn't have paid with those odds either. But next time, it will be different." She grins over. "You'll be able to get a dozen cats and buy a house big enough to hold them. World's youngest cat lady."

"I do not want to be cleaning litter boxes for a dozen cats. And can you imagine the shedding? Not to mention the smell." I shudder.

"Pfft. You're going to be rich, girl. You can hire someone to clean those boxes and brush those cats and vacuum up the fur. Ten *million* dollars."

"Before taxes."

She lowers her shades to goggle at me. "At that level, who cares about taxes? Even with the lousiest advisor, you'd walk away with five mil. Ms. Jimenez says you should clear seven. Seven. Million. Dollars. You can do anything you want."

I nod, staying quiet, trying not to think about that.

"You could go to med school after all," she says. "Or, with that kind of money, if you invest it right, you wouldn't need to work."

"I'd still work."

"Of course you would. You'd go stir-crazy otherwise. But you could go to med school and become a doctor and not give a damn what kind of wages you're pulling in. You wanted to be a small-town GP. You could do that."

"I want to focus on Mom first."

She squeezes my knee. "Okay, I'll take a hint and stop dreaming for you. Let's dream for me instead."

I smile. "Three kids, a dog, and a house in the country?"

"Of course. Should I add a guy to the mix?"

"Nah. You can rent one."

Her laughter fills the tiny car. "I just might do that." She glances over. "Did I tell you that Ms. Jimenez already wired me five grand?"

"*Nice.*"

"Do you know where it came from?" She doesn't wait for an answer. "My asshole brother."

"Uncle Mark?"

She nods. "Dad left me the dining room set, which your aunt Ellen has always had her eye on. So we agreed on a price, and I now have five grand burning a hole in my pocket. Wanna know what I'm doing with it?"

"Buying five grand in booze to get us through the next month?"

"Ha! That'll get us through the first week. And don't worry—I'm not pushing the money on you. I know you were able to rent out *your* apartment and negotiated to pay a portion of your mother's tab."

"I did. So what is the money for? A splurge, I hope."

"Kind of. If you consider it a splurge to make the cottage habitable."

I arch a brow at her.

Her voice goes serious. "No one's used your family cottage in fourteen years, Sam. No one has used *any* of the cottages."

Because after my father killed a local boy, my family didn't dare stay there. I'd like to see that as proper respect for their grief, but if my grandfather gave a shit about that, he'd have left the property to the dead boy's family—or to the town itself.

My grandfather had always been the biggest local donor. He stopped after my dad died. It wasn't just Mom and I who betrayed his favorite child. Paynes Hollow did, too. We were the founding family, damn it. There's a long tradition of rich folks getting away with murder. The fact that we weren't granted that courtesy is, apparently, unforgivable.

I realize Gail is waiting for me to say something, and I pull from my thoughts to focus.

"No one has used the cottages . . . ?" I say, and then her meaning hits. "What state are they in?"

"I asked Ms. Jimenez, but she wasn't sure."

"She only knows that I need to stay in mine—the one my parents used." I look over sharply. "Considering what my father did, are we sure the locals didn't burn it? I wouldn't blame them."

"There's a caretaker, and he says the cottage is still standing. No loopholes there, I'm afraid. However, 'still standing' isn't the same as 'habitable.' But it will be. I have five grand to spend. With any luck, Ikea will deliver. If not, I'll pick up what I can in my car."

I thump back against the seat. "Because I'm not allowed to leave the property for more than an hour, once a day. I should be grateful for that concession. Otherwise, if you weren't there, I couldn't exactly count on the locals to bring me food. Not unless it's poisoned."

She shakes her head. "People will feel nothing but sympathy for you, Sam. You were a child."

The child of a killer. Gail always forgets that part. I can't.

This was one of the things I had unfairly blamed my mother for. To me, we should have moved across the country, where no one knew our names. Instead, we went back to Syracuse, with me attending the same school where everyone knew what my dad did. My mother was a teacher, like my father. Why couldn't she take me somewhere and homeschool me?

It wasn't until much later that I understood Mom *couldn't* leave. Her father was in Syracuse, suffering from the same ailment she has now. Her mother had taken off for Florida when the disease first appeared, leaving Mom to care for him. He'd been at the stage where a move would have been unbearably traumatic. Combine that with the fact that she had a good teaching job and a good support network in Syracuse, and I understand why she didn't leave.

But staying in the same neighborhood and going to the same school meant I endured years of whispers and bullying.

Oooh, you cut off Sam Payne in the lunch line? Don't you know what her dad did? You took your life in your hands.

Uh, Ms. Chu, do you really think you should give Sam Payne a scalpel to dissect that frog? You know what her dad did, right?

I shake it off. I won't need to worry about what Paynes Hollow thinks of me. I might be allowed to leave for an hour a day, but I don't plan to. I won't take any chance of getting in a fender bender or being stuck in a checkout line and losing the property.

I can do this. I *will* do this. I will beat my grandfather at his game. Win the property. Make sure my mother gets all the help and comfort she deserves. Quietly give money to Austin Vandergriff's family. Donate to Paynes Hollow, if they'll let me do it anonymously. I will fix everything that my father and grandfather screwed up.

Will I fix my own life, too? Is med school finally in my future? Even thinking about that makes me anxious. I'll focus on the rest.

I will be okay. However this turns out, I will be okay.

Nothing at Paynes Hollow can hurt me worse than I've already been hurt. The only ghosts there exist in my mind, and I've dealt with them so far. Maybe, as much as I hate to give my grandfather any credit, this summer really will help.

See the property for what it is: a piece of land and nothing more.

See my father for what he really was: a good dad but a monstrous person.

One can be both, as hard as that is to accept.

Maybe, after this summer, I will finally accept it.

Gail bypasses the village of Paynes Hollow. I don't even realize she's done it until I see a familiar Private Drive sign and frown, wondering how I missed all the landmarks. Because she took a route that didn't exist fourteen years ago. The last community we drove through was unrecognizable—a vacation-home development from the past decade or so.

Even this road leading to the property isn't what I remember. For one thing, it's paved. For another, there are a whole lot more No Trespassing–style signs on the trees lining the road.

Back when we stayed here, there was just that one discreet Private Drive sign, meant for outsiders who might mistake the lane into our property for a regular road. Locals had been welcome to camp on the property and use the west side for fishing, swimming, and boat launching. But now there are endless signs—NO TRESPASSING, PRIVATE PROPERTY, NO LAKE ACCESS, NO THROUGH ROAD, PROTECTED BY SECURITY. There's even a gate.

"Huh," I say. "Looks like it's locked. Well, we tried. Time to go home."

Gail passes me a key.

"Damn it," I mutter. "What about the caretaker? I don't want to get shot opening the gate. We probably should turn around."

"I wish," she says. "I'm guessing the caretaker is some local oldtimer. Hopefully collecting the big bucks from my father's estate while never setting foot on the land. It's not as if Dad would have known."

I shake my head. "Your father probably paid him a hundred bucks a month and expected GPS proof that he was driving around the property every day."

"Sadly true. We'll meet him tonight, according to Ms. Jimenez. My plan is to relieve him of his duties, with full pay, of course. I don't think we want some old guy wandering around with his hunting rifle."

"Oh, I don't know." I swing open the door. "If I'm shot by the caretaker, is *that* a loophole?"

"Probably not."

I head to the gate. The lock is new, and that gives me pause. Gail was joking about the elderly caretaker who never bothered to come out here, but this lock suggests she might be right. I imagine the lawyer calling to warn him that we're coming today, and he rushes out to put a lock on the gate, look as if he's been doing his job.

Doesn't matter. I don't *want* an attentive caretaker—like Gail said, we'll be giving him the month off, with pay of course. But I do like the idea of some old codger conning my grandfather out of a caretaker's pay.

Beyond the gate, the road is overgrown on both sides, bushes and trees crowding in with barely enough room for Gail's tiny car to pass. I remember Mom grumbling about how fast the brush grew, and Dad would be out here early the first morning, making sure it was clear for her grocery run.

I swallow hard. Then I heave open the gate and—

Pain stabs through my hand, and I drop the gate with a hiss. I hold out my hand as a line of blood opens up across my palm, the skin splitting.

I curse and squeeze my fist, only to have blood drip from it, huge drops hitting the ground. I stand there, transfixed as the blood disappears in the dry earth, and the wind sighs in something like relief.

Home.

She's home.

I shiver and open my hand to see a wash of blood with a bright red line across my palm. Time wavers, and I'm four or five, running to the cottage, my hand clenched, blood dripping from it. Dad sees me and drops his book as he jogs off the porch to meet me.

"Oh, honey, what happened?" he says, peeling open my hand to see the line across it.

I shake my head and mumble something.

He folds my fingers over the injury. "Come on inside, and let me get that fixed up. Then you need to show me where it happened. There must be something sharp."

Except I didn't remember where it happened. I didn't remember anything but seeing the cut on my hand, the blood dripping into the parched earth, hearing the wind whisper and then running, running as fast as I could for my father.

No, there was something else. I thought I saw—

"Oh my God." Gail runs over and grabs my wrist. "What happened?"

I start to say I don't know, still caught in the memory, but then I come back to myself and wave at the gate.

"Damn gate bit me," I say, trying for lightness.

"I think I have bandages in the car."

"Nah, a tissue will be fine. I just want to get to the cottage. See what we're dealing with."

She nods and hands me a tissue from her pocket. As she heads back to the car, I squint into the shadows cast by the overgrown bushes. Then I shake my head, clasp the tissue, and follow Gail.

Five

We continue up the lane, and I wince with every branch that scratches the car.

"I'll trim those," I say.

Just like Dad used to do.

I bite my lip and look out the window. Through a break in the thick bushes, I see an old tire on the ground, a rope still attached to it.

"Higher, Daddy! Higher!"

I look away sharply and clasp my hands in my lap.

Today will be the hardest, but I'm going to face these ghosts head-on. No hiding in the cottage. I'll walk the property and let the memories flow, and as difficult as that will be, it's better than cowering in a run-down shack.

I'm actually glad that the cottage will be in disrepair. Fitting. A reflection of our ruined family. I need to see the damage as a project. The beach is probably full of trash, and I imagine no one obeyed those No Trespassing signs. It'll give me something to clean up. Maybe I shouldn't bother—the developers won't care—but keeping busy will be good. Between that and work, the month will zoom by.

Gail and I can give this place an extreme makeover. Exorcise the past that way. Get rid of that tire swing. Refurnish the cottage. Put bright-colored beach chairs on the shore. Just the two of us, enjoying a beach vacation while renovating a run-down cottage. Working remotely during the day and drinking beer by the campfire at night.

By the time we turn the last corner, I'm lost in my plans, determined—

The cottage appears. It doesn't leap from the bushes or anything so dramatic. Gail is driving dead slow around that last curve, the road pitted and rough, and the cottage appears as if someone slowly draws back a curtain, revealing one sliver at a time.

The porch railing. Then the front corner and then the entire thing emerging into the bright late-August sunshine.

The cottage is exactly that. Cottage, cabin, camp, whatever you want to call it. Not a beach house. Not a summer house. My grandfather's money was old money. He was descended from European settlers who moved to America in the early waves, making a homestead here along the banks of Lake Ontario. They did some farming, but their business was in trade, establishing a port a little farther down.

That kind of generational wealth doesn't mean grand beach houses and sprawling estates. It means owning the most desirable land and keeping it as a vacation getaway with small and rustic cottages for your own personal family camp.

"It's about the land," my grandfather said when my uncle Mark wanted to tear down his cottage and build one of those fancy beach houses. "Harris understands that. His wife understands that. Even their little girl understands that. It's about the land."

I'd been so proud when I overheard that conversation. Yes, I understood. It *was* about the land—the glorious endless forest and beach that was all ours. Our family compound, where I could run to my grandmother's cottage for breakfast and back to my own for lunch, with a shared barbecue on the beach for dinner. Where I could ride my bike to town and everyone knew me and the shop owner snuck me sweets and ice cream. Where I could explore the forest trails all day and walk along the lakeshore at sunset. The only thing I couldn't do was swim alone, but that made sense, and I was still allowed to fish and wade to my knees, and Mom would take me swimming off the platform and Dad would take me canoeing along the shoreline.

It's about the land.

Except that wasn't what my grandfather meant. He meant the value being in the land itself, and as a child, I took that metaphorically. To me, the land meant a king's ransom of adventure. But he meant the actual value.

Ten million dollars.

For land that held three rustic cottages and a storage shed.

I don't see the shed or the other cottages. That's part of the design. Trees separate the buildings enough that we could pretend we were here alone.

All I see now is our cottage.

And it looks exactly as I remember it.

A plain rectangular building with a full-length front porch. As boring a piece of architecture as one could imagine. All-natural construction, the wood weathered, as it's been for as long as I can remember.

It looked exactly like this each summer when we rolled up, and then Mom and I spent the day unpacking our clothes and food while Dad brought out all the touches that made the cottage our own: my bike, the porch chairs, the box of lawn games.

One year Dad had added something new to the front door. A custom wooden sign with painted caricatures of him and Mom and me, our names below each. Mom had gently asked if we could hang it inside. She didn't like the idea of announcing that they had a little girl, complete with her name.

Best not to tempt predators.

Except the predator was inside, sleeping beside her.

I swallow hard.

"Sam?" Gail says softly, and I realize the car has stopped and I'm sitting here staring at the front door after she's already climbed out.

I push open the door with more force than necessary. Then I stride up onto the porch.

"It looks in decent shape from the outside," Gail says as she fumbles with the key ring. "That's a good sign. Structurally sound. They always were. As basic as possible, but sturdy enough to withstand all Lake Ontario can throw at them." She pauses and glances over. "I'm babbling."

"Babble away." I lean my head against her shoulder. "I'm glad you're here. I know I argued, and you probably didn't feel welcome, but I do appreciate it."

"You didn't want me to feel obligated. I get it. But this was my choice." She takes a deep breath. "Ready?"

I push open the door without answering. Then I stride in and—

The whole world stops as cold rushes through me.

I'm standing in my childhood summer home.

Not the building it used to be in. My actual home.

Nothing has changed.

Nothing has changed.

I'm in the kitchen, on the mat where we were supposed to wipe our feet—or our shoes, but mostly our feet, because mine stayed bare until Labor Day. There's a towel hanging on the wall for wiping them if they're muddy or wet, and it's the same towel it's always been—my threadbare Lilo & Stitch beach one.

In front of me is the vintage yellow Formica kitchen table that Aunt Ellen turned up her nose at. It's set for dinner, with equally bright primary-color stoneware, the plates draped in cloth napkins because Mom hated the waste of paper ones.

Ready for dinner. Just as it had been that last day.

Mom liked to set the table for the next meal after the last one was cleared, and that day, I'd helped her. Then I'd gone to wander. Dad was out chopping wood. I'd been heading to see him when Mom called me in—she'd realized we were out of burger buns for dinner and did I want to come to town with her? I did. We climbed into the car, and as we were leaving, we spotted Dad, and I waved. He'd been distracted, didn't seem to see me.

We'd gone to town, only Mom started talking to Mrs. Smits, and I got bored and asked to head home. She'd said okay, and I'd run the whole mile, raced up our lane and spotted Dad in the forest, digging a hole—

I yank myself back. My gaze snags on a black shape hanging on the back of a kitchen chair.

Dad's cardigan. Still on his chair. Where he'd left it that morning.

"What the hell?" Gail breathes behind me. She walks past, gaping around. "What the *fucking* hell?"

I don't think I've ever heard my aunt use that word.

She turns to me, and for a second, she doesn't seem to see me. Her eyes are wide, her mind someplace else, her breath coming quick.

Remembering her brother. Remembering all the times she'd stayed with us, in this cottage, when it looked exactly like this.

Her arms go out to me, but I pretend not to see them, turning away and tossing my bag into the corner.

"Sam?" she says.

"We should bring in the groceries."

"Sam? Please."

"Well, look on the bright side. At least we don't need to worry about fixing the place up." I run a hand over the little table by the door. "Not even a speck of dust. It's like he sealed the building in plastic wrap."

I look around. "I'm impressed. I mean, seriously impressed. It's perfectly preserved, right down to my artwork on the fridge." I walk over to the pencil sketches of deer and squirrels. "They aren't even yellowed. Grandpa must have had them archived and put back up, exactly as we left them." I whistle. "Next level, Grandpa. This is some truly next-level bullshit."

Gail doesn't answer, and I squirm. I try not to be so scathing around her. Whatever my grandfather had done, he was still her father. I understand the pull of that loyalty better than anyone.

I'm about to say I'm sorry when I see her eyes brimming with tears. Now I'm the one reaching out, and she falls into my arms, hugging me tight.

"I am so sorry, baby," she says. "I have always known what my father is, and I have spent my life fighting against the urge to hate him. Making excuses for him. But this is inexcusable. This is . . ."

She trails off. *Sadistic.* That's what it is. My grandfather had always been cruel, but this is pure gleeful sadism. I truly cannot imagine how much work went into preserving this time capsule for me. Because it was always for me. For the day when my grandfather died and I came back here, sentenced to spend a month in this twisted memory of my perfect childhood with my perfect dad.

How much joy had he gotten out of imagining this moment? Me

walking in, expecting a ruin, instead rocketed back to my last day here? He wouldn't be around to witness it, but he must have spent joyful hours imagining it.

You twisted old fuck.

All those times my grandfather swore my dad was innocent because his very nature meant he couldn't be guilty.

There wasn't a cruel bone in Harris's body. You know that, Veronica. Samantha knows that.

No, Grandpa. There must have been cruelty there, a darkness, and there is no doubt where it came from. Just look in the mirror.

How many people at my grandfather's funeral said what a good man he was? My dad had been better at hiding his darkness from those who loved him. My grandfather hadn't bothered. It was those who cared about him who'd suffered.

"You aren't staying," Gail says, herding me out the door before I can protest. She yanks it shut behind me and locks it with a decisive click.

"Gail . . ." I say.

"No," she says firmly. "He is not getting away with this."

"So the property goes to strangers who don't need the money?"

"No, the property goes to the person who deserves it most. You. We are going to screw that old bastard over, and I hope to God he'll be watching us do it."

"There are no loopholes—"

"Yes, there are." She turns to me. "I've had ideas. I didn't want to tell you, in case you got here and things weren't so bad, because my ideas require some work."

She walks onto the driveway, and I follow.

"The first thing is that we switch phones," she says. "There are no cameras. No eye in the sky. The only thing that tells the lawyer you were here is your phone. I'd love to leave it on the table and go, but it'll need to show you moving around. So I'll take it and stay here."

"You can't—"

"I can. I will stay, and you will go. I have a list of hotels where you can get a room, all within a half hour's drive. We'll book under my name."

"What about the caretaker?"

"We're giving him the month off, remember? At worst, someone will spot me from a distance and think it's you. I'll wear one of your ball caps to hide my shorter hair."

"Gail..."

"We'll put a security alarm on the gate. Oh, and I'll replace the lock. If someone comes to check on you, the security system will alert us and the locked gate will slow them down."

"Then you'll call me, and I'll sneak back?"

"Why not?" Her jaw sets. "You're allowed to leave for an hour. If you can get here in thirty minutes, that's perfect. We'll say you took my car for an errand."

I sigh. "No, Gail. I appreciate the offer, but it's not worth the risk."

"We can do this, Sam. Screw my father. You will spend the month—"

"Right here," says a voice, making us both jump. "Ms. Payne will spend the month here."

A figure walks from the trees. I can't make him out at first. Just a tall figure with a masculine voice, slinging what looks like a backpack off his shoulder. Then he steps out of the shade, coming into the sunshine.

He's a few years older than me. Tall and lean. Dressed in jeans and a flannel shirt that's too warm for late August, though he's rolled up the sleeves. Sandy beard and shaggy light brown hair. I can't see his eyes behind his sunglasses, and the beard doesn't help me see his face, but something about him looks familiar.

"May I help you?" Gail snaps. "This is private property."

"Yep. It is. I believe Ms. Jimenez mentioned a caretaker?"

"That's you?" Gail sounds surprised.

"That's me." His voice is flat. "I am the caretaker of this property, and for the next month, the caretaker of Ms. Payne herself. Making sure she doesn't... What was it I heard you say? Have her live off the property while you stay and pretend to be her?"

Gail's jaw set. "If you heard that, you were mistaken."

"Yeah, don't think I was. But it won't work anyway. You forgot about this." He unzips the bag and pulls out something with a black box and strap.

"An ankle monitor?" Gail's voice rises.

"Worn one, have you?"

"I'm a social worker," she says coldly. "I have seen them. You are not putting that on my niece."

"Well, then she's not getting the . . . what is it? Ten million dollars from the sale of this place?" He hefts the monitor. "This is one of her grandfather's stipulations."

"No one mentioned an ankle monitor," I say.

"Seems your lawyer left the dirty work to me." He holds out his phone. "Go ahead and call her. You'll be wearing this, and I'll be monitoring it. Small price to pay for ten million, I'd say."

"Look," Gail says. "I don't know who you are but—"

"The caretaker. You mean my name? Right. I forgot that." He turns to me and removes his sunglasses. "You don't remember me, do you, Samantha?"

"It's Sam," I say reflexively. "And I'm sorry. You look familiar, but it's been a very long time."

"We only met a few times. You knew my brother, though. He was about your age. I'm Ben." He meets my gaze. "Ben Vandergriff. Austin's older brother."

Six

My breath seizes in my throat as I force out words. "I—I—I'm so sorry. I—"

"Here's the deal, Samantha," he interrupts, shades back on, his voice ice cold. "You do not get to mention my brother. You do not get to mention your father. You do not get to mention what happened here. Bring it up, and you will wish you hadn't."

"Whoa!" Gail lunges between us. "I understand what happened to your family—"

"Nope, I don't think you do."

Gail continues, "You're right. We cannot imagine what you went through—"

"Don't."

"But you will not threaten Sam. For God's sake, she reported her own father for what he did to—"

"Gail?" I cut in, fisting my hands to control my shaking. "Could you wait for me inside, please?"

Her eyes flash, mouth opening to argue.

"Please?" I meet her gaze. "I'd like to handle this."

I watch as her jaw clenches and unclenches several times before she nods abruptly and goes inside the cottage.

I turn to Ben. "I will not mention any of those things while you are here. However, *you* will not threaten me. If you do, I will speak to Ms. Jimenez. Whatever my grandfather intended for me to endure, it doesn't include being alone on a remote property, threatened by the caretaker."

"That wasn't—" He snaps his mouth shut and gives his head a sharp shake. "Fine. I was out of line, but you get the gist of it. Just don't talk to me about *enduring* anything. This is a rich-people game with a ten-million-dollar prize."

"Which is the only way I get anything. Ten million or nothing, and my mother—"

"—is sick. Early-onset dementia. I've heard, and I'm sure she needs special care, but I'm not the person whose shoulder you want to cry on, Samantha."

"I never said—"

"If you *endure* living on the best damn land in the county for a month, you're set for life. You know what I get? Three months' severance." He cuts me off when I open my mouth. "And don't offer to pay me to let you live off-site. You aren't the only one with family to look after. My father had an accident after my brother died."

He sees my expression. "Oh? You didn't know that? Yeah. Two days after the funeral. Drank until he could forget he just buried his thirteen-year-old son, got in the car, and hit a tree. He hasn't been able to work since. But your grandfather—generous guy that he is—came to the rescue. He offered to help my parents and pay me full-time wages if I took over as caretaker for the property here. Sweet deal for a sixteen-year-old kid. But then it came time to go away to college and . . . Sorry, no, if I quit—or subcontracted the job—my parents would lose their payments, too. Still, I kept telling myself that surely when the old bastard died, he'd make provisions for us, and I could get the hell out of this town. Now he's gone, and I have one last task: babysit the girl who'll inherit this place, for which I'll get three fucking months' severance. Oh, but he will provide that pension for the rest of my father's life. Unless I renege on the deal. Then my dad gets nothing."

I stand there, processing all this, my mind reeling. My grandfather *made* Ben Vandergriff look after the land where his brother died? Where his brother had been murdered by my father?

"That's—that's—" is all I can manage.

"Your family," he says. "That is your family, Samantha. I don't care if you promised me enough to pay that pension for my dad. I wouldn't take it. I'll earn that spiteful bastard's money by making sure you fulfill his stipulations to the letter. And if you get cabin fever, stuck out here in the middle of nowhere?" He meets my gaze. "At least *you* got to leave fourteen years ago."

There's nothing more to say after that. Ben Vandergriff isn't my secret route out of this, and I would never ask him to be, after what he's gone through. I can only console myself with the knowledge that he has no stake in this otherwise. Whether I go through with it or not, he gets paid—and his father's care is covered. He only loses out if he helps me cheat or refuses to see this through.

As for what he does here, the overgrown state of the place suggests he's not a gardener. Apparently, his job is patrolling the property once a day and maintaining my parents' cottage and the shed. If a tree falls across the driveway, we can call him to clear it away. If we see campers, we can call him to escort them off. Otherwise, he patrols on foot daily, and he will stay out of our way.

I do ask whether the pruning shears and chain saw are still in the shed, so I can clear the driveway. For that, I am told that I will, under no circumstances, be doing anything of the sort. Gail drove through just fine, and the only cutting tool around is the old hatchet, which I can use for chopping firewood. Apparently, Ben doesn't want the daughter of a murderer having access to too many sharp implements.

Gail and I call Ms. Jimenez about the ankle monitor, and we get a lot of "Oh, didn't I mention that?" but the upshot is that I need to put the thing on while Ben is watching, and it doesn't come off for the next month. It will alert him when I leave the property and when I return and those two times better be less than an hour apart. So I strap on the monitor, supervised by Ben.

After Ben leaves, Gail and I argue. With every passing moment, my grandfather's deal gets worse. Not only staying on the property, but in a cottage frozen at the moment my world shattered. Not an elderly caretaker we could pay to skip his patrols, but the older brother of my father's victim, who has been victimized in his own way for the past fourteen years. Not being confined to the property by my easily faked phone GPS, but with an actual ankle monitor. Oh, and in case we considered redecorating the place, we can't. According to Ben—with Ms. Jimenez confirming—I'm not allowed to even buy new bedsheets.

Gail wants to leave. She's worked out how much money she'll get and how much of that I'd need for Mom. She's even calculated a sliding scale. She can give me enough to pay for Mom's care fully for five years, which provides the breathing room needed to get back on my feet. Then she'll subsidize Mom's care until the end. She doesn't point out that the life expectancy for early dementia maxes out at about twenty years after symptoms first appear. We know the statistics, and we never discuss them.

I understand what Gail is saying, and I am so grateful for the offer, but I refuse. Categorically refuse. The more torture my grandfather piles on, the more walking away feels like surrender.

I won't give the bastard the satisfaction, even if he's not here to witness it. I won't give Uncle Mark and Aunt Ellen and Caleb the satisfaction of seeing me fail. I want to say I'm not including Ben Vandergriff in that, but I keep seeing the contempt on his face.

I already planned to help his family with that ten million. I will still do that, more than ever now that I know their situation. If Ben doesn't want any, then it can all go to his parents.

It's not just about showing everyone I can do this. It's also about not being indebted to Gail. I'd always feel the guilt of knowing I took away part of an inheritance she deserved.

It's *one* month. On a dream property. If I view it through Ben's eyes, I really do seem like the sort of whiny rich girl who considers it torture if she's forced to fly overseas in economy. I'm not physically being hurt. I'm not confined to the cottage. I'm not expected to subsist on stale bread and water. In fact, when I go into my old bedroom, I find an envelope with three thousand dollars in it, and a note that it's for "expenses." With that, I can pay the remainder of Mom's August bill, and I'll be eating better than I have in two years.

I will get through this, and when I come out the other side, my life will be changed forever.

By dinner, we've hit the awkward-truce stage. Gail insists on staying, despite me declaring I can handle this. I insist on staying, despite her declaring I shouldn't *need* to handle this. No one would ever know we were related, huh?

Mom always said I didn't just look like my aunt—we also share similar personalities. Even before the disease dug its claws in deep, Mom would occasionally call one of us by the other's name.

Sometimes I look at Gail, and I see a flattering reflection of myself, and other times, I see an uncomfortable one. Gail gives so much, and I admire that . . . but I also wish she'd think of herself more. I commend her strength in overcoming my dad's betrayal and then her husband's, leaving her for another woman. But I'd like to see her let down her guard more and admit how much she's been hurt.

Pot, meet kettle.

Tonight, though, our shared stubborn streak means we don't completely give up the fight. But our dislike of confrontation means we don't keep arguing either.

We set the dispute aside and eat dinner and then find other things to focus on. For Gail, that's work. For me, it's meal planning. One thing we don't have in common? Our cooking skills. Gail is all about takeout and ready-to-eat. Here I take after my mom. I want home-cooked meals, and I'm happy to make them myself.

I'd hoped for a bonfire to celebrate our first night. We'd unofficially planned on it, with Gail bringing beer and canned cocktails and me packing marshmallows and sticks. But darkness starts to fall and she's on a call with a client, so I quietly head out by myself.

It turns out to be later than I thought. Darker, at least. I really should have found wood after dinner. Better yet, I should have had Gail stop to grab some from the dozen "firewood 4 sale" spots we'd passed along the back roads.

I scrounge up some dry sticks, which will make perfect kindling. But I want a fire that lasts more than five minutes. That requires logs.

I peer into the pitch-black woods. Yeah, I don't want a campfire *that* badly. Even as a kid, I only went in the forest during the day. When I think of entering after dark, my heart picks up speed, and a memory flashes, someone grabbing my arm.

"Uh-uh, Samantha. Stay out of there at night. You know the rule."

Samantha. My grandfather.

He was right, though. That was the rule. Always had been.

Past dark, we all had to stick to the bonfire area between the cottages. No going in the forest. No going for night swims.

I remember that moment, standing on the edge, peering into the shadows, Grandpa holding my arm.

"What's in there?" I asked.

"The headless horseman."

I turned, and . . . was he smiling? It wasn't the smile I remember from later, the predatory one when he'd tell my mother he'd be happy to help with our bills—she just had to say she knew my father hadn't murdered Austin.

That day, his smile glittered, along with his blue eyes, but it was a mischievous glitter.

"The Headless Horseman from Sleepy Hollow," I say.

"*Paynes* Hollow. The original. Our horseman."

I tilt my head. "But if he's ours, why can't I go in the forest and see him? He won't hurt us."

"Mmm. Best not to take the chance. If you stay in the light, he'll know you're a Payne. In the forest?" He shrugs his wide shoulders. "We wouldn't want him to make a mistake."

"What would he do if he caught me?"

Grandpa leans down. "Have you forgotten the story?"

"He's supposed to be looking for a head, to replace his own. But how does he take them? His was supposed to have been blown off by a cannonball, but he's not going to use a cannon."

Grandpa laughs. "You've thought about this far too much, little girl."

"But also, in the story, we're never sure there's a horseman, right? That's what my dad says. It's probably Bram Bones, trying to scare Ichabod away."

"Your father is too much of a teacher. Always pulling stories apart and ripping out the magic. There's a horseman, and he's out there, looking for his head, ready to take yours instead."

"But mine wouldn't fit. He's a grown man—"

"What's going on here?" It was Mom, bearing down on us. "Did I hear you trying to scare her, Douglas?"

My grandfather straightened. "We were having a bit of fun. Samantha wanted to know why she can't go in the forest at night, and I was teasing about the horseman."

"But it doesn't make sense," I pressed. "A horseman would explain why I can't go in the forest, but not the lake. He isn't *in* the water."

"She's got you there, Dad," a voice said. It was my father, walking over, his arms loaded with wood.

Mom said, "We don't go in the lake at night, Sam, because we can't see. An undertow could grab you, and we'd never notice you going under. As for the forest, while most of the people who camp here are just ordinary people, some have problems. They can be dangerous, especially around children. We don't want you getting hurt."

They can be dangerous, especially around children.

I rub the back of my neck and shake off the memory. That's going to keep happening, isn't it? Memories of my life here. Memories of Dad. But it'll be worst at the beginning, as it all rushes back. Eventually, I'll settle in, those old memories played out.

For now, I need wood, and that means getting the old hatchet.

I have the keys in my pocket—there'd been an extra set in the cottage. I fish them out as I head for the shed.

To get there, I need to pass my uncle's cottage. My grandfather's and ours have a view of the shore, but my uncle's is farther back among the trees. My dad was the oldest, the heir. A ridiculously outdated concept to me, but not to my grandfather. He got the best cottage, and Dad got one almost as good. My uncle had to make do with one that only caught a sliver of lake view. As for Gail? She didn't get one at all. She was just a girl.

As I head toward Uncle Mark's cottage, I'm aware that I really should have brought a flashlight . . . or at least my cell phone. I can see—it's not fully dark—but once I pass into even the sparse trees, I need to keep my hand outstretched so I don't bash into anything. The thing I almost bash into is the cottage itself.

When my hand hits the porch railing, I stop short and frown. The trees never used to come up to the porch. But now saplings crowd in.

Under my fingers the wood is damp, and when I pull back, bits of wood come with them. I reach out and touch the railing. Rotting? I run my fingers over it. Yes, it's definitely rotting.

I remember Ben saying he was charged with maintaining my family cottage. I thought he specifically mentioned that one to clarify the devil's bargain my grandfather made—that Ben had to maintain the house where his brother's killer had lived. But from the looks of this porch, he'd meant exactly what he said. Ben had been hired to maintain *our* cottage. This one—once used by the son who is still alive—could rot.

I shiver and make my way along the porch. The shed is about fifty feet in that direction. When I reach the end of my uncle's cottage, I catch a break with the cloud cover, and I can see the shed ahead.

I take one more step, and something skitters inside the shed. I stop. The sound comes again, not from the dirt floor but the wooden walls. A squirrel racing into the eaves as it hears me coming.

I square my shoulders and continue on. I've spent six months in an apartment with so many mice that my cat had lost interest in catching them. I'm fine with a squirrel in the eaves.

I'm almost at the door when another sound comes, this one stopping me in my tracks.

A grunt and a shuffle. Someone moving.

I flip my back to the wall and press up against it. Then I scan the forest, as if I'm actually going to be able to see a person in the darkness.

I strain to listen, but everything's silent.

I didn't hear a person out here. As overgrown as my uncle's cottage was, the shed is one of Ben's responsibilities, and there's a ten-foot cleared gap all around it. I might not be able to see into the forest, but I can see what's right here, and it's just me and the shed.

I wait another minute, letting my heart rate slow. I must have imagined the grunt and the shuffling sound. Or I heard my own breathing and movement, which is embarrassing, but proof that I'm freaked out. Either way, I am very clearly alone.

Still, as I edge toward the door, I'm grateful there aren't any security cameras to watch me creeping along. Even when I reach it, I do a weird twist so I can undo the padlock without turning my back on the forest. I throw open the door and reach inside for the light switch.

Like the rest of the buildings, the shed is hooked up to electricity. I never thought much about that as a kid. I lived in a world where electricity was a given. But now I realize it would have cost a small fortune to hook up these buildings.

My ancestors might have liked to act like they were just regular folks with regular cottages, but my great-grandparents made sure to hook their new cottages up to electricity and install septic beds. I mean, we were Paynes. We weren't actually going to rough it.

I hit the switch and wait for the usual flicker before the light comes on. When nothing happens, I toggle the switch a few more times.

Darkness.

Well, shit.

Guess I really did need that flashlight.

I peer past the door, listening. Nothing. There's no one there and never was.

I open it wide, in hopes of letting in enough light to see the hatchet. The moon is in the right direction, and it's currently cloud-free, so I just need—

Something moves inside the shed.

My heart stops for two seconds, until I curse under my breath. Yes, something's moving . . . because I already heard a squirrel.

But this didn't sound like a squirrel.

My fingers tighten on the open door. Nothing of any size can be in here. The door was locked.

Still, how badly do I need that campfire? I'm just being stubborn, aren't I? I decided I wanted a fire, and if I forgot to prepare wood during daylight, that's my own fault, and I will rectify the mistake.

I shake my head. I'll have a bonfire tomorrow when Gail can join me. I'll spend part of the day building piles of tinder and logs. And I'll figure out why the light isn't working—

A grunt. A shuffle. Feet shuffling on the dirt floor.

From inside the shed.

That is not a squirrel.

I'm frozen, trying to peer through near darkness. My eyes adjust and—

There's something less than ten feet away. It moves toward me, and a figure takes shape, and my gaze rises to see a human head and dark liquid eyes glinting in the barest hint of light through the open door.

I wheel and run. My brain screams for me to look back and see what I'm running from, that I can't race blindly into the forest or I'll bash into—

My hands hit a tree, wrists snapping with the force. I spin around to face whatever's behind me.

Nothing's behind me. In the moonlight, the shed door stands open.

I blink at it. Then I cautiously move around the big tree until I can see my uncle's cottage and the road beyond.

I take one last look at the shed.

Then I run.

Seven

"There's someone in the shed," I say as I burst through the cottage door.

Gail looks up from the table, where I'd left her on her work call. "What?"

I struggle to catch my breath. "I went to get the hatchet. Ben said it was in the shed. There's someone in there."

She pushes the chair back as she rises. "In the shed?"

"Yes." I take a deep breath and slow down. "There's a person in the shed. A man, I think. Someone tall. That's all I could see. The light isn't working, and I forgot to grab a flashlight." I take another breath as I fight to calm down. "It must be a squatter. With no one living here, someone found a dry place to sleep."

"Was the door unlocked?"

"I used the key in the padlock, but I didn't check to see whether the hasp was fastened." I pause. "No, if someone shut the door from inside, the latch couldn't have been shut, and it was. There must be another way in." I fidget with the keys. "I definitely saw someone, Gail. I wasn't imagining it."

"I never said you were."

"I thought it was a squirrel moving around. Then I heard a grunt that sounded human and saw a human figure and eyes. That's when I ran."

"Thank God," she says, coming over to squeeze my forearms. "You're right. It's probably a squatter. But that doesn't mean he isn't dangerous. Living in the shed? What the hell is that caretaker doing?" She shakes her head.

"The question is what are *we* going to do," I say.

"Call the police, of course." She takes out her phone.

"Do we really want to do that?"

Her brows rise. "Uh, yes. There's a stranger living on our property."

I lower myself into a kitchen chair. "If you think that's the best way to handle it, go ahead. But my guess is that the guy's long gone, and the local law enforcement is Sheriff Smits, who is not going to appreciate being called out at this hour for a squatter."

"We met Sheriff Smits at the funeral, right? If he was there, he can't hold a grudge for what happened here."

"He was there because his wife used to be friends with my mom. I could never get a read on the sheriff. I just know that I don't want him writing me off as a hysterical city girl . . . and ignoring my call if I really need help." I pause and give myself a hard shake. "That's silly. You're right. We should call him."

Gail envelops me in a hug. "No, I get what you're saying. It's awful being back, but at least we can hole up here, shop in the next town and not need to interact with the locals. I'm sure most of them are sympathetic, but you don't want to take any chances. Not after that asshole caretaker."

I tense. "Ben—"

"—is the brother of Austin Vandergriff, and I'm being unkind. Uncharitable, too. I wouldn't say this to anyone else, Sam, but whatever Ben has gone through, his behavior toward you was unacceptable. I can understand him blaming you when he was a teenager, but he's a grown man now. My point is that if you don't want to call in the police for this, we won't call them."

She walks to the door. "We'll lock up tight, and keep our phones handy. I also . . ." She glances over her shoulder. "I brought a gun." Before I can react, she says, "I've had one for a few months. I didn't want to tell you, but remember when I was having problems with that client? I . . . may have downplayed it."

"What?"

She waves a hand. "It wasn't a big deal, but my coworkers said it was finally time for me to get a gun. So I did, and I brought it here." She glances toward the door. "It's in the trunk."

"I don't have any problem with you owning a gun, Gail. I do have a problem with you *needing* one, though."

"It's over. He moved out west."

"Okay, well, if you brought a gun, I'm going to suggest that maybe keeping it in your trunk kinda defeats the purpose."

Her lips quirk. "You think?"

"Nah, it's fine. If we're beset by angry townsfolk, we'll just ask them to wait while you find your car key."

She rolls her eyes. "My keys are right . . ." She turns and scans the counter. "Uh . . ."

I point to the ring, hung on the coatrack. "Bring your gun case inside. I just hope you don't have a key for that, too, or we're really in trouble."

She swats my shoulder, retrieves the keys, and heads out to her car.

I'll be sleeping in my old bed. I hadn't wanted to do that, but the only other option was my parents' bed. It's a two-bedroom cottage, built back at a time when you could expect all the kids to bunk down in one room, at least for the summer. I'd considered the sofa bed, but it wasn't comfortable even back then, and if I'm going to be here for a month, I'll need to get used to my old room. The problem isn't how difficult that will be—it's how easy it is. I settle in, and the sheets smell of the laundry detergent we always used. It's my actual old bedding, too—plaid flannel sheets with a quilt made by my grandmother.

I keep thinking of how much work my grandfather went through to reconstruct my childhood summer home, how long he'd been planning this. He must have had the linens professionally stored, and he even made sure they were washed in the right detergent after they were taken out of storage.

I'm going to stop mind-boggling at that, and instead, I'm going to find satisfaction in it. All that painstaking work, and it's not going to make a difference. He said he wanted me to remember "the truth," and maybe that's what all this is for. He's convinced that if he immerses me in sensory memory, I'll recall some critical fact.

Oh my God, I was wrong all along. I saw my dad burying a dead deer, and mistook it for Austin Vandergriff's body, which happened to also be on our property, murdered by a crazed camper! It was all a horrible coincidence!

At best, this re-creation is a desperate old man's delusion. At worst, it's a vindictive bastard trying to punish me from beyond the grave. Re-create the scenario so it'll all be too much, and I'll flee, to spend the rest of my life knowing I could have been rich . . . if only I'd been stronger.

If that's his plan and he's watching, he's going to be disappointed. I'll leave still knowing my dad is a killer but with the money to help my mother.

You lose, Grandpa.

I *will* pay a price in mental torment and emotional trauma, but I've *chosen* to pay it, and that makes a difference.

I slide into that bed, with my old stuffed cat Blinky, feeling those warm sheets, smelling the freshness of them, and I am a child again. Safe and loved and enjoying my perfect summer break.

Tears spring to my eyes, but I don't even stay awake long enough to cry. I'm in my old bed, and it is so damned easy just to close my eyes and drift off. Before I do, the last thing I hear is the memory of my parents talking in the kitchen, as they always did after I went to bed. Dad is saying something and Mom is laughing and the little girl in me smiles and cuddles down with her stuffed cat and falls asleep.

I startle awake to the sound of hooves pounding hard dirt. I wake, gasping, ears straining until I realize what I thought I heard and I have to laugh under my breath.

The headless horseman rides again.

I shake my head. Of course, there's no sound of hoofbeats once I'm awake. It's just me and Blinky and the ticking of my old alarm clock.

How many times had I woken in the night and sworn I'd heard hooves? My cheeks heat as I remember how I'd rush out to tell my parents.

I heard him. The horseman. I heard him outside.

Mom had always fretted at that. My grandfather's stories were clearly giving me nightmares. Dad said no, listen to my voice, look at my face. I *wanted* to see the horseman.

He was right, of course. Maybe it's because "The Legend of Sleepy Hollow" was such an old story, like a fairy tale, set too far in the past to be frightening. Maybe it's because the story is—let's face it—a little ridiculous. New schoolteacher comes to town and sets his hat on the girl from a wealthy family. His rival tells him the horseman story and then chases him and throws a pumpkin at him. Oh, I know, the ending is supposed to leave that open to interpretation, but even as a child, I never envisioned an actual horseman throwing his actual severed head. The implied explanation had been clear to me.

The Headless Horseman of Sleepy Hollow was as fake as a Scooby-Doo mystery. I wanted *our* horseman to be different.

I wanted the magic.

I smile to myself and walk into the living room. It's warm. Normally, we'd open the windows facing the lake, but I can't do that if there's someone squatting on the property.

Gail and I will check out the shed in the morning. If someone's been living in there, I can hope that once he realizes the property is occupied, he'll leave. If that seems unlikely, I'll need to tell Ben. That'll be awkward, but he *is* the caretaker. I'll only contact Sheriff Smits if the squatter seems dangerous.

I hate to drive someone off. That's such a rich-landowner thing to do. There's plenty of space. But Gail and I are two women surrounded by acres of forest, with no neighbors for a mile. We can't have a strange man camped a few hundred feet away.

We'll figure it out. For now, the windows stay shut, which is making for a very stuffy night. At the very least, we need to invest in fans.

I head for the front window. I'll crack it open enough to get a breeze and cool off. I'm reaching down to do that when I spot lights on the water.

I squint. I'm wearing glasses—I have contacts during the day. My glasses, though, are several prescriptions out of date. I can see lights on the water, but that's it. Boats? I squint more. No, I don't see anything floating on the surface. Even the lights seem to be under it.

Okay, that's weird. Lights *under* the water?

I briefly wonder whether I'm actually awake. After Dad died, I'd started sleepwalking. Mom kept finding me in his office at home, wandering around as if looking for him. Once she'd found me out back in his toolshed.

I'd gone to therapy then, with someone Gail had recommended, and my therapist had explained that the sleepwalking was a manifestation of my trauma. I haven't done it in over a decade, but every time I see something questionable at night, that's my first thought.

I peer at the lights. It must be something bioluminescent under the water. I'll need to look that up in the morning. For now, it's kind of cool. It'd probably be even cooler if I were wearing my proper prescription. Or maybe it wouldn't be. Put on my contacts, and I might realize I'm just seeing reflections from light pollution.

I pull open the window. And the stench of something dead blasts in on the breeze. I fall back, hand to my nose. Then I quickly shut the window.

I'd forgotten that part of cottage life—the smell of decomposing critters. Of course, I used to get that in my apartment, too, when Lucille would actually bother to kill a mouse and leave it under the sofa. Dead mouse, though, smells a whole lot less than dead deer or dead raccoon.

I shiver. There must be a carcass between here and the lake. Add cleaning that up to my to-do list. One advantage to having been med-school-bound is that I'm not freaked out handling a dead animal. I used to find them fascinating, crouching to examine them and identify what I could. My own childhood anatomy labs.

I stand at the window as sweat dribbles down my temple. Lights dance under the water, and I really do hope it's not a trick of the light. It's so pretty. I'm tempted to slip outside and get closer, dead-critter stink and all. Except there's more than a dead critter out there. I don't want to bump into the squatter.

I sigh, take one last look at the lights, and head back to bed.

"Do not open the window," Gail says, by way of greeting, as I walk into the kitchen the next morning, drawn by the smell of coffee.

"Still stinks out there?"

Her brows rise.

I yawn and take a mug from the cupboard. "I got up last night and made the mistake of opening a window for a little air. Something's dead outside. I'll clean it up."

"Isn't that a job for the caretaker?"

"Nah, I've got it." I pour a coffee from the pot. "We might need to do something about the headless horseman, though."

Another brow lift.

I add cream and sugar to my coffee before saying, "I heard him last night."

A moment's pause, and then she bursts out laughing. "I remember you hearing him every summer, and it was adorable. Oh! There was that one time when you talked me into staying up half the night listening for him."

"And you heard him, too."

"Uh, yeah . . . About that . . ."

"You were humoring me, weren't you?"

"Well, no. Not exactly." She leans against the counter. "Remember all those times you said I smelled like skunk? It wasn't skunk."

"You smoked weed as a teen? I am *shocked*." I stir my coffee. "It does explain the smell, though. I was seriously worried for your hygiene. Or the possibility of an illicit relationship with a skunk."

She throws a pot holder at me.

"As for the hoofbeats," I say, "I woke up thinking I heard them and then nearly laughed loud enough to wake you. I was a weird kid."

"You were adorable. Still are."

"You're just saying that because I offered to clean up a rotting animal."

She raises her mug, and I clink mine against it.

"I know you don't do breakfast," I say, "but I will be cooking eggs. Right after I clean up that mess."

"You do know that most people would put that off until *after* they ate?"

"It's better to do it on an empty stomach."

She makes a face.

I gulp half my coffee and set the mug on the counter. "Step one, clean up the mess. Step two, make breakfast. Step three, work. And at some point this morning, I want to check out the shed."

"Can I bring my gun?"

"If you promise not to point it at me."

She gives me a thumbs-up as I pull on my boots. Then I grab a garbage bag.

"What about a spade?" she says. "That'd be in the shed, right?"

I pause. "Shit. Yes. So maybe we move up the shed investigation. Let me take a look at what we're dealing with first. If it's a small animal, the bag will be enough."

I rifle through our open boxes until I find disposable gloves. I snap on a pair and swing open the front door.

"Oh God." Gail slaps both hands to her face. "Go! Quickly!"

I shake my head, step out on the front porch, and stop.

There's something on the steps. Something red and pink and brown.

"Hey!" Gail calls as I start forward. "Shut the door!"

I keep walking, my gaze fixed on that lump. Flesh. That's what I'm seeing. Fur and flesh and bone.

"Hey!" Gail says behind me. Then, "What the hell?"

I don't know what it is. A dead animal. That's for sure. But it's not . . . Something about it . . .

What the hell am I seeing?

I stop short. There's a head. A rabbit head. Staring at me. But it's . . .

I struggle to process. All the parts are there—a head, legs, a body—but it's not making sense. Then I see why. The rabbit has been ripped apart, every limb and the head torn off, but then . . .

The torso is splayed on its back, belly ripped open, organs arranged around it. The legs all protrude from inside that open chest cavity, paws sticking up. And in the middle is the head, perched there, staring at me with empty eye cavities.

My mind rockets into the past, to a squirrel, carved up and left for me—

I let out a small whimper, arms wrapping around myself as I shake.

A noise sounds behind me. I don't even need to look to see what it is.

My aunt, retching her coffee onto the porch.

Eight

I make the call to Sheriff Smits. Gail is in shock, sitting on the sofa, her legs drawn up. When she realizes I'm on the telephone, she says, "I can do that," but I pretend not to see her. I need to do this.

I can't let her see how that dead rabbit affected me. I'm shaking inside, a quivering, sobbing little girl who just found a squirrel in pieces and knows she can't tell anyone, knows she needs to bury it before anyone thinks she would do such a thing. Everyone knew she liked poking around dead things.

I could tell Gail what happened all those years ago, but what good would it do? She'd only be more determined to get me off this property, and it's not as if the same person can be responsible. I need to shush that terrified child and deal with it.

I don't even speak to Sheriff Smits. It's an answering machine—an actual old-fashioned machine.

"Sheriff Smits," I say. "It's Sam Payne, up at the Payne place. We arrived last night. Someone . . . left something on my front steps. A prank, I think, but it's a mutilated animal, so I wanted to report it. I also think someone might be living in our shed. The two could be connected, of course. If you get a chance, could you swing by? My aunt and I would appreciate it." I leave my phone number. Then I hang up.

* * *

Sheriff Smits arrives just over an hour later. I meet him at the parking pullout before the road reaches our cottage. Gail has a video-chat appointment, and honestly, I'm relieved to be doing this on my own. Yesterday with Ben proved that she's too ready to jump to my defense. I don't want the locals of Paynes Hollow thinking I need protection from them.

"Sheriff," I say as I walk over, hand out. "Good to see you again."

He shakes my hand. "I heard about your grandfather's will. Hell of a thing. You and your mom deserve this place."

"Thank you. I intend to get it. For both of us."

"Good."

He starts to say something else, but then someone climbs out of the passenger side.

"You met my daughter, Josie," Smits says.

"That's Deputy Josie," she says with a smirk, tipping her wide-brimmed hat. "Pleased to meet you, ma'am."

Her father rolls his eyes affectionately. "She likes to act as if she's just helping her old man out, and didn't spend four years taking criminology in college."

"Nice," I say, extending my hand.

Smits snorts. "*Nice* would have been her accepting the job she was offered with the feds instead of coming back here to a post she could have gotten out of high school."

"Ignore him," Josie says. "My boss feels the need to make sure everyone knows how well-educated his deputy is, and my dad just likes to brag. Good to see you again, Sam. I was planning to check in later today, bring the welcome pie Mom baked."

"Sorry to call you out," I say.

"Not at all. I just wish you didn't need to. Your message said someone left a dead animal on your doorstep."

I nod and lead them over. "It's under that," I say, pointing at a garbage bag stretched on the ground, weighed down with rocks, after a turkey vulture swooped in. I put on gloves and reach down for the plastic. "It's a rabbit."

"Seems to be a bumper year for them," Smits says. "We've had them all over the roads. There was a coyote cleanup early this spring, and that's cut back on natural predators."

He's gently telling me that a dead rabbit outside my cottage isn't unusual. I don't comment. I just gently pull back the bag.

"Yikes," Josie says, her hand flying over her nose and mouth. "That's a mess."

"Something tore that rabbit up good," her dad says, hunkering down.

Some*thing*. Not someone. Between the turkey vultures and the impromptu covering, it's no longer obvious how the body had been arranged. It just looks like a dead rabbit, which settles the butterflies in my gut but doesn't help convince the sheriff.

I tell him what it had looked like.

"Huh," he says.

"My aunt can confirm that," I say. "We should have gotten a photo, but we weren't exactly thinking about that."

"I can imagine." He rises from his crouch, rubs his mouth and looks around. "Well, it's definitely not a natural death."

You think? I bite my tongue and keep my expression neutral, but Josie gives a soft snort.

"Could have been predation," he says. "You have a couple of bald eagle nests on your property. Nice to see them in the area again. They might rip a rabbit up like that. Maybe leave the pieces in a way that makes it seem like a deliberate arrangement."

I open my mouth, but he beats me to it with, "Or it could have been deliberately arranged, as you said."

I shove my hands in my pockets. "After what my father did, I wouldn't blame anyone for not wanting any Paynes around."

He tilts his hat back and scratches his forehead. "I think folks are good at understanding that one bad apple might spoil a barrel, but that doesn't apply to people. All I've heard is sympathy for what you went through." He looks at me. "No one blames you, Sam. At all."

Guess he hasn't spoken to Ben Vandergriff.

He turns to Josie. "I'd like you to swing by once a day, check on Sam and her aunt."

"That's not nec—" I begin.

"Got it," she says. "At the very least, having the local police coming and going will make people think twice about harassing you. Or trespassing on the property. You said you thought someone was in your shed?"

"Someone *was* in there. Last night, I went to get a hatchet and saw him."

Her head snaps up, as if I have her full attention. "*Him?* A man?"

"The size suggested a man. I heard a grunt and the shuffle of feet on the dirt floor, and then I saw a figure. I took off. I don't know whether he chased me. I don't think so."

Smits mutters under his breath. "Useless son of a bitch."

"Dad . . ." Josie's voice warns that we can hear him.

"You know who it was?" I ask.

"No," Smits says. "I mean your dam—your caretaker. Have you met him?"

"Uh, yeah. Ben Vandergriff. Austin's . . ." I swallow. "Older brother."

"That was your grandfather's way of making amends, I guess. The kid should be grateful, but instead, he does a half-assed job, and now you have a squatter living in your shed."

"Ben's thirty years old, Dad," Josie says. "He's not a kid."

"Then he should stop acting like one." Smits exhales. "I know I sound awful, snapping about a young man who lost his brother, but that boy wields his family tragedy like a baseball bat, hitting anyone who comes into range." He looks at me. "I hope he was decent to you."

I go to say something neutral, but my expression must answer for me, because Smits shakes his head. "He was an ass, wasn't he?"

"Dad . . ." Josie says. To me, she says, "Ben's fine. His bark is much worse than his bite. The point right now is that you have someone living in your shed and you walked in on them at night." She shivers. "I don't think I could have stayed here after that."

"I have my aunt, who has a gun." I quickly add, "A legal handgun in a locked case."

Josie taps her hip. "I've got a gun, too, and I still wouldn't have stayed."

"I'm not sure the man is living there. That's just a guess."

Her hard look says this isn't the point, and I have to bite my cheek to keep from laughing. Now that I know who she is, I keep seeing the little girl who tagged along and tried so hard to keep up. Having her giving me shit is adorable . . . which is not the reaction she wants.

I nod solemnly. "We just didn't want to call the police our first night here."

"And seem like a couple of nervous ladies from the city?" Josie shakes her head. "Don't think that. Please. If you're concerned, call. This isn't the big city. Peak tourist season is past, and things have slowed right down. No drowning scares. No campers reporting strange noises in the night. No hikers who didn't make their rendezvous."

"No false alarms from city folks," Smits says.

"We are, however, fully trained officers," Josie says. "We can handle an intruder, and we should be the ones handling it. If you're worried we'll overreact, don't be. Out here, we know that whoever is in your shed is probably just a drifter passing through. We'll act accordingly. Now remind me where that shed is, and let's take a look."

The shed is empty. We're all in there with flashlights. Josie spent a couple of minutes fussing with the shed light switch, until her father grumbled again about Ben's incompetency, and she abandoned it.

There's no one in the shed. Nor is there any sign that someone has been squatting in there.

"I definitely saw someone," I say. "I heard them and then I looked up and saw eyes and the outline of a figure in the dark."

"You didn't have a flashlight?" Smits asks.

My cheeks heat. "No. City-girl move, I know. I decided to have a bonfire, realized I needed wood, which meant I needed a hatchet . . . so I tramped out here without a flashlight. I have completely forgotten everything I knew about cottage life."

"It'll come back," he says. "But yes, always have a flashlight. Even in the daytime, these woods can get dark."

"As for wood," Josie says, "there's a place just down the road. The kids sell firewood at the end of the drive, but if you go to the house and ask, I'm sure they'll cut you a deal on enough to get through the month."

"Thanks. Gail will check it out. I'm pretty much stuck here."

When she frowns, I lift my leg to show the ankle monitor. Then I realize how that might look—especially to cops—and hurry on. "It's part of the will."

"Your grandfather—" Josie begins, staring at the monitor. "That's messed up." She pulls back. "Sorry. He's still your grandfather. I shouldn't judge."

"Oh, it's plenty messed up," I say. "But I am determined to win this last little game of his. My mom really needs—" I clear my throat. "Anyway, I can only leave the property for an hour, so I'm probably not going to take the chance."

"You need anything, you call Josie," Smits says.

"We're fine. Gail isn't under any restrictions. But yes, we will get that firewood, and we will start carrying flashlights—or at least make sure I always have my phone with its light."

"About this fellow," Smits says. "You said you looked up and saw his eyes. Any idea how tall he was?"

"Maybe six feet?"

"Eye color?"

I remember those eyes, dark and liquid, reflecting like an animal's. I can't say that. "It didn't register. Sorry."

"Don't be sorry. Just be sure to keep the shed locked, and tell the Vandergriff boy to do the same."

I don't say that the door seemed to have been locked. I probably should, for Ben's sake, but I can't give Smits any more reason to think I imagined it.

I'm sure that's what he does think already. Just like he thinks the dead rabbit was killed by a predator. I really should have taken a picture. By the time he saw it, the poor creature was nothing but a jumble of guts and body parts. Had I found it like that, I'd never have called him.

Had I found it like that, I would never have flashed back to—

I wrap my arms around myself to stop my shaking.

I didn't know what to expect from Sheriff Smits. All I recall of him is a taciturn man who reminded me of a cowboy, rangy and rawboned, with his sheriff's Stetson. Even that impression fades behind the overwhelming memory of him behind a table at the station, his elbows on it as he leans forward to get down to my level. I'm shivering uncontrollably despite the summer heat, and Mom's there with her arms around me as Smits asks me to tell him what I saw.

I suppose, looking back now, he'd been kind, gently and patiently walking me through my statement. To me, though, he'd been huge and terrifying.

Now he is again being kind and patient, but I know he's humoring me. So I can't admit the door was latched—and probably locked. In the daylight, I can see that there are no holes big enough for the intruder to have entered through. But I know what I saw, and I saw a person.

"Dad?" Josie says from across the shed.

He clears his throat meaningfully. She rolls her dark eyes. "I'm not calling you 'Sheriff' in front of Sam. That's for the tourists."

He grumbles but walks over to where she's bent, shining her flashlight beam on the dirt floor.

"Huh," he says.

"A footprint," she says as I come over. "Large enough to be a tall adult male."

I crouch where she's indicating, and see with relief that she's *not* humoring me, pretending a smudge in the dirt could be a print. It's a very clear footprint.

"It's from a bare foot," I say.

"Hmm," Smits says.

Josie says, "Yeah, that's not good. A boot could be Ben. A shoe could mean someone was poking around, looking for something to steal. Or just passing through, wanting a place for the night. A bare foot is more troubling."

"But it is summer," I say. "Bare feet aren't that unusual. And he could have removed his shoes to sleep."

She wags her flashlight at me. "Don't downplay this. Yes, you make a good point, but we don't want you presuming your intruder is just a hapless camper . . . and finding out otherwise."

"I know. A lack of footwear could suggest mental issues. Gail is a social worker."

"Ah. Good. That helps." Josie straightens. "So someone *was* in here. Hopefully, they're long gone, but you do need to speak to Ben."

"Tell him to get off his ass and earn his pay," Smits says.

"Dad . . ." Josie says.

"Don't 'Dad' me. That boy is paid very well to take care of this place, and what does he do? Lets two of the cottages rot and leaves the shed open for squatters."

"I think the cottages rotting was my grandfather's idea," I say.

Josie passes me a grateful look. There's clearly friction here, between Josie, her father, and Ben. Are Josie and Ben a couple? And her father disapproves?

"Maybe so," Smits says. "But you still need to ride his ass and tell him to do his job. And don't look at me that way, Jo. Every other kid in this dead-end town gets out as soon as they can, and he stays. Not a lick of ambition, that one."

"I'm right here, Dad."

His brows rise in question.

She continues, "Uh, your daughter? Who also stayed in this 'dead-end town'?"

He waves a hand. "That's different. You left and got your degree and chose to come back. You have a future. You're just taking a breather while you figure out what you want to do."

She rolls her eyes at me. "Sure, that's it. I'm just training for my big move to the city."

"You are," Smits says.

"Well, since I *am* in training, let me take photos of this."

Nine

The Smitses are leaving. Sheriff Smits insisted on doing an hour-long walk of the property, which I begged off from to get some work done. They didn't find anything, but Josie still promises to do a daily sweep, over my objections. After her dad is in the truck, she comes back to where I'm outside the cottage, watching them go.

"You okay if I still bring that pie later?" she says. "I know you're working."

"I don't have set hours. I just need to get my time in. Pie would be great."

Her face lights up. "Mom makes the best."

"I remember that."

"Good. Then I will be here with pie, which is totally a good-neighbor-plus-business call and not because I'm desperate to talk to another woman under thirty."

I choke out a laugh. "Your dad wasn't exaggerating then? About all our generation leaving?"

"He was not." She leans one hip against a tree. "The town is fine economically—in the summer, we're booming more than ever. But if all the young people leave . . . ?" She shrugs. "We get a lot of retirees moving in these days. It's not the same."

"I can imagine."

"Even the tourists are aging up. People our age can't afford time off work plus vacation expenses."

"I hear you. This will be my first getaway since college. And I'm still working."

"We get some young families," she says, "but those moms aren't exactly hanging out at the bar, chatting up socially starved local girls. So, if I come on too strong, let me know. I just . . ." Another shrug. "I probably remember you better than you remember me. So I may get a little overeager."

"No worries." I wave at my ankle monitor. "With this, I won't be hanging out in the bars either, but I could use some company."

"Good. I can provide that. But yes, the under-thirty-five crowd here is pretty much me and Ben, and he still treats me like I'm twelve, so it does get lonely." She lowers her voice. "And that was an awkward segue to the subject of Ben. Please don't listen to my dad. Ben's a good caretaker. I don't know the details of his deal with your grandfather, but even if Ben resents it, he does his job. The shed was an oversight."

Guilt strums through me, and I hedge with, "I'm not even sure he left the shed open. Gail or I might have."

"I'll mention that to my dad. Get him off Ben's back." She glances over at the car. "I should go. I'll see you this afternoon. I really am looking forward to having you back, Sam. I have good memories of those times, chasing after the older kids, especially you and—" She stops short and flushes. "Well, you know."

I nod somberly. "I do. I'll see you this afternoon."

I have good memories of those times, chasing after the older kids, especially you and—

I know what Josie had been about to say, and why she'd cut herself off.

Especially you and . . . Austin Vandergriff.

Ben's little brother.

How much does Josie remember? How much did she understand back then? Not enough, I realize.

And I'm glad of that.

To her—to everyone—Austin Vandergriff had been my friend. Always part of our group of kids, hanging out with me, always with me.

But it hadn't been like that.

It hadn't been like that at all.

I work alongside Gail until Josie comes by late in the afternoon. Then we both take a break. Gail seems ready to leave us alone, but Josie insists she join us for pie and coffee, and the three of us have a good time, settling in and maneuvering around awkward first-time conversation to find points of contact and relax into them.

Before Josie goes, she suggests coming by at the same time tomorrow, doing her round of the property and then we can finish off the pie. I happily agree. Josie isn't the only one starved for company her own age. When I moved away from Chicago, I left behind all my college and work friends. In Syracuse, I hadn't had time to make new ones—too busy with work and Mom, letting Gail fill the friendship gap. But it's nice to chat with someone who isn't related to me, and when I say I'll look forward to seeing her tomorrow, I'm not just being polite.

After Josie leaves, it's shopping time. I've made up a list for meals. And that's when Gail and I have our next fight.

"No, I'm not coming along," I say. "I don't want to take a chance leaving the property."

"And I don't want to leave you here with some barefoot drifter sleeping in the shed."

"There was no sign that he's been sleeping in the shed."

"What about the other cottages? Did they check those?"

I pause. "No one thought of it."

"Right. So he could be in there. I'm not leaving until we're sure he's gone."

"Then we're going to starve, Gail, because I can't risk being two minutes late getting back and have Ben Vandergriff jump to call Ms. Jimenez, and I lose out on ten million dollars because we got stuck behind a tractor."

Her mouth firms in a hard line. "This business with the Vandergriff boy is ridiculous."

"Ben isn't a boy. He's only six years younger than you."

She continues as if I hadn't spoken. "I want to explain the situation to the lawyer. You are trapped here, and your jailer is a man who apparently holds you responsible for something your father did."

"What my father did was *murder* his brother." I catch her flinch. "Sorry."

"No, you're right. I'm not saying Ben doesn't have a reason to hate our family, but neither of you should be forced into this situation. I will speak to Ms. Jimenez."

"And get Ben fired? Lose the pension his dad receives if Ben sticks this out?"

"Well, maybe Ben should have thought of that before he was rude to you."

I laugh. I can't help it. "Rudeness is not a capital offense, Gail. If I complain to Ms. Jimenez, then I seem like exactly the spoiled brat Ben expects. And if I cost him his payout, he has more reason to hate me . . . and retaliate."

"So we're stuck with him?"

I squeeze her arm. "Let's see how this goes. As for the groceries, it's better that you leave while it's still early and full light."

She hesitates.

"Even if I didn't see anyone in the shed, it doesn't mean no one else is on the property, Gail. It's three hundred acres with a mile of beachfront. Those piddly signs at the gate aren't stopping anyone who really wants to hike or camp here."

"We should start patrolling."

"And if we find someone? We tell them it's private property, and they say so what?" I shake my head. "Let's leave patrols and possible confrontations to the armed deputy."

"I think you should learn how to use my gun."

"Okay."

Her eyes narrow. "Don't humor me, Sam."

"I'm not. I agree. For now, while you go shopping, I'll stay locked in the cottage with the windows shut and the curtains pulled. Worst case?" I waggle my phone. "We have excellent cell service here. I'm not stranded in the middle of nowhere."

She exhales. "Fine. I'll go. But you're staying inside."

"Only if you promise to bring back s'more fixings and have a bonfire with me tonight."

"Deal."

Gail has been gone for almost an hour when a footfall hits the front steps. My head jerks up from my laptop. I didn't hear her car drive in.

A floorboard on the deck creaks. I get up to go meet her, help with the groceries. Then I pause.

I promised to be safe. That means not rushing out when I can't see through the window—the perils of having shut the curtains.

I wait for the sound of her key in the door. When it doesn't come, my heart speeds up, and I pull out my phone to check my friend tracker. It spins for a second. Then I see her emoji at the gas station in Paynes Hollow.

I tilt my head. Had I really heard someone out there? A footfall and a creaking board aren't exactly proof of life. I'd been working away, oblivious to my surroundings. Maybe I just heard a random noise.

A board creaks again.

Someone is there.

On the porch. *Not* knocking on the door. Just standing there.

I rise and creep toward the front window. I'm hoping to sneak a peek, but Gail pulled both the blind and the curtains. Making sure no one can see me alone inside also means I can't see anyone on the porch.

Yet I can tell someone is there. A shadow darkens the blind, visible only from this close.

I swallow and back up to the kitchen, where I take a knife and wrap my fingers around the handle. Then I return to the window and ease the side of the curtain until I can see.

A man stands on my porch, with his back to me. All I can make out is what looks like a dark gray T-shirt. Then he turns, and I fall back, dropping the blind and banging into a chair.

"Samantha?" he calls.

I pause. "Ben?"

"Open the damn door. I don't have all day."

I have the door halfway open before realizing I'm still gripping the knife. I go to put it down . . . and then reconsider. Just because it's Ben Vandergriff doesn't mean it's okay.

I think about the person in the shed. The dead rabbit. Intellectually, Ben Vandergriff makes an excellent suspect, and yet my gut says no. He doesn't match the figure in the shed.

I tug open the door, and his gaze goes straight to the knife in my lowered hand. "I hope you're not trying to cut vegetables holding it like that."

"You ever think of knocking?"

"I did knock." He leans toward the screen. "You know what I didn't do, though? Leave the fucking shed open."

I push the screen door, making him step back as I join him on the porch. "I never said you did."

"Yeah? Tell that to Smits. Guy called to tear a strip out of me."

I set the knife on the railing. "I never said you left it open. In fact, I told Josie that I didn't think you did. I'm sorry if the sheriff called you. I'll straighten that out."

"Better yet, don't be calling Smits when you get spooked. Taking care of this place is my job."

My brows shoot up. "One, you never left me any contact information. Two, you made it clear what your duties are and that you don't do more. Three, I did not 'get spooked.' There was someone in the shed—there's still a footprint. I didn't call the sheriff after that either. I called him after I found a dismembered rabbit stacked in front of the stairs."

His face screws up. "What?"

I explain about the rabbit. When I finish, he shoves his hands into his pockets and rocks back, muttering under his breath.

"It was deliberate," I say. "By the time Sheriff Smits arrived, it'd been disturbed—by a turkey vulture and then me covering it to protect it from turkey vultures. So it looked like a random pile of parts. Sheriff Smits thought it was a bald eagle kill."

Ben snorts. "Craig Smits is a cop, not a forest ranger. Eagles pick up rabbits and carry them off. You'd find blood and fur. Maybe not even that much. We had coyotes until the hunt, but there could still be a few. They don't kill like that either."

"The rabbit was dismembered. And not eaten."

"Hmph." He looks around. "You hear anything last night?"

"No."

"But you saw someone in the shed."

"Yes. There aren't any signs of squatting, though. Just a bare footprint." I peer up the road. "Gail mentioned checking out the other cottages. Make sure someone isn't staying in them."

Another grunt. Then he starts down the stairs. "Come on." A pause. "Bring the knife."

I can't tell whether he's joking, and I don't care. I grab the knife.

Ten

Ben heads to my uncle's cottage. It's down the lane by the shed, and I suspect he'll want to divert to the shed first. He does, and I follow, watching as he checks the lock and heads inside. He flicks the light switch on and off.

"That wasn't working last night either," I say.

He doesn't even grunt an answer to that. Just takes out his keychain and turns on a penlight. I walk to where I saw the print, and I point at it, saying, "Here's the footprint," but he only shines the flashlight around the rest of the shed, searching and saying nothing. Then he finally makes it over to where I am, as if getting there on his own. He looks at the print. Then he puts his own foot beside it.

"Larger than yours," I say. "What size are you, nine? That would make these . . . Ten, eleven maybe?"

He finally deigns to speak. "I was just showing you that it wasn't me."

"I never thought it was."

He looks at the door. "You say it was latched?"

I nod, realize he can't see that with his light shining the other way, so I say, "Yes. I put the key in and turned it, but I can't say for sure it was locked. Definitely latched. I know that means someone couldn't get in unless they were locked in. I didn't see any other entry points."

He walks to a spot and kicks at the dirt. When the light passes over it, I see a hole dug under the wall.

"Concrete's crumbling here." He points his light directly at the hole now. "Mentioned it to your grandfather. He never replied."

"That looks small, though. I'm not sure even I could crawl through."

The light shines up to my face. "You arguing *against* an explanation for how someone got in with the latch on?"

"No, I'd just rather . . ." I try not to fidget. "I know I saw someone, and I'd rather have a possibility that proves it."

"Don't need to prove it to me. You're the boss. You say you saw someone? I follow up." He rises and heads for the door. "I'll fill that hole and replace the lock."

"If you need to buy anything, I have money in the cottage."

"There's a petty cash account with the lawyer. I'll bill for repair time. I need authorization for any big jobs, like hiring someone to repair the concrete. But I can handle this."

He walks out. I follow, and he heads to my uncle's cottage.

"I was told not to touch this," Ben calls back as he jabs a finger at the cottage. "Not this one and not your grandfather's." He continues to the porch. "His exact words were that I wasn't being paid to maintain them, which implies I could have, on my own time. Didn't bother."

"I don't blame you."

His shoulders tense. Okay, not the right thing to say. He isn't explaining so I can absolve him. He's just getting it in before I can make a Smits-style sarcastic comment.

I follow him onto the porch, and a board cracks under my weight.

"Watch your step," he says without turning.

I narrow my eyes at him, well aware that he can't see it. Then I get my first look at the cottage.

"It's boarded up," I say.

"Yeah. Years ago, people heard they were empty and decided that meant free lodgings. I got permission to board them up."

"Even ours?"

He paces along the porch, checking the boards, and I think he isn't going to answer. Then he says, "The windows on yours were boarded.

Door had to be left open so I could clean it. I installed a few locks before I found one that kept people out."

"The . . . redecorating," I say carefully. "Putting it all back the way it was . . ."

"Not me," he grunts. "The place was empty when I started working here. All I did was keep it clean. Then, the day after your grandfather died, I got a message from the lawyer to let a truck in. They must have put everything back."

He passes me and heads back to the ground level. Then he circles the cottage, tugging at boards and peering at the nails holding them on.

"The boards are secure," I say, "and the nails are old. That means no one has pried them off and reattached them."

"I can open it up later, take a look inside, but I don't see any sign that someone's been in here."

"Agreed."

Without a word, he heads back up the road. We pass my family's cottage and continue on to my grandfather's. As soon as we draw near, I see it's in the same condition as my uncle's. The porch is rotted, but the windows and door are securely boarded.

This time, I wait as Ben circles. Then I hear a curse from the back and go around to find him pulling back the branches of a bush that's grown up against the house. Under that bush, a window has been broken, boards pried off.

"That's not recent," I say. "Not if the bush grew over it."

"I haven't checked in a while," Ben says. "It's been years since anyone even tried breaking in."

I realize he thinks I was blaming him for not seeing it. "I mean that no one is in there now."

He still yanks the bushes off. Then he clears the broken glass, grabs the sill and heaves himself up and through. When he disappears inside, I move closer. It's the spare bedroom, with a long window low enough for me to see inside. Or it *would* let me see inside if the interior weren't pitch black.

I really do need to start carrying around my phone. Or ask Gail to grab me one of those keychain penlights like Ben has.

Speaking of Ben, he's vanished into that darkness. I consider. Then I check that the sill is clear of glass and climb through. When I'm in, enough light filters through for me to see.

The spare room is as I remember it. Except, unlike our cottage, it's been left to rot exactly as it was. There are two twin beds, with moldering quilts. Dust covers everything, and I stifle a sneeze as I walk in.

It looks like it did that last summer, right down to the paperbacks piled on the nightstand, left there for guests by my grandmother. I bend to read the titles: *Eat Pray Love, Shopaholic, Twilight, The Time Traveler's Wife.*

All popular titles from around the time we were last here. My grandparents never came back. They hadn't been at the cottage when my father . . . When it happened. They never spent the whole summer—the humidity was too much for my grandmother's arthritis—and they'd been home in Syracuse. This was how it looked when they left earlier that month . . . and they'd never returned.

I'm standing there, staring at that stack of books, when I remember something and ease open the nightstand drawer. There's a flashlight inside. All the cottages have them in the bedrooms, for the frequent power outages. I'm sure the batteries are long since corroded, but I flick the switch and then startle when the light comes on.

I carefully shine the beam around the room, half expecting the light to flicker out with any movement, but it stays on, and I head into the next room.

All three cottages have the same floor plan. There's no bedroom hall—just the two bedrooms and bathroom coming off the main room, which stretches from the kitchen at one end, through the dining room, to the living room. I enter just past the kitchen and look around for Ben. There's no sign of him, and I have a wild image of being trapped in here as he slipped out to board up that one open window. That's a testament to how spooked I am, however much I'm trying to hide it.

A light moving in the bathroom leads me to Ben, and he walks out, not seeming the least bit surprised to see me there.

"Nothing," he says. "Someone obviously broke in, but it was years ago. I don't even see tracks in the dust. Don't see anything obviously missing either. Must have just been looking around." He walks past me. "Got a lot of that a decade ago. All that urban-spelunking shit."

"People exploring abandoned buildings."

"Yeah. With the history here . . . ?" He trails off with a shrug. "But it was a fad. They lost interest years ago."

He heads back toward the spare room. I shine my light around. It lands on the door to my grandparents' room. I glance toward Ben again. Then I push open the half-shut door. Footprints in the dust show where he'd walked in for a few steps, looked around, and then left.

I'm about to do the same when I spot an open book on the right-hand nightstand. My grandmother's side of the bed. I smile and walk over to see what she was reading. Old-school historical romance with a classic clinch cover, a busty maiden in the arms of a half-dressed pirate. That makes me laugh softly under my breath, old memories sweeping back, me tracking down Gail to find her in the forest, devouring one of my grandmother's romance novels. How she'd turn bright red when I caught her and stammer some explanation about liking history.

I reach to pick up the novel, my smile turning to a grin as I plot where I'll leave this book and what Gail will say. But when I step toward it, my foot falls and I pitch forward, my knee knocking hard into the nightstand as I yelp.

By the time Ben arrives, I'm standing on one foot, cradling my knee.

"There's a broken board," I say. "I was grabbing that book."

His flashlight beam lands on the cover. "Interesting choice."

"I like pirates. Especially half-naked ones."

"Not judging." His light sweeps down. "Huh."

"What?" I follow his beam and see that I was wrong. The board isn't broken. It's missing.

The light moves on, and when he gives another "Huh," I track the beam to a second removed board at the foot of the bed. He carefully skirts it as he rounds to my grandfather's side.

"Two more here," he says.

"Someone looking for treasure," I say. "Or more of my grandmother's romance novels. I always did wonder where she stashed them. Gives a whole new meaning to pirate booty." I pause. "Well, they already gave a whole new meaning to pirate booty, but that's another story."

He doesn't even crack a smile. Just crouches to shine his beam into one of the holes. I do the same with another board. Underneath the wooden plank, there's just a gap with joists before the solid layer of the structural floor.

"There's a crawl space underneath," I say.

"Yes. I know. I'm the caretaker."

"I just mean that I don't know what someone would be looking for under the floorboards. Any storage would be down below."

"That's hidden and locked." He rises and goes into the bathroom. I follow, and he pushes aside the moldering mat to show the crawl space hatch. There's a built-in lock, just like the one in our cottage.

"What's down there?" I ask.

"No idea. I don't have the key." He rises from checking it. "And before you ask, I did mention it to your grandfather. Just like I mentioned clearing all this shit out before it rotted. He never answered."

"I wouldn't have asked why you never went down there," I say. "I know Sheriff Smits . . ."

I trail off, not sure how to finish that.

"Smits thinks I'm a lazy kid who can't bother doing more than I absolutely have to." He brushes past me. "I don't much care what he thinks of me. We had run-ins when I was a teen, and that fixed his opinion for eternity."

"Does anyone know . . . ?" I struggle for the right words. "The, uh, terms of your employment."

"No one's business. I told you because it's your business, being the new owner." He slows, as if realizing something. "It's between us. Smits is the only one who expects me to be grateful for my job here and, like I said, his opinion isn't changing."

"Okay."

He's moving fast, and I need to jog to keep up as he heads back into the spare room. When he reaches the window, he turns, considering before saying, "That stuff with Smits, back when I was a kid, it had nothing to do with my job here." Another pause. "Also nothing violent. Just angry teenager shit."

"Got it." I glance back. "But about that crawl space. I have the key for ours, and it probably works in that one. Should we open it?"

"For what?"

"See what someone might have been searching for."

He snorts. "Knock yourself out. I've got work to do." With that, he climbs through the window and walks away, leaving me behind.

When we reach the cottage, Gail's back and panicking because she didn't find me inside, where I was supposed to be. Seeing me with Ben doesn't exactly calm her fears. Nor does the fact that he just walks past her without even a greeting and continues down the road.

"What was that about?" she asks when he's gone.

"Ben heard about the guy I saw in the shed. He wanted to check it out. Then we looked in the other cottages, to be sure no one was squatting in them."

"And?"

I grab a grocery bag from the hatchback. "Uncle Mark's place is boarded up. So is Grandpa and Grandma's. Except theirs had the boards removed from a window."

She stiffens.

"It wasn't recent," I say as I pick up a second bag. "A bush had grown over the opening. We still went inside. No sign of anyone in there for years, but when someone did break in, they'd torn up floorboards in the bedroom."

She frowns over at me as we head to the cottage. "Looking for what?"

"No idea. I thought you might know."

"I can't even imagine." She waits as I balance a bag on my knee while I open the door. "No, I *can* imagine actually. Someone probably thought your grandfather stashed money there and didn't come back for it. Everyone around here figured the Paynes were rich."

"Uh, they kinda were. Still are, compared to the locals."

She flushes. "Right. That was insensitive."

I hold open the door for her. "No, I get what you mean. They thought the Paynes were still loaded rather than middle class stretching toward upper. It might not even have been locals. The whole town is named after us, after all. Someone hears the Paynes abandoned their cottages in a hurry, after a family tragedy, and they might think we left something valuable behind. But whoever went looking, Ben thinks it'd have been years ago, which means it's not connected to our trespasser."

"Good. Now if you want to get dinner going, I'll do a little more work and then give you a shooting lesson."

"Sure."

She eyes me. "Is that a 'yes' kind of sure, or an 'I'm agreeing but plan to distract you later' kind of sure?"

"It's a yes. At the very least, the sound of gunshots should scare off anyone on the property."

"Good point. All right then. Dinner. Shooting. Bonfire. Our evening is planned."

Eleven

After my shooting lesson, we reach my favorite part of the plan: the bonfire. I'd made an easy dinner—mac and cheese with sausages—and gathered kindling while it cooked. Gail had picked up a load of firewood. The kids apparently really are children, who weren't home, but their mom said she'd tell them we'd like to buy in bulk. That means I don't really need the hatchet I brought from the shed earlier, but I use it anyway, splitting some logs and chopping up kindling before the brief lesson. Now we have a full-on bonfire going, which is a little warm for the weather, but we're enjoying it from a distance. I'm popping s'mores like I didn't just eat dinner a couple of hours ago. I'm also on my second canned cocktail. Yep, this is how I handle stress—sugar and booze.

We've been out there for an hour before I realize Gail's beer is nonalcoholic.

"Whoa," I say, lifting the can. "Did you grab this by mistake?"

"No."

My brows shoot up. She's silent long enough that my heart races.

"Gail? Is everything okay?"

"I booked the appointment this morning," she blurts.

My heart thuds so hard I struggle to breathe. "You're sick?"

"What?" She peers at me through the dancing shadows. "Sorry! That came out wrong. I booked the IVF appointment."

"What? Oh my God. Really?" I vault out of my chair and hug her so fast she startles with a laugh.

I hug her again fiercely before I return to my chair. "So you're finally moving forward."

"I am. Even after I found out about the money, I kept shifting the goalposts. Wait until I know whether it's anything serious with Carlos. Wait until I know how much the treatment would cost. Then wait for the actual money to come in. Yesterday, I realized I don't want to wait. Carlos is out of the picture and the money is coming, and it's enough. If I wait, I'll just keep raising more obstacles when the truth is . . ." She looks at me, her eyes glistening. "The truth is that I'm just scared. I want a baby so much, and I'm afraid the IVF won't work. Afraid I'm doing the wrong thing for a child, raising one alone."

"But you aren't alone. You have a niece, who will be the best nanny and big cousin ever."

She reaches out and when I extend my hand, she squeezes it. "I know that, Sam, but I also don't want to give you one more responsibility. One more reason to not go to med school. One more reason to stay in Syracuse."

I meet her gaze. "I am not going anywhere for the next couple of years. That gets you through the pregnancy and babyhood. Then, yes, I might go off to school, but I'll come back, and by then, it'd be because I want to, not because you need help."

"I want you to have your own life, Sam. The way it should be at your age. Out dating. Out with friends. Not working eighty-hour weeks and still barely scraping by."

"By the end of the summer, that will be in the past."

When she nods, I eye her. "That wasn't another thing you were waiting for, was it? To be sure I'd get the money and wouldn't need any of your inheritance?"

"No, no, of course not."

She's lying. I can see that. But I only wag my finger. "Good. And if you were, then I hope making that appointment means you realized I can do this. I can and will stay here until I earn this place."

She reaches to squeeze my hand again. "I know."

I'm adjusting in my lawn chair when something catches my eye. "Did you see that?"

"See what?"

I rise, squinting at the dark lake. "A light. On the water."

"That'd be Canada."

"Ha ha." Yes, Canada is across the lake, but across from us is cottage country, like here, and it's nearly fifty miles away. We aren't seeing lights from that.

I rise and start toward the beach.

"Sam?"

"I saw lights out there last night, and I could swear I just saw another one." I continue walking, crossing the hundred feet toward shore. "There! Did you see that?"

Gail rises from her chair. "A light, you said?"

"Right."

"Like a boat?"

I slow as I near the water. I can call this a beach, but it's hardly the kind of sandy shore where you pop up an umbrella. It's rough, sand interspersed with driftwood and grasses.

I stand on the edge and peer out. The lake is empty. While the occasional vessel goes by, we're too far from a marina to see many pleasure boaters. Fishing boats are farther out, and not out at all by this hour. Lake Ontario is calm, water gently lapping at the shore, and I see nothing except ink-black water.

"I saw two lights under it," I say. Then I peer up at the sky. "Could it be stars reflecting down? Bright ones?"

"Maybe?" Gail moves along the shore, craning to see what I do.

"I don't see them now." I shove my hands into my pockets. "Pretty view, though, isn't it? We should get out for a swim tomorrow." I glance over at her. "Hey, the canoe is still in the shed."

Her gaze drops to my ankle.

"Right," I say. "I can't leave the property."

"We'd be fine if we stuck to the shore. And just went to the end of the property."

I shake my head. "I'm not taking the chance that they can say the property ends at the shoreline."

"Maybe a quick swim? The monitor is waterproof."

I don't answer. I'm trying very hard to see the bright side of my "house arrest." It's summer, and I'm at the lake. But part of being at the lake is swimming and boating and going into town for ice cream.

I shake it off. I'm being immature, pouting because I can't do the things I did as a child. There is plenty I can do, along with work I need to do. If I can pull this off—which I will—I can go to the damn Caribbean this winter if I want. Enjoy the beaches there.

I'm turning away when something rises from the water's surface. Seeing it out of the corner of my eye, I spin, and it disappears.

"Did you see that?" I say.

"The lights?"

"No, something popped up." I point. "You can still see the rings where it went down."

"Oooh." Gail cranes to look where I'm pointing. "Otter? We used to get them all the time when I was a kid."

"I don't think so." I mentally replay what I saw. It had looked like a head. "It was bigger. Maybe twice the size."

"Huh. The back of a fish? Breaching and diving back under?"

"Maybe."

I walk closer. Water laps at my bare feet. I'm wearing shorts, and I start to wade out, but Gail grabs my arm.

"No swimming at night," she says.

I roll my eyes. "I'm wading."

"Still off-limits. You know the rules. The undertows here can be wicked."

I look over at her. "Have you ever felt one?"

"No, which is why I'm still alive to talk about it."

Her tone is light, and I suppress the urge to argue. Why ruin our good evening fighting over something I don't even really want to do? It's just . . .

I look out to where I saw something pop up.

Don't go in the water after dark. It isn't safe. Undertows.

People often talk about undertows in the Great Lakes, and they *are* a thing—rip currents that can pull you off your feet. But if I fell where

I am, with the water barely over my ankles, I'm hardly going to get dragged out into the lake. Yet we grew up hearing that.

Don't go in the water after dark. Yes, that includes wading. No, it doesn't matter if you're only up to your ankles. Just don't do it.

I stare out at the lake.

"Fire's dying down," Gail says. "It should be small enough to pull our chairs closer."

After one last look, I take the hint and follow her back to the bonfire.

That night, I toss and turn, haunted by memory and nightmare. Again I wake imagining I heard hoofbeats, and again, once I'm up, everything is silent. I curse under my breath and toss a few more times before rising, putting on my glasses, and heading into the living room.

We've left the windows open. It was too hot and stuffy with them shut, though Gail made me promise to keep my bedroom one closed. At least in here I can breathe, and I move to the window and inhale the night air, thankfully free from the stink of rotting rabbit.

The lake is dark. No lights on it. No lights shimmering beneath the surface. A quiet and still night.

After a minute, I ease open the door and walk onto the porch to properly enjoy the summer night—and calm my nerves from the unsettling dreams. I lean on the railing and lift my face to the sky. When I open my eyes, I'm gazing out at endless stars, and that makes me smile. Living in the city for so long, I've forgotten what the night sky looks like.

I'm standing on the porch, drinking it all in—the starry sky, the pine-scented air, the distant hoot of an owl—when lights appear under the water. I blink, certain it's the aftereffect of looking at the stars. But even after a few blinks, the lights are still there, seemingly right below the surface.

I head down the steps. From here to the lake, it's open land, kept clear, and I can walk easily across it in the moonlight. Soon I'm at the water's edge. The lights are still there, three or four of them, bobbing under the surface. I squint, as if that will help me see better, but again, my out-of-date prescription means my vision is less than twenty-twenty.

I peer into the sky. While I do see bright stars—probably actually planets—they aren't clustered the way these lights are.

It must be something bioluminescent. I meant to look that up and forgot. Maybe I could ask Ben. He's lived here all his life.

Uh, no, I'm not asking Ben anything. I'll ask Josie.

I'm turning to leave when I notice something off to my left. Marks in a patch of sand between the tufts of grass. They look like . . . footprints?

Earlier, we'd walked straight from the fire, which is to my right, and these are to my left.

I walk over and peer down. Bare footprints head inland, the sand slightly damp, as if someone was out swimming.

They're roughly my size. Could they be mine from earlier? Gail and I had both been barefoot.

I put my bare foot down beside the print.

It's about a half inch smaller and narrower.

Gail wears a size larger than me. I know that, because she grumbles that I'm able to borrow her footwear but she can't squeeze into mine without getting blisters.

That print didn't come from our feet.

And the prints are still wet.

I start to shiver. I've been trying so hard to explain what's been happening. Someone in the shed? A dead animal on the steps? Lights under the water? Footprints on the beach? There are a dozen logical explanations, and none of them have anything to do with what happened here before, when my father killed a boy. A boy who . . .

I swallow and struggle to shake it off. What happened back then wasn't strange or inexplicable. It was all too real and too human. And yet, seeing those strange and inexplicable footprints, I start to shake, and memories whisper up from the dark hole where I've stuffed them.

In the memory, it's early morning, and I've snuck out to run down to the beach. On a TV show, I saw kids getting up early to look for beach shells, and I'm too young to realize that was the ocean, not a lake, so I race down at dawn . . . and see prints on the sand. Bare footprints going into the water. I'm frowning at them, confused, when a hand lands on my shoulder.

"What are you doing out here?"

I look up, but that part of the memory is lost, and I don't know who has me, fingers lightly gripping my shoulder. "Why are there footprints going into the water?"

"Come inside. You know you aren't supposed to be out here at night."

"It's morning. Why are there footprints—"

"Someone must have been here. That's why you never come out here alone. People think they can use our beach. People who might hurt you."

People who might hurt you.

But it wasn't those people who hurt me. It wasn't those people who left mutilated small animals for me to find, who knocked me down and threatened to—

I step back sharply and take deep breaths.

I'm letting this place carry me away. Drag me into its darkest memories when the good memories outweighed them twenty to one.

But it doesn't work like that—loading all your memories onto a scale and saying the good outweigh the bad.

What happened here, what I saw my father doing, wasn't the kind of memory you can ever balance with good. Add in what happened before that . . .

My breath quickens.

I need to get inside. I'm worried about these footprints . . . and so I'm just going to stand here and tumble into memories while someone might be lurking on the property?

I'm turning away from the lake when something rises from the water. I freeze, my breath stopping.

What I'd spotted out there earlier hadn't been an otter or a fish. I knew that. Now I'm seeing it again, maybe twenty feet away. A dark semicircle, like the top of a head.

A human head? Is that really what I'm saying? That there's a person out there?

It looks like a seal or sea lion, but we don't have those in the Great Lakes.

Debris? Some kind of container? Maybe a small beer keg? No, it looks like the top of a head.

My gut tells me to run, but I find myself rooted there, squinting, wanting a logical explanation. Needing one. Knowing there is one. There *must* be.

The object starts to move my way, stopping me short, my heart rate accelerating.

That's not debris. And it isn't moving in the current. It's swimming, ripples flowing out on either side. But I can still only see what looks like the top of its head. Whatever it is can breathe underwater.

A memory rises. My grandmother telling me she'd once seen a seal here, on one of the first visits with my grandfather. Everyone had told her she was imagining things—my grandfather had teased her mercilessly. But then someone said harbor seals have been spotted in Lake Ontario, having come in from the St. Lawrence River.

The head rises, and I exhale in relief. It's a seal. I can see the dark cap over a lighter face, with huge liquid eyes and—

I step back. My brain keeps trying to arrange what I see into a seal's features. A furred head, dark on top, lighter below, small dark snout. Even as part of me screams that it doesn't look right, that logic center keeps reassuring me it fits.

Then I see shoulders. Human shoulders and a human neck and a human head. Dark short hair frames a thin, pale face. Only something's wrong with the face. The eyes are huge liquid pools, like a seal's. And there's a dark patch where the nose should be, like a hole gaping into a dark and lipless mouth.

Bone. I see bone through that hole. More bone on the cheeks, patches where the flesh is gone. Gray skin. The skin of the drowned.

I slowly back up as my brain screams that I'm wrong. I'm exhausted. I'm freaked out. I'm seeing things.

The figure continues to rise from the water, its naked pale body covered in gaping but bloodless wounds. My gaze flies back to the face and—

My heart stops.

I know that face.

It turns my way, and those eyes, those huge, liquid eyes burn with hate, a hate I know as well at that face, and before I can stop myself, I whisper, "Austin?"

Austin Vandergriff. I am seeing Austin Vandergriff. The boy my father murdered.

I turn and run. I run as fast as I can, brain screaming for me to stop, that this isn't Austin, cannot be Austin. But I keep going. I race up the steps and onto the porch and into the house, slamming the door behind me and locking it.

Then I run to the window and look out.

Nothing.

I see an empty stretch of land from here to the lake.

No sign of the figure that rose from the water.

No sign of Austin Vandergriff.

Because it wasn't him. Could not be him. Even if my fevered brain could imagine him drowned and returning from the lake, coming for me, always coming for—

Stop.

I rub my hands over my face, glasses tumbling to the floor.

Austin didn't drown. He didn't vanish into the lake. My father tried to bury him, but his body was found and given a proper burial. I know all this.

Am I sure?

It wasn't as if I'd been here for the funeral. Wasn't as if anyone told me what happened after I gave my statement.

I fumble my way to where my phone's plugged in on the kitchen counter. When my fingers tremble, mistyping on the keypad, I take two deep breaths. Then I try again.

Austin Vandergriff. Paynes Hollow. Funeral.

My page fills with results, my stomach clenched as I see my father's name peppered among them. I force myself to click on a local article titled "Funeral Held for Austin Vandergriff."

My gaze skims over the words, landing on the ones that matter. Body recovered. Postmortem examination. Laid to rest. Paynes Hollow Cemetery.

I lean against the counter and shut my eyes.

There. It wasn't him.

Of course it wasn't. Because even if Austin had drowned—which he did not—he's dead. He's been dead for fourteen years.

"Sam?"

That startles me so much I nearly drop the phone. Then I realize it's Gail. I walk to her bedroom door and crack it open. She's sitting up, one hand pulling out an earplug.

"I thought I heard you," she croaks, still obviously half asleep. "You okay?"

"Just getting a glass of water."

She nods and slides back down onto the bed. I shut the door and look at the window.

What happened out there?

I don't know.

I only know that I did *not* see Austin Vandergriff.

I shut the front windows and return to bed.

Twelve

"Sam!"

I startle awake to Gail's panicked scream, and I half roll, half fall out of bed. Then I race in to find her at the open porch door, hand over her mouth.

"What's wrong?" I run toward her. "What happened?"

She points. I follow her finger but see nothing except that open stretch of grass and sand, like last night.

She saw him. She saw—

"Down there," she says. "I didn't mean to scream. It's just . . ."

I step out and even without my glasses on, I can see a heap of fur and blood and bone. My brain goes wild, that girl gibbering in terror. Austin was here. Last night. He did this. I squeeze my eyes shut and force myself to retreat for my glasses. Then I walk out onto the porch.

Again, it takes a moment for my brain to resolve what it sees. I'm thinking of the rabbit from yesterday, and this doesn't look like that. Because it's not. The fur is white and brownish red and the head is—

Fox. I'm seeing a fox. My stomach roils, those old memories surging, that terrified girl peeking out.

I push her back and firmly tell her this is not the same.

Am I sure?

After what I saw last night?

I shush that little girl. Calm myself. Analyze and deal with it, and whatever happens, do not let Gail see how this affects me. Be the rational, former premed student who can deal with this.

At first glance the fox seems whole. It's lying on its stomach, all the body parts where they should be. Except it's been dismembered, like the rabbit, and all the internal organs laid with a small gap from where they should be attached, like a macabre puzzle, the pieces waiting to be pushed back together.

"I'm calling Sheriff Smits," Gail says. "Take photos of it. He's not going to be able to brush this off as a bird kill."

I turn.

"What?" she says, a little belligerently. "Don't tell me not to call him, Sam. Someone did this. A *human* someone."

"I know. Just . . . don't demand he come running out. We'll notify him, and I'll take pictures, and he can come at his leisure."

She grumbles, but I know she sees my point. If we demand an immediate response to a nonemergency, we run the risk of him not hurrying when it is urgent.

"You call then," she says. "I need a shower."

She stalks back inside and then stops, looking over her shoulder. "I'm sorry. That was snippy. I'm angry with whoever is doing this and taking it out on you."

"You're shook. I get that."

She peers at me. "And you're not?"

How do I answer that? Inside, I'm trying so hard not to freak out.

"Sam?" Gail steps outside and envelops me in a hug. "You're obviously in shock. Let me handle taking the photos while you call the sheriff."

I hug her back. "No, I've got it. Former premed student, remember?" I'm about to also remind her how I'd been fascinated by the anatomy of dead animals as a child, but I stop, a little voice inside whispering that won't help. It's why I couldn't tell anyone what Austin did, in case they blamed me. Then, after what my father did? In high-school biology labs, I'd always pretended to be repulsed by the dead critters we had to dissect. Because if I treated it in the proper way—as an interesting science specimen—I knew what my lab mates would say.

Sam Payne, daughter of a killer.

Instead, I say, "I'm sickened that someone did that to a fox, but I'm okay with the gore. I got used to it in my undergrad classes. You go have your shower."

Sheriff Smits arrives just after we finish breakfast. Josie isn't with him this time, and that makes me nervous, as if he left her behind so he could tell me I'm paranoid. If that was his intention, it doesn't happen, probably because it's impossible to blame the dead fox on any predator who doesn't walk on two legs. I don't even need the photos, though I still show them.

He rubs his mouth. "I'm sorry, Sam. I can't imagine . . ." He shrugs. "Well, I just plain can't imagine what would make someone do that."

My father murdered a local child, I want to say.

But Smits means that he can't imagine a person mutilating an animal to send a message to the killer's daughter.

"Someone wants me gone," I say.

He hunkers down, prodding the fox with a stick. "No sign of a bullet or trap. Of course, the, uh, damage could be hiding that. Might also have been found this way." He quickly says, "Found dead, I mean. Not found like *this*."

He keeps prodding as he talks. "Someone finds a dead fox. Hit by a car or died of natural causes. Chops it up as a message." He sighs and shades his eyes to look up at me. "Not that it makes much difference, I guess."

"Well, using the corpse of a dead animal is different than killing it."

He keeps studying the fox, his gaze on it as he says, "I know you're under orders to stay on the property. Part of your granddaddy's will, apparently. I can't say much about that, except that it's another thing I can't quite wrap my head around. But, if I understand correctly, if you leave the property, you don't *get* the property." He looks over at me. "That right?"

I nod. "I need to be here for a month, and I can't leave for more than an hour."

He shakes his head and mutters something under his breath that sounds like "rich folks." I can imagine how my grandfather's stipulation seems to him. Like some kind of game show, the rules set by an old man with too much money.

He continues, "So if someone scared you off, you'd forfeit. Who gets it then?"

"Ah. I hadn't thought of that." I lower myself onto the porch steps. "It goes to distant relatives I've never met."

"What about . . . ?" His gaze shoots to the house, where Gail works inside.

"No," I say adamantly. "My aunt already received her inheritance, and she's here to help me get mine. Otherwise, she'll insist on giving me part of hers for my mother's care. Gail would gain nothing by scaring me off."

"Isn't there another brother? And a cousin? Didn't come here much?"

"My uncle Mark and my cousin Caleb."

"Bet they aren't too happy about you inheriting. Especially the cousin. You two are the only grandchildren, aren't you?"

I nod. "Both Mark and Caleb got a share of the house, like Gail. It was split three ways. They're also not in line to inherit the property if I fail, though."

Smits shrugs. "They could contest it. Easier to do that if it's going to distant relatives. Might also not matter whether they inherit, if they're upset enough. How do they feel about this?"

My answer must show, because he nods. "Could just want to scare you off so you don't get it. Being petty. Jealous. Let me ask around town, see whether anyone's been through who looks like your uncle or cousin. Even your aunt."

I nod. Can I imagine Uncle Mark or Aunt Ellen doing this? I look down at the fox and shudder. No. Caleb, though? Scaring me off so I don't inherit, just to be vindictive.

Oh, yeah.

Especially if he'd somehow heard what happened all those years ago.

"Let me clean this up for you." Smits waves at the fox. "Then I'll take a walk around. See what I can see."

Sheriff Smits stays for another hour, while I work inside with Gail. I don't mention his theory that one of our relatives could be behind this. I need to think on that.

While Smits investigates, I try to work, but my mind keeps sliding back to last night.

How do I explain what I saw?

The obvious answer is that I was dreaming. I'd seen a figure in the shed, with dark "liquid" eyes, and then I saw Austin coming up from the water with similar eyes. Clearly a dream. Except I woke with sand on my feet, and Gail mentioned me getting up last night.

Could I have been sleepwalking again?

Being back here could trigger it. Combine sleepwalking with a nightmare about Austin Vandergriff. Was that a thing? Could you be partly conscious while sleepwalking, your environment impacting your dreams? That must be possible—I would have been partly conscious while sleepwalking as a child, if I kept going places where I might find my father.

Maybe I should contact that old therapist. I'd liked her, and I'd gone to her for years, until we couldn't afford it.

Can I afford it now?

Silly question. No, I cannot.

I take a deep breath, close my laptop, and say to Gail, "I'm going out. Can you see how the sheriff is doing?"

She nods distractedly. She's filling out some kind of form, and while I don't mean to spy, I glimpse enough to know it's a medical form for IVF. That makes me smile, and I squeeze her shoulder as I go past.

When I reach the porch, Sheriff Smits's pickup is gone. He must have finished and didn't have anything new to tell us.

I look out toward the lake. Then I find myself slowly heading there, caught between compulsion and reluctance. I continue to the spot I'd been in last night. I can see my footprints in the sand, the clear signs of me walking one way and then just the balls of my feet as I ran for the cottage.

There are no other prints.

What did I expect? The still-wet footprints of a thirteen-year-old boy chasing me? A *dead* boy chasing me?

I stare down at the empty expanse of sand and shiver, arms wrapping around me. Before I can process what I'm doing, I'm heading into the forest. I keep walking until my feet automatically find a path. After a few hundred feet, I turn onto a smaller trail, almost overgrown.

I walk until I see the massive maple tree. Then I stop, calm my breathing, and walk around the trunk, fingers on the bark as if to steady myself. By the time I get to the other side, my breathing has picked up again.

I don't want to see it still here.

And what do I want? To have imagined it? Imagined all of it?

No, I just want it gone. Erased by time and the elements.

It is not gone. It's right there, a spot where the bark had been chipped away and a picture carved in the open space. It's little more than a stick figure. A girl with pigtails, her hands raised to her chest, holding something there. At the bottom, the initials: A.V.

Time flickers, and I'm twelve, staring at this picture carved into the wood, hearing footsteps behind me.

"Do you like it?" Austin says.

I don't answer. I know better. I don't even look over at him. I just stare at that picture, trying to figure out what it is. I know *who* it is—who it always is. But what does it depict? I'm afraid to guess.

"It's you," Austin says. "You're trying to pull out the knife."

My breath catches, and my gaze flies to the figure's torso. I see it then. She's holding something sticking from her chest. A knife. Blood drips down. Drops of blood that he's painted bright red, the only color on the carving.

I don't look at him.

I set my shoulders, lift my chin, and start to walk away.

He grabs my arm. I yank free, and stumble. My foot slides, and I fall to the ground. I scramble to get up, but he kicks my leg out from under me.

"You're kinda stupid, aren't you, Sam?" he says. "I tell you not to ignore me, and you keep doing it. I make that"—he points at the picture—"to *show* you why you shouldn't ignore me, and you still do it."

My hands clench at my sides. "I want you to leave me alone."

"Or what? You'll tell your mommy? You know what she'll say—that you shouldn't be mean to me. I like you, that's all. I just don't know how to show it."

My face flushes. That's what everyone says when I complain about Austin following me around.

He likes you.

He's a nice boy.

Just play with him.

That's all he wants.

I swallow. That's how it started. Everyone thought it was cute. We were just kids, after all. He had a crush. Nothing wrong with that.

As much as I'd hated being around Austin, I'd given in. I'd been a good girl. I'd been a nice girl. I played with him and made sure he was included when the summer kids played together.

Only this year things changed. He didn't want me playing with the other kids. He didn't want me *talking* to other kids. I ignored that. I might have been forced to play with Austin, but that didn't mean I liked him, and now that we weren't little kids anymore, I decided I could stop hanging out with him. So he'd started doing things like this. Carving pictures of me in trees. Me stabbed. Me hanging. Me dead.

My gut told me that this was different. My mom wouldn't make me play with him if I showed them this.

But what if they did? What if Mom didn't see what I saw and said it was just a crush?

I could tell Dad. He'd always said that I didn't need to play with Austin if I didn't want to, and if I showed him these pictures and told him about the dead squirrels—

"Sam."

I jump, slingshot back to the real world as I spin around. For a moment, time stutters, and I'm turning to see thirteen-year-old Austin looming over me. Only it's not Austin. It's Ben. And he's standing back, frowning.

"Hey," I manage to croak, hoping my voice won't shake too much with a single word.

I move to the side quickly, away from that tree, away from the picture. But even as I do, his gaze shoots to it.

"You saw that?" he says.

I nod mutely.

"He carved that," Ben says. "Austin."

"I know."

Ben crosses his arms. "It's you, isn't it."

"I . . . I don't know."

"It is. It's you holding flowers."

I blink and look at the carving again. I see what he does—a girl seeming to hold something to her chest, vestiges of red paint around the knife seeming like flowers.

"He liked you," Ben says. "Liked you a lot."

I stiffen so fast it's almost a convulsion. Then I turn, and I do what I tried to do with Austin all those years ago. I walk away.

Unlike Austin, Ben doesn't come after me. He doesn't say a word. He just lets me leave, and once I'm out of his sight, I run all the way back to the cottage.

Thirteen

Josie comes for coffee, and we finish the pie. Gail doesn't join us. She'd been out for a walk earlier, and then something urgent came up, and she's been in her room ever since, working.

While Josie and I eat, I tell her about the break-in at my grandparents' cottage. I make it clear that I'm not reporting it to her—it happened years ago. But I suspect she'll find the removed floorboards more interesting than Ben had. I'm right. She's all over that, and we eat the pie while joking about all the things that someone might have been looking for.

"So, are you going to check out the crawl space?" she says.

"I plan to. I shouldn't do it alone, for safety. Ben obviously wasn't interested." I hook my thumb at Gail's closed door and raise my voice. "And my darling aunt recoiled in horror at the thought of crawling through a window."

I wait for Gail's rejoinder, but she must have her headphones on, because nothing comes.

"Are you hinting for law-enforcement backup?" Josie says, waggling her brows.

"Nah. Well, maybe. Kind of. Mostly just someone to make sure I don't fall through the hatch and get trapped there. But only if you'd be interested. Honestly, I'm sure I'm exaggerating the danger. I could do it myself. Gail would happily stay outside, within shouting distance."

"No, I *want* to do it. Check out an old crawl space? One that could hold whatever those intruders were searching for? Hell, yeah. Even if it's just old camp stuff, it'd be a treasure hunt."

"Okay. Good. Maybe on the weekend then?"

"Why not now?" She pauses. "Right. You have work. This is just a break."

"I could do it now if you can. Like I said, my work schedule is flexible."

She rises from the kitchen table. "Great. First thing we need is flashlights. I have a good one in the car. Strong light plus a stealth baton for fighting off the invading mice and squirrels."

I get up. "I'll clear these while you grab—"

Her phone buzzes. She takes it out and curses under her breath. "My dad." She pulls a face. "I mean, the sheriff. Technically, I'm on shift, and he needs me to follow up on a call."

"Tomorrow then?"

She lights up. "Yes. Tomorrow. I'm off, and free all day. I'll give you time to work, come by for our coffee break, and then we'll check out the crawl space."

"Perfect."

I walk Josie out. Then I prepare the bonfire for tonight. We're out of kindling, so I drag in a fallen branch to chop up, only to realize the hatchet isn't where I left it.

I look around, in case I'd put it somewhere else. I haven't.

Frowning, I go inside. Gail is still in her room with the door shut. I hate to bother her if she's working, so I wash the plates and mugs Josie and I used, while listening for Gail to move around, indicating she's taking a break. A half hour passes with silence from her room. I fix her a coffee and the last slice of pie, and rap on her door.

"Snack delivery service!"

When she doesn't answer—and I can't hear her typing—I start getting nervous. I knock again.

"Coming in to check on you," I say. "Stop me if you don't want that."

I open the door to find her lying on her bed, eyes closed, headphones on. I start to back out, presuming she's napping, but she opens her eyes.

"Snack?" I say, thrusting out the mug and plate.

She shakes her head as she silently removes the headphones.

"Have you seen the hatchet?" I ask.

A weird look crosses her face.

"Gail?" I move into the room. "You didn't get bad news, did you? About the IVF? Shit, not about the inheritance, is it?"

She pats the edge of her bed for me to sit.

"Uh, this sounds bad," I say, trying to keep my tone light. "If it's about me using up all the hot water, I'm sorry. Like I said this morning, I need to remember how small that tank is. Five-minute showers."

"I think I underestimated how hard this would be for you, Sam."

"Uh . . ." I mentally struggle to switch gears.

"Being here. With all these memories." She sits up straighter, crossing her legs. "It was wrong of me to expect you to do this."

I frown. "You *didn't* expect me to do this. You tried to stop me."

"Maybe that was the problem. I made you feel as if you couldn't handle it, and you needed to prove you could."

Irritation flares. "That's not it at all."

She scoots over and takes my hands in hers. "Then why are we here, Sam? Why are we spending a month in a place where your world fell apart?"

I pull from her grip, and my voice hardens, even as I struggle against it. "*We* don't need to be here, Gail. You chose to come, no matter how hard I argued. You don't need to stay. Come visit me on weekends. I can do this."

"But why are *you* doing it? It's for me and your mother. So I can keep all my inheritance for the IVF and you can afford to buy your mother whatever treatment might help. You're doing this for us. But what about you?"

"I'm fine."

She meets my gaze. "No, you're not, Sam. You're pretending that you are, but you really aren't."

I try not to shift in discomfort. I think of my sleepwalking hallucination last night. I think of being spooked in the shed. I think of my flashback at the tree carving.

Still, none of that means I'm *not* coping. It's *part* of coping. I'm remembering what happened here, and I'm dealing with it. Isn't that what I'm supposed to be doing?

"I'm okay," I say. "It's tough, but I think I really do need to face this, and that's what—"

"The shed was locked, Sam." She blurts the words and then rubs her face. "I didn't mean to say it like that."

I pull back, hoping my voice doesn't cool too much. "If you've just realized that it was latched—and possibly locked—when I saw someone in there, I know that. I realized it right away."

"And you told Sheriff Smits that?"

"I wasn't giving him any more reason to think I was imagining things, so no, I didn't tell him. But I did tell Josie. I also told Ben, who pointed out a hole where the concrete is crumbling."

"I saw that hole, Sam. No one could get in there. I also saw how the door latches. There's no way someone got inside and re-closed it."

"Then I was imagining seeing a person," I say coldly as I rise from the bed. "I don't think I was, but does it even matter? I didn't call the sheriff for that."

"Where were you last night?"

I blink. "Last night?"

"When I woke up. You seemed as if you'd just come in."

"Because I did. I saw the lights again."

"The lights . . ."

Her low murmur raises my hackles, and I snap, "Yes, the lights in the lake that you didn't see earlier that evening. More proof that I'm stressed? Who knows. But I didn't freak out over someone in the shed. I presumed it was a squatter. I didn't freak out over the lights. I'm guessing they're something bioluminescent. If I am imagining them?" I shake my head. "What does it matter? I apologize if I spooked you by saying I saw someone in the shed. That was not my intention."

"You were looking for the hatchet."

"When I went to the shed the other day? Yes."

"I mean just now. You were looking for the hatchet. That's what you said when you came in."

Once again, I need to pause as I mentally shift again, following her back to the top of the circle. "Uh, yeah. Have you seen it?"

"It's in the shed."

"Oh? Ah. You used it and put it away properly. Thank you."

"I didn't put it there, Sam."

I frown. Then my stomach clenches as the answer hits. "You think whoever cut up that fox used our hatchet? Then they put it in the shed." I pause. "But the shed's locked. No, Ben must have left it open."

Gail gets up and walks to the door. When she leaves, I hurry after her. She continues to the front door and walks through. I hesitate, confused, and then follow.

"Gail?" I say.

"The hatchet," she says. "I think you need to see it."

"Okay."

She's moving fast, even in bare feet, and as I jog after her, sticks bite into my soles and a voice whispers that something is wrong.

Something's wrong with Gail, and I should not be following her to the shed.

I keep going back to that conversation on the bed, the strangeness of it. Now I'm jogging after her in my bare feet, which is normal for me, but Gail is the sort who wears her flip-flops to the beach.

When she reaches the shed, she lifts the lock. "This is how I found it."

"Locked. Okay."

She takes out her keys and opens it. Then we go inside. She instinctively flicks the light switch, only to mutter in frustration when she remembers it doesn't work.

"Do you want me to run and grab—" I begin.

She walks inside before I can finish. I wedge the door open and follow. She marches to a corner, takes out her phone, and shines the light on the hatchet, propped against the wall.

"Okay, that's the hatchet," I say. "Is the point that I forgot I put it in here? Because I didn't. Ben has a key, too. If he found it lying around, he could have realized that's not very safe when we're concerned about a trespasser."

"Take a closer look, Sam." Her voice is tight and strange.

I walk over and shine my own cell-phone light on it. There's blood on the blade, and when I bend, I see bits of reddish-brown fur.

My breath catches and my voice wobbles as I rise. "Someone did use this to cut up the fox."

"Yes."

"You think it was Ben? But why would he leave the blood and fur on it?"

"What's down beside the hatchet, Sam?"

Frowning, I follow her light to some kind of fabric on the shed floor. I prod at it with my foot and startle when I see what it is.

"My gardening gloves," I say. "I used them yesterday, when I was pulling some weeds."

"Ben didn't take those gloves. They wouldn't fit him."

"Okay, so . . . ? Whoever cut up the fox used the gloves and hatchet I left outside. They also presumably have a key to the shed—or know how to pick the lock."

Gail's gaze pierces into mine, searching, her shoulders stiff. Then she slumps. "This is my fault."

"What's your fault? That?" I wave at the hatchet and gloves. "I'm the one who left them out."

"You shouldn't be here," she says. "What my father did to you is horrific, Sam. Cruel in a way I can't fathom. But he knew you'd come here and try to spend the month. That you *had* to, with your mother's situation. And I didn't stop you."

"I'm an adult, Gail. You couldn't have stopped me from coming here. And I don't understand what that has to do with . . ." I wave at the hatchet.

"Oh, baby." Her eyes fill, tears spilling as she reaches for me.

I slowly back up. "I'm very confused and a little scared. What is going on?"

"You should never have had to come back here, Sam, and I understand how badly you need to leave. To get away without it being your fault."

"I really do not understand—"

"No one would blame you if you left now. After seeing someone in the shed. After finding a rabbit and a fox mutilated on our front step. No one would blame you, but honey . . ." Her eyes meet mine. "I *never* would have blamed you."

"I don't . . ." I trail off, my chest constricting as I realize what she's saying. "You . . . you think I did those things? I *mutilated*—"

"The animals were already dead. That's what Sheriff Smits said."

"So?" I say, my voice rising. "You seriously believe I staged all this as an excuse to flee?"

"We don't need to talk about this. We can just go."

"I don't want to go. I've made that clear. I'm spooked by what's happening—"

"Not nearly enough," she murmurs.

"What's that supposed to mean?"

When she doesn't answer, I say, "You're implying that I've been *too* calm? That the fact I'm trying very hard not to show you how freaked out I am is proof that I did this? That the fact that I don't want to leave is proof? I stayed calm so you *wouldn't* insist I leave. I *faked* it."

"Because you don't want to be responsible for us leaving. You knew after those dead animals I'd make the decision for you."

I want to scream. She's not hearing me. She's made up her mind, and she's not listening. I take a deep breath and focus on logic.

"So, according to you, I mutilated a dead rabbit," I say. "Then I must have cleaned the hatchet, because you saw me using it yesterday. But when I chop up a dead fox, I leave blood and fur on the blade and the gloves, and I put them in the shed. Where Ben is almost certain to see them when he fixes the light or the hole."

"You made a mistake because you're upset and not thinking straight."

"Nope, pretty sure I'm the only one here who *is* thinking straight. I admitted that the shed had been latched—and maybe locked—when I saw someone inside, even though that suggests I imagined it. I asked whether you'd seen the hatchet. I was confused when you said it was in the shed. How does any of this suggest I'm responsible?"

"Because you're under a lot of stress. You might not remember doing it. Your mother said that after your dad died, you sleepwalked—"

"And went looking for my father!" I shout, my eyes stinging with tears. "Not cutting up small animals!"

I want to say more, scream more, shout that I cannot believe she would think I'd do this. Instead, I turn and I stride out of the shed and then break into a run.

Fourteen

I run through the woods, blinded by tears. This is a nightmare. A terrible dream where the one person who still sees me—really sees me—could accuse me of something so horrible.

I've had so few people in my life I can trust. There'd been many at one point. Back when I was a child and believed everyone around me loved and cherished and understood me.

Then the person who'd loved me best murdered a boy and killed himself, and something inside me—some capacity for trust—shattered. I'd seen my grandfather for who he really was, self-centered and cruel. My grandmother for who she was, kind but ineffectual. Even Gail had retreated, nursing her own pain, but at the time, it felt like rejection. All I had was my mother, who was always—even before the disease took hold—only half there, and I felt as if she'd betrayed me, too.

I came to trust my mother again, and then lost that part of her. I also came to trust Gail again, and that's who I clung to. No matter what others thought of me, how badly my extended family treated me, Gail knew me.

And now she thinks I would carve up animals and scare the shit out of her because I'm too proud to just admit I want to leave. That I would frighten her, file false police reports, disrupt everyone's life . . . just so I can escape while saving face.

When I reach the porch, I stumble. My knee cracks down hard on the step. Hands grab me and I spin, fighting them off, but she grips my arm tighter. Something whines in the distance, and I look up sharply, but it's just the wind picking up.

"Sam," Gail says. "Please. I don't blame you—"

"You think I wasn't sufficiently freaked out by those animals?" I say, wiping my free hand over my tears. I meet her gaze. "What you saw was what I wanted you to see. To look calm while I was melting down because it's not the first time this has happened."

She blinks. "Not the first time . . . what?"

"Someone has done that. Left me chopped-up animals as a warning."

"Someone has been doing that to you at home?"

"No. *Here.* Someone did that to me here." I lock my gaze with hers. "Until my father killed him."

I wrench from her grip. I get onto the porch, and she grabs for me. I dodge, only to smack into the railing, and when she tries to steady me, I rip out of her grasp. She lets go too fast, and I fall to the porch as the wind whips past, sand blowing everywhere.

"I am so sorry," Gail whispers. "I didn't mean—"

I scuttle backward when she steps toward me.

"Sam—"

"Just leave me alone." Tears blind me. "Please. Leave me alone."

I use one hand to pull myself up, the other outstretched to ward her off.

"If you think I mutilated those animals, then you don't know me at all," I whisper.

"I do know you, Sam. The trauma—"

"Trauma makes me cry myself to *sleep*. Trauma made me *melt down* when I saw those dead animals. Trauma did *not* make me chop them up. The obvious conclusion is that someone left that hatchet and gloves for one of us to find and blame the other. If I'd been the one to find them, I would never, for one second, have thought you did it."

Tears stream down my face, and she blurs behind them. "Because I know you."

"Sam..."

She reaches for me again, and all I see through my tears is the blur of her as I stumble back, smacking into the wall hard. I wrench from her grip, stagger into the cottage, and slam the door behind me.

Once inside the cottage, I go straight to my room and stay there. When Gail tries opening the door, I wedge a chair under it. When she tries talking to me, I put on my headphones. I tell her to go away. Just go away and leave me alone. Eventually she does.

It takes forever for me to fall asleep. I'm hungry, having missed dinner. I need to pee. And I know I'm being immature hiding in my room, but I can't face her. The thought of it makes me break out in a literal cold sweat. Even when I start to drift off, I'm tormented by memories of Austin Vandergriff, of the things he'd done that last summer.

It started with carving my death scenes and leaving dismembered animals in all my secret spots. Austin never pretended he didn't do it. That was the point—for me to know. Then came that final carving, the one I still shake thinking about.

A carving of *me*, lying in pieces, like the squirrels and rabbits he'd left.

Finally, it seems late enough to slip out. I'm turning my doorknob when I see the light shining under the door. I tense in a near spasm, every cell in my body preparing for flight, my brain screaming that I can't face her, can't risk the damage to my paper-thin sense of self-worth.

Gail questioned how I could hide my reaction to those animals so well. But I've had practice, so much practice. I've perfected the art of seeming perfectly calm while inside, I'm this cowering, terrified child.

When I say my mother was always half there, I don't mean she was vague and absent-minded. She was just always partly someplace else, unknowable to me as a child. High walls, I realize now. Maybe some trauma in her own past. But after my father died, she maintained that stiff upper lip for my sake, and I mistook it as a sign that she needed me to do the same. To stuff my grief and confusion into a deep hole and present the face that others—including her—seemed to want.

I know better now. I understand how deeply she'd been hurt and how much she wanted to be strong for me, and how she never needed—much less wanted—me to tamp down my trauma until it exploded in the battles of my teen years. But now, through Gail, I also see how others could misinterpret my stoicism as a disturbing lack of emotion.

The point is that I do feel, and I am that terrified child again, afraid of leaving this room no matter how much my stomach grumbles or my bladder screams. I ease the door open just enough to peek out, hoping Gail just left a light for me. Instead, I see her on the sofa, knees up, reading on her phone.

I close the door and retreat.

It's past midnight. She has to go to bed soon.

I'm lying there, awake and waiting, when I hear her moving. I hold my breath. I just need her to get into her room. From living with her as a teen, I know my aunt's routine. She'll hit the washroom first to scrub her face and brush her teeth. Once she's in her room, she'll stay there.

Footsteps creak across the living room. I tense, worrying they'll come my way.

Go to bed. Please. It's late.

When they grow softer, I exhale under my breath. Moments pass. Did she go to bed? I don't think so—the bathroom is right beside my bed. I'd hear her in there.

"Sam?"

I jump and stiffen.

Footsteps patter to my door. "Sam? Are you up? I see your lights on the lake."

I stop breathing as my heart clenches, and something in me shrivels. She's placating me. Treating me as if I'm still a small child.

Oh, you heard hoofbeats in the forest? Let's go investigate! Wait, is that a print on the ground?

"Sam?"

I don't answer. I don't even breathe. After a few moments, her footsteps recede, and I yank the covers over my head . . . and fall asleep.

I wake the next morning to a banging at the front door. With my brain still foggy—why do I need to pee so badly?—I stumble from my room and then stand there, blinking.

The front door is open.

The sound I heard wasn't a knocking—it was the screen door banging in a strong lake breeze.

I back up as I stare at that open door, remembering that I saw someone in the shed. Because I *know* I saw someone in the shed.

That sends everything else tumbling back. Yesterday afternoon. Me looking for the hatchet. Gail—

Even as my chest seizes, I back up toward her door, because no matter how hurt—how fucking *devastated*—I am by her betrayal, I am not going to race out and leave her with an intruder.

The cottage is silent except for that screen door slapping. I back into her bedroom door, twist the knob, and retreat inside. Only as I do that do I realize I may have just stepped into the room *with* the intruder. But if he's anywhere near my aunt, I'm sure as hell not running.

The room is dark, blind drawn. But it's silent and still. I ease the door shut and move backward toward her bed.

Then I pause.

Gail already thinks I'm losing my mind. Now I'm showing up at her bedside to protect her from my "imaginary" trespasser?

I don't care. The front door is wide open, and I am not taking any chances.

I reach her bed and turn slowly, keeping part of my attention on the closed bedroom door. My mouth opens to say her name. Then I realize the bed is empty.

I check the bed, as if those wrinkles in the covers could be my aunt. They are not. I look around, but there's no place else for her to be in here.

I run from the room, forgetting that there could be an intruder. No, not *caring* about an intruder, because the front door is open at six in the morning, and my aunt is gone.

As I race for the front door, every horrible thought whipping through my head, I notice something. Or rather, I notice something missing.

Gail's flip-flops.

They'd been by the front door, on the mat where she leaves them. I know they were there yesterday, because I'd noted them when she went out barefoot.

Gail's shoes are gone. A kidnapper is not going to stop to let her put on footwear.

She wasn't dragged out by a stranger. She left.

My heart jams into my throat, and I want to curl in on myself.

My aunt has finally had enough of me.

She's gone.

My breathing picks up as I fight to control the rising dread and pain, the voice that screams I've finally done it. I'm too damaged. Too needy. The last adult in my life has left. The last *friend* has left.

I clench my fists.

Get a grip.

It's dawn. She probably went for a walk on the beach, and my doom spiral only proves she's right and I'm not doing nearly as well as I pretend. But I know that, don't I? I'm more fragile right now than I've been in years.

I step onto the porch. "Gail?"

No answer. It's light out, but just barely. Do I really think my aunt—who never rises a minute before her alarm—has decided to go for a dawn beach walk? That's my kind of thing, not hers.

Maybe she's really gone.

Without her car? It's parked right outside, and when I back up, I can see her keys where she left them, on the kitchen counter.

"Gail?" I call inside. Then I step out and try louder. "Gail?"

The only answer is the slapping of the screen door behind me.

Fifteen

It's nearly eight o'clock now. I've walked to the beach. I've taken one of the trails. And I've called. That's where I start and where I end, with constant calls. Gail's phone goes straight to voicemail. I've texted. I've left messages. Nothing.

I'm sitting on the front porch when my brain finally calms enough to think beyond the last hour, and I bolt upright.

The lights.

Last night, she came to my door and said she saw my lights on the water. I'd withdrawn under the covers and presumed she'd go to bed. But what if she didn't? What if she'd gone out?

And didn't come back in.

That would explain the open door far better than thinking she'd gone for a predawn walk and forgot to close it. What if, last night, she'd seen the lights and stepped out, thinking it was just for a moment, and then . . .

I race toward the beach. Earlier, when I'd searched it, I'd come from the road. Now, going straight from the cottage, I stop short.

My aunt's flip-flop prints are right there, in the dew-damp sand. She's walking toward the beach. Unhurried. In two spots, she seems to stop, the prints scuffed as if she'd stood there and peered around before continuing on.

Like me the night before. Seeing lights on the water and drawing closer until—

Until I saw that head pop up, seal-sleek.

I shake it off. Of all the things I saw, that was the one I definitely imagined. Dreamed in my sleepwalking state. But I'd spotted the lights several times, so Gail could have seen those.

She wasn't lying to lure me out of my room. She actually saw something.

Her footprints get closer and closer to the water's edge. Then they stop and—

My breath catches. I'm staring down at my aunt's prints, multiple sets, as if she'd paced and then headed to the west. She got about ten steps and—

And I don't know what I'm seeing. It's a mess of marks in the sand. My aunt's prints veer left, as if she'd been heading back to the cottage. They're deeper, farther apart, only the balls of her feet sinking in.

Like my own footprints from the night before. When I'd been running.

Her prints only go a few feet, though, before they're ground into a mess of disturbed sand. Two more of her prints to the west, running leaps in that direction and then—

And then the ground is chewed up, a roiling mass of sand, dirt, and ripped-out grasses. I stand there, staring down. Then I see more marks, heading toward the water.

Drag marks.

I recoil fast. No, this is not what it looks like. My paranoia is interpreting them in the most disturbing way. Yes, they're my aunt's footprints as she investigated the lights. Then she heard the door banging, realized she hadn't shut it and ran back. Her footprints seem to end, but that's only because the ground is harder here.

As for that scuffle, it had nothing to do with Gail. Just some animals fighting in the same spot. Maybe an eagle swooping down on some small critter. What did Ben say? That if an eagle attacked, we'd only see blood and fur, if that much. On sand, we'd see signs of a struggle. The drag marks are an eagle landing. Or maybe an osprey.

I justify. I justify *madly*. And yet I cannot look at these marks without seeing my aunt being hauled out into the lake by—

By what?

The drowned body of Austin Vandergriff?

I did not see Austin. I am not seeing my aunt's final moments, dragged into the water by a dead boy.

So where is she?

I head inside and look for her phone. She keeps it in a wallet case and carries it shoved into a pocket, like I do. She has a laptop bag, and that's still in her room, along with her laptop. There's no sign of her phone.

I try calling it again and still get voicemail. That had panicked me earlier, but now that I'm thinking it through, I remember seeing her scrolling through her phone late last night. She probably didn't charge it. She goes out, pocketing it, but not realizing it's almost dead.

A thought hits, and I lift my own phone, hitting buttons as I check her last known location. It's from a few hours ago, and it's nearby. I zoom in and walk in the direction of the dot. That takes me out the door and down toward the beach and—

I stand on the water's edge, looking at the dot out somewhere in front of me.

In the lake.

I swallow and back up fast, shaking my head.

The GPS isn't precise, especially not out here. Still, I wade into the water, phone lifted, trying to gauge where it's showing me.

I'm in to my knees, and on the screen, my blue dot has barely moved. Her last-known indicator is far out in the lake. Which means it's wrong.

Unless—

No, it's wrong. Like the time I was fourteen, and Mom and I had a big fight, and I'd stormed off. When she checked my location, it apparently showed me walking in the middle of a highway, and she'd suspected the worst.

Of course I hadn't been walking down the highway. I'd been a half mile away on a hiking trail.

Gail's last known location is somewhere on the property. That's all I can really say.

I check the time of that last ping. Seven hours ago. So just past one in the morning.

Did that mean she went out to see the lights? Maybe. That'd been closer to midnight, but her phone could have died around one, maybe even after she'd gone back inside.

Except she's not inside.

I retreat to the porch, sit on the step and bury my face in my hands. I keep hearing Gail from yesterday, seeing the way she looked at me, that combination of fear and pity. Thinking I'd mutilated those animals and—

I swallow.

I'm trying very hard not to panic because I don't want her strolling back from a walk, finding Sheriff Smits in our yard and me in hysterics, babbling about footprints and drag marks and her phone signal in the lake. I don't want to prove she's right and I'm losing it. But in stifling the whirling fear, am I also doing what she accused me of? Reacting too calmly?

She thought I cut up those animals and "hid" the hatchet—

My head snaps up. The shed! Yes! Where might Gail go this morning? To the shed, for another look, to think this through while I'm sleeping.

I'm halfway there before I remember the keys. I pause, ready to run back. But if she's there, she'll have opened it with her keys.

Except her keys are on the counter.

No, I'm actually not sure she put the cottage and shed keys on that ring. After my overheated brain spends much too long deciding, I continue running for the shed. I reach it to find the door shut, and yet I still check the padlock, as if she could somehow be in there with it latched. It's locked.

"Gail?" I back up and look around. "Gail!"

Tires crunch on the road, and my heart sings. Even as my brain says this can't be Gail—her car is beside the cottage—it also comes up with explanations. Her car wouldn't start, and she walked to Paynes Hollow for help because her phone was dead.

Does this make sense? Of course not, but I cling to it as I run back to the cottage. I'm halfway there when a much more plausible explanation hits, and I skid to a stop.

What if those tires were the sounds of Gail leaving? If she'd been outside, thinking things through, and then saw me running about like a madwoman and realized she should leave. She waited until I was gone and now she's fleeing.

Fleeing me.

No, she wouldn't do that.

She thinks I carved up—

She thinks I'm traumatized. She's not afraid of me.

Am I sure?

I break into a slow jog, and soon I see Gail's car where she left it. On the other side is a familiar pickup.

I race around the cottage just as Sheriff Smits is climbing from his truck. The morning sun is in his eyes, and he shades them as he looks my way.

"Morning," he says. "Sorry for the early visit, but I wanted to check on you girls. See if anyone left any more grisly presents this morning."

I shake my head. "Nothing, but my aunt's gone."

"Oh?" He's still shading his eyes, trying to see me. "Left early for . . ." He trails off as he turns toward her car.

"No, she's missing. Gone. I don't know where."

He's walked into the shade of the cottage, where he can see my expression, and he stops walking. "Missing?"

The words tumble out. "I was up at dawn. The screen door was banging. She was gone, and at first, I thought someone kidnapped her, but her sandals are missing. I can't find her. Her phone's dead. There's been no signal for hours. There are footprints on the beach, and her last signal was from the lake and—" My breath catches so hard it nearly doubles me over. "The water. An undertow. A riptide. I never thought about—"

"Sam?" His hands land on my shoulders. "Take a deep breath."

I pull back. "No, you don't understand. There are footprints. Hers. Then drag marks." I turn and run toward the beach. "I can show you."

He follows, and I run until I reach the first prints, and then put out a hand to stop him.

"They start here," I say. "She's wearing her flip-flops. You can see how she's walking, just strolling along."

"Okay..."

I'm well aware of how I sound, like a kid playing detective, but I can't stop myself. I need him to understand.

"Then here." I point. "She stops and seems to start running toward the cottage, but something happens. See it there? The scuffle of footprints?"

"Okay..."

"Then over here. These lines in the sand. They're like drag marks, right?"

He walks alongside them and says nothing, just crouches for a better look.

"Here's her last known location." I hold out the phone. "Around one in the morning. It's—it's out on the water. I think she was walking along the beach and the undercurrent grabbed her. Or she saw a rogue wave and tried to run."

"Rogue wave..."

My jaw sets. "They happen. My grandfather told us about one."

"I'm not arguing, Sam. I'm working it through."

I look out at the lake. A hand squeezes my shoulder, and I glance up through teary eyes to see Sheriff Smits. He seems ready to pull me into a hug, but then settles for another awkward shoulder squeeze.

"You don't think that's what happened," I say.

"I'm really hoping it's not. Can I see that locator again?"

I pass him my cell. "The blue dot is my phone. The icon is Gail's. It shows the time and location of the last ping."

He examines it. Turns toward her icon, holding the phone up and walking toward the water.

"GPS isn't very accurate out here," he says.

"I know, and I could be misinterpreting everything, but that doesn't explain where she is." I wave at the forest. "She hasn't come out to even stroll along the beach since we arrived. She never walked the trails alone when we were young. Gail isn't outdoorsy. At all. I can't imagine her being struck by the urge for a moonlit stroll."

"You said she has a gun."

I pause, taking a moment to process the segue.

He continues, "What if she saw your trespasser and took the gun outside to talk to him? I certainly hope not—for her sake—but do you know where she keeps it?"

I take him inside. As I do, I point out the empty mat where she keeps her flip-flops and then I show him her keys on the counter, which I now see do include the cottage and shed keys. We go into her room, and I pull the gun case from under her bed. It's closed and locked. I have the combination, so I use it and open the box to reveal the gun.

Smits looks around the room. Then he heads into the main area and looks around some more. "You said the screen door was banging?"

I nod as I join him. "In the wind this morning."

"So she went out, expecting she wouldn't be gone for long. Probably around midnight. Any idea why?"

"I . . ." I swallow. "We had a bit of a fight last night."

His eyes narrow. "A bit of a fight?"

"An argument."

"Did it come to blows?"

"What? No."

"There's a bruise on your leg, Sam. A fresh one."

"She caught my arm to talk to me, and I yanked away and fell. That's all. Afterward, I retreated to my room. She came to the door, probably around midnight, saying she saw lights in the water. I'd been seeing them."

"Lights on the water?"

"Under it. Something bioluminescent, I presume. Anyway, she hadn't seen them, and last night, she said she did. I figured she was humoring me."

"Because you'd argued. Over what?"

I shrug, hoping my face isn't reddening. "Just being here."

"She wanted to leave?"

"She thought I did. I don't. Like I said, it was just a little tiff." *Liar.*

"I headed to bed early partly to stop fighting, but mostly just because I was tired." *Liar.* "But yes, I figured she was humoring me about the lights so I went to sleep. I didn't hear her leave, but I also wasn't listening for it."

He nods, thoughtful, and then says, "Getting a closer look at the lights would explain why she'd be out at the lake."

I swallow, fighting to control my racing heart. "Yes."

He leans back, thumbs hooked in his belt loops. "I'm really hoping there's a simple explanation here, Sam. Maybe she went for a walk after looking at your lights. Maybe she fell and twisted her ankle."

I need to force out the words. "But you don't think that's what happened."

"I don't know," he says firmly. "Even if she was pulled into the lake by an undertow, she very well may have come up on shore somewhere else. Exhausted by the fight, having lost her cell phone, she passes out."

"Okay. That makes sense. So now . . . ?"

"Now we search. Let me get Josie and my other deputy here." He starts walking away, taking out his phone. "I'll call in that lazy-ass caretaker, too."

I step toward his retreating back. "Don't bother Ben with this."

Smits snorts and lifts the phone to his ear. "Ben should be bothered a little more often, if you want my opinion. He's coming. Doing some work for once."

Sixteen

I really don't want Ben Vandergriff here. Ever again, if I have the option. But apparently, I don't even have the option of not summoning him to help search for my aunt, and when I realize that, I'm ashamed of my impulse. Yes, Ben makes me uncomfortable. Not Ben himself, but his connection to Austin, the reminder of that, the fact that he thinks Austin and I were friends and I cannot set him straight. I can't set anyone straight, but especially Ben, who may be an ass but doesn't deserve to have his good memories of his brother tainted.

Yet with Gail missing, I must be grateful for every bit of help. So I only raise that token protest and then shut up. Smits calls Josie, and tells her to notify the other deputy. He also leaves the Ben-summons to her, which is probably for the best.

After that, Smits and I walk up and down the beach. We don't go far, and when we hear the car engines, Smits returns to the cottage while I keep looking.

Five minutes later, the sheriff's whistle brings me jogging to join them. Josie watches me with obvious worry and offers a tentative hug, whispering, "We'll find her." The other deputy—a middle-aged man introduced simply as Danny—nods sympathetically my way. Ben just watches me, suspicion rolling off him.

"Okay, so we're splitting up," Smits says. "I do not expect trouble, so we don't need the buddy system. Except for Sam. She'll go with Ben."

Ben and I squawk in almost perfect unison.

"I can take Sam," Josie says.

Her father shakes his head. "I know you'll search properly, and I know Sam will try. But if Ben's by himself, he'll just plunk his ass down and tell us he covered his quadrant."

"Remind me why I'm here again?" Ben says.

"Because the daughter of your goddamn employer is missing. On the property where you are supposed to be taking care of things."

I open my mouth to say that this isn't Ben's fault. But everyone knows that, and if I say so, it'll sound as if he *could* be blamed.

Smits and Danny will take the beach, one heading west and one east. Josie will take the west side of the cottages. Ben and I get the east, including the shed. That's where he heads first. I tell him it's locked, but he just keeps walking. That's fine—I want to check it anyway.

It's only as he's opening the shed that I remember the hatchet and bloody gloves, and I hurry inside to warn him. He's going to see that. Then I'll need to explain and—

There's no hatchet. Both that and the gloves are gone.

Did Gail move them?

There's no sign of Gail in the shed. Ben does a full round with his flashlight. Then he leaves and heads for the trail. He's walking west, toward the road, and I'm about to stop him when I see my uncle's cottage ahead.

Ben circles the cottage, hunting for signs of entry. He tests the boards and the doorknob and peers at the windows. He even hunkers down to check the base of the porch, in case there's a hole or gap there. Then, without a word, he carries on.

We're walking through the forest, along one of the trails, when I can't take the silence anymore.

"I'm not sorry you were called in," I say. "I'll take all the help I can get. But I am sorry that Sheriff Smits is being an asshole."

"He has to be. Otherwise, I'd die of shock and you'd be down one searcher."

"I don't understand what his problem is with you."

"None of your business, Samantha."

I let it go for five steps. Then I say, "It's Sam. You know that. You're being a jerk, and I'm asking you to stop."

"In all correspondence with your grandfather, he refers to you as Samantha."

"Because *he* was being a jerk. That's the word for someone who insists on calling you by a name you don't like, Benjamin."

He shakes his head and keeps walking. Every few steps, he'll stop and peer into the forest, and I really don't know what Smits's problem is, because I'm sure Ben would search just as thoroughly without me here.

We've walked another fifty feet, both of us scouring the sides of the path, when he says, "There's no riptide. It's a lake."

"Don't argue semantics. Undertow. Riptide. Giant wave."

"Giant wave?" He turns so I can see his eye roll.

"My grandfather said the waves can get up to thirty feet high."

"In a storm. Waves require wind, *Sam*."

My cheeks heat, and I snap, "Fine. You're right. So maybe Gail just walked into the water and drowned. Driven to it by the hell of being locked up here with me."

He keeps walking. "My point is that I don't think your aunt drowned. It makes no sense. And, yeah, I heard that shit about footprints and drag marks, but I can give you a dozen explanations for what would look like drag marks."

"So she just left? That's what you think?"

"I think you two should have damned well let me camp out when I asked."

My face screws up. "You asked to camp here?"

He turns to study me. "Your aunt didn't tell you?"

I shake my head.

"After you saw someone in the shed and got that rabbit on the front porch, I said I should stay on-site at night. Camp in front of the cottage. She refused. She said you both didn't want that."

So she made the decision without asking me.

The wrong decision?

While I do not want Ben Vandergriff living outside my door, if he had been there last night, would he have seen Gail? Heard her if she got into trouble? She might not even have ventured out knowing he was there.

"You think whoever I saw attacked my aunt," I say. "Hurt her."

"Nah. I'm sure she's fine. Just fell and twisted her ankle. Or maybe sat down and drifted off."

A chill runs down my neck, those words echoing something deep in my brain, memories I'd presumed long forgotten.

It's the day Austin Vandergriff disappeared. Mom and I are joining the search party in the woods behind the Vandergriff house. Ben's there, an acne-pocked teen standing by himself, staring down at his sneakers as Sheriff Smits explains the search procedure. First, though, Smits reassures us that Austin was probably fine.

"Maybe he fell and twisted his ankle. Or sat down and drifted off."

Does Ben know he's parroting those old words? He could be mocking me. My aunt disappears just like his brother, so he says the same thing, while clearly meaning my aunt has met a similar fate—murdered and buried in a shallow grave.

But there's no sign of mockery in his voice or expression. He doesn't seem to realize he's repeating Smits, the words bubbling up from his own subconscious.

Fell and twisted her ankle.

Sat down and drifted off.

Another memory bobs below the surface, one too deep for me to pull up. I'm maybe five or six, my hand stretching up to hold my father's, and we're . . .

I struggle to draw out the memory. We're in town. Dad's talking to someone. A woman? Discussing a tourist who'd gone missing. A camper? A hiker? The woman's voice.

Oh, he's fine, I'm sure. All this fuss over nothing. Fellow probably stumbled and broke his ankle. Or just drifted off and had a nice nap. That's if he even disappeared from here. Could have been anywhere from here to the highway.

The email from my grandfather flashes back, that podcast link he sent me.

"Paynes Hollow: The Bermuda Triangle of Upstate New York?"

I give myself a thorough shake, glad that Ben has resumed walking, his back to me.

I'm inventing connections. My aunt, Austin Vandergriff, some random hiker. As for breaking an ankle or falling asleep, those are the most likely scenarios in any disappearance like this, where there's plenty of countryside to wander but not enough to get lost in.

We're walking on a smaller trail when a voice calls "Ho!" from somewhere to our left. It's Danny, the deputy assigned to this side of the lake.

"Got something!" he shouts.

I start to run. I race full out, even as Ben shouts for me to slow down, watch where I'm going. I ignore him, dodging through trees, the path abandoned as I run on a direct course to Danny's voice.

My foot catches a half-buried branch and I go flying face-first, sprawling onto the forest floor. I leap up and get two running steps before my ankle gives out.

Fell and twisted her ankle.

I vault back to my feet.

"Sam!" Ben snaps. "Stop!"

When I ignore him, he catches me around the waist. Maybe that should ignite a wild panic. Maybe it should remind me of all the times his brother grabbed me, threw me down, kicked me, slapped me. But I don't have that visceral connection. That was Austin. This is Ben. I had never confused the two.

"Slow down," Ben hisses at my ear, and his tone impatient but not unkind. "It's okay. Just slow down before you hurt yourself."

"I need—I need—" I can't get the words out, and I angrily wipe at my tears.

"You need to see what Danny found. I get it. But you're not getting there if you fall and impale yourself on a damn branch. Now you've done something to your ankle."

I hiccup a half-hysterical laugh.

Fell and twisted her ankle.

"Take my arm, and we'll keep moving. Just don't expect me to carry you. I don't do that shit."

My laugh now is a wheezy snort. I take his arm, my own shaking, and I put a little weight on his so we can move faster. In twenty steps, we're at the shore. I spot Danny maybe fifty feet away, holding something out in the other direction, where Sheriff Smits is approaching. My gaze drops to the beach, looking for my aunt. There's no sign of her.

Smits reaches Danny first. He looks at something in Danny's hand and then takes it and turns to us as we approach.

"Sam?" Smits says gently. "Do you recognize this?"

He holds it up. It's a pink and blue flip-flop.

Twisted with weeds from the lake bottom.

I'm in the cottage. Josie is with me, fussing around the kitchen, brewing coffee I won't drink. I'm huddled in the corner of the sofa. Someone—Josie? Ben?—brought me a sweatshirt when I wouldn't stop shivering. It's not mine or Gail's. I don't know where it came from, but it's huge, and I've pulled it over my knees as I sit there, rocking.

Oh, everyone has assured me that the weed-covered sandal means nothing. Gail could have taken off her flip-flops to walk in the sand, and they got pulled out and caught some floating weeds before drifting back to shore. It's not evidence that she drowned and sank, her sandal catching on the weed-choked lake bed before sliding from her dead body.

That didn't happen, Sam. Not at all.

They're going to widen the search. Take out the boats. Get a diver. They're sure she's not out there, drowned, but that's what they'll do. Just in case.

Time stutters, and the next thing I know, I'm sitting there holding a mug of cold coffee and Sheriff Smits is asking me a question.

"Sam?" he says. "I need to know how you want this handled."

His tone says it's not the first time he's asked.

"Handled?" I croak.

"How public would you like me to go with this? It's still early in the search, and the media wouldn't necessarily broadcast it under normal circumstances, but . . . with your grandfather and your connection to Paynes Hollow . . ."

He's dancing around something, and it takes a moment for me to understand. If he declares Gail a missing person, he can ask for the public's help finding her. But will that do any good, if we're reasonably sure she didn't just wander off? And if the regional media gets hold of it—daughter of Paynes Hollow's founding family disappears under mysterious circumstances—how long will it be before my grandfather's will and its stipulations are public knowledge? Resurrecting my father's crime and clarifying who is currently living—alone—on the property?

"Can Gail *be* declared a missing person?" I ask. "Doesn't it take forty-eight hours?"

"Not if she disappeared in circumstances that suggest she didn't just walk away."

"Would going public help?"

He chews that over, and I realize I'm putting him in a tough position.

"No, right?" I say. "It would do more harm than good."

"I believe so, but I am going to make this your call."

"You'll keep searching?"

"Of course." He seems affronted by the question. "I'll still call in others, including people with boats. I know someone with sonar. That might help. I will also notify nearby police departments."

I nod. "That's enough. Thank you."

"Josie will stay here with you."

I open my mouth to protest, but Ben beats me to it.

"Why?" he says. "She can leave, can't she?"

Josie frowns at him. "I'm fine with staying."

"I mean Sam," Ben says. "No one's going to expect her to stay after this." He looks at me. "Right?"

"I . . . I have no idea. I presume I need to stay—"

"When your aunt has disappeared? With a trespasser on the property?"

"We aren't considering that a likely scenario," Smits says.

"Why not?" Ben says. "Sam reported seeing a stranger. Her aunt disappeared with the front door left wide open." He waves it off.

"Fine. I'll call the lawyer. I'm sure this means Sam can go home and still collect her inheritance."

As he makes that call, my heart thuds. Part of me would love to hear that it's over. But part of me panics at the thought of leaving while Gail is missing. It would feel like abandoning her.

I withdraw into my thoughts and tune out Ben's phone call. After a few minutes, Josie says, "Sam?," and I look over to see everyone waiting for me.

"I'm putting Ms. Jimenez on speaker," Ben says. "Just so no one thinks I'm making shit up."

His voice is as empty as his expression, but his eyes are dark with anger. Is the lawyer saying I'm done? That I get my inheritance without—in Ben's opinion—earning it?

"Ben has explained the situation to me," Ms. Jimenez says over the speaker. "Sam, I am so sorry to hear about your aunt, and I am truly hoping it is a misunderstanding and she's simply wandered off. But, with Sheriff Smits involved, I understand that the authorities consider it a disappearance and that you wish to know how this affects your situation."

"Sam didn't ask," Ben says. "I did."

"Be that as it may, the answer, I'm afraid, is no. You must remain there for the full month. The only exception comes if you yourself are in dang—"

Ms. Jimenez cuts herself short with a throat clearing. "As I said, anything that happens to your aunt would not change the will. However, were she to be found in need of medical care, obviously you would be able to get that. If you must leave the property for a length of time, for anything that falls within a set of criteria—such as you or a family member requiring urgent medical attention—you may do so and make up the time at a doubled rate."

"You mean for every day Sam's gone, she has to spend two more days here," Josie says.

"Yes. And the situation must be fully verifiable."

"Back up," Ben says. "You started to say that there's an exception if Sam herself is in danger."

A pause long enough that he leans over to check the phone. "Ms. Jimenez?"

"Yes."

"Would you please elaborate on that?" Ben's voice takes on a tone I haven't heard. Gone is the irritation and the sullen I-don't-give-a-shit. It's crisp, focused, professional.

"No," she says.

"I need you to elaborate, Ms. Jimenez," he says. "Under exactly what circumstances—"

"They are complicated, and I do not wish to risk misunderstanding."

"So send me a copy. I'm sure I can figure it out. I know a little legalese."

Sheriff Smits makes a noise that I can't decipher. Mockery, I'm sure.

"I cannot do that, Mr. Vandergriff," the lawyer says.

"Don't," I say to Ben. "Please."

One brow lifts. He opens his mouth, but before he can speak, I say, "It's better if I don't know. If *no one* knows."

His brow furrows, and frustration rises in me.

"She doesn't want to tell me," I say, "so I can't cheat. Or someone else can't decide to cheat for me."

Josie nods. "Like if the will says there's an exception if you're shot. Maybe I'd decide to help out by shooting near you. Or if it says you're exempted if you're seriously injured, you might injure yourself to get the money."

"Yes," I say. "So let's drop this."

"Thank you," Ms. Jimenez says. "Also, I must point out that if you did obtain an exception, it would only be under extreme circumstances, and even then, it would be heavily scrutinized. Not by me. I am not your enemy, Sam, however much it might feel like it right now. What I'm doing is interpreting the will for you in the strictest sense, to keep your uncle—or other relatives—from challenging it. But they will challenge any exception, so that is a last resort."

I thank the lawyer and go into my bedroom, where I resume the same position I'd had on the couch, sitting up with my knees pulled in, my chin on them.

After about twenty minutes, Sheriff Smits knocks. Even making the effort of speech is really too much, but I don't want to be mistaken for rude or ungrateful, so I say, "Come in."

He opens the door only a crack. "Just letting you know I'm leaving to continue the search. We'll be taking boats out further down and coming back along the lake. Josie will stay here."

I straighten my legs. "I'll be fine. You need her searching. I can help, too."

"We're going to have you two search the property."

I swallow. "Right. I can't leave. But Josie should—"

"She should stay here to help, and in case Gail comes back."

"Right. Okay."

He says he'll be in touch and starts to close the door before stopping. "Sam?"

"Hmm?"

"Don't give up hope. We have no idea what's happened here."

"Okay." I pause, and then add, "Thank you, sir."

"Craig. Call me Craig."

"Thank you."

Josie and I spend the rest of the day searching the property. My gut says it's pointless, but I can't stop, even when she suggests I take a break.

Ben is long gone. Took off as soon as Sheriff Smits forgot about him, I'm sure, and I don't blame him. This isn't his responsibility.

Mrs. Smits drops off dinner. We don't see her—we just go inside to find a cooler and reheating instructions. After we eat, I'd planned to resume searching, but all my drive has vanished, and I just want to curl up in my bed again.

"You should head home," I say to Josie. "I'm just going to sleep."

"Then I'll stay here while you do."

"You don't need—"

"We don't know what happened to your aunt," she says, meeting my gaze. "Hopefully nothing, but you did see an intruder."

I slump into the sofa. "I'm not even sure about that anymore. I was, but . . ." I trail off and shrug. "Who knows."

"If you want to sleep, do that. If you want to do anything else—play cards, dig up a board game, talk—we'll do that. Failing everything else, there's always the treasure hunt in your grandfather's crawl space." She stops and winces. "And that was insensitive, wasn't it? Sorry. I'm just trying to come up with a distraction."

"That would actually be a good one." I look at her. "Are you up for it?"

"I think that's my question. If you are, I am."

"I am."

Seventeen

We have Josie's cop flashlight, which is ridiculously heavy with an equally ridiculously strong beam. My best flashlight from the house looks like a candle flame beside it. I also take a couple of old beach towels, and she raises her brows at that, but high-fives me when I spread them over the windowsill with its slivers and bits of broken glass.

We crawl through. She takes in her surroundings with that gajillion-lumen flashlight, as I continue on to the bathroom.

"Ooh," she says when I move the bathroom mat aside. "That really is a super-secret hiding space."

"More like a place to stash the booze off-season. My da—" I clear my throat. "My family always said the only thing people would break into our cottages for was the leftover booze. We didn't keep anything else here."

"What about your gran's pirate booty?"

I smile. "She'd say they were welcome to it, and would hope they enjoyed it as much as she did. The alcohol is another story, especially if the local kids decided to pour something else in to cover up the theft." I make a face. "Sorry. You're one of those local kids."

She shrugs. "It's a trick used by teens everywhere. Add a little water and food coloring to hide the missing booze. Also, full confession, as teens, my friends and I knew all the summer cottages where owners kept the key under the back mat and a shit ton of booze in the cupboard. We never bothered watering it down, though."

"I used to sneak my grandfather's crème de menthe up here."

"The stuff that tastes like sweetened mouthwash? Ugh. How old were you?"

"Eleven? Twelve? It was a very small amount—like a quarter of a shot—that I poured on my ice cream. Told my parents the shop in town had mint syrup. Which worked very well until the day my mom asked for some on hers. After some confusion, Mrs. Cooper said they were out of it."

Josie laughs. "Mrs. Cooper is the *best*. My mom really didn't like me having sweets, so Mrs. Cooper would tell her that I'd used my snack money for apples."

I smile and unlock the crawl space hatch. When I tug it open, dust flies up, and we fall back, coughing.

"Forget strong flashlights," Josie says. "We need gas masks." She leans forward and makes a gagging noise. "And not just for the dust. Something died down there."

"A lot of somethings, I bet." I ease onto my haunches. "You want to abandon ship?"

"Never." She pulls her shirt up over her nose and mouth. "Ready when you are. Just . . . leave the hatch open."

"For ventilation? Or escape?"

"Both."

I wasn't kidding about the booze in the crawl space. That's the first thing we find—two plastic milk crates full of half-filled bottles. We heave those out, and Josie jokes about distributing them in all the local teen bonfire spots. There are a few unopened bottles of wine and one of scotch, and I tell her she's welcome to those. She says her parents will appreciate them, especially after the extra aging.

Otherwise, the crawl space is full of household stuff. The outdoor furniture and lake toys always went in the shed. Down here are things like the hibachi grill, sleeping bags, and boxes of old sheets and dishes that my grandmother was too thrifty to throw out and my grandfather was too stingy to donate.

The crawl space itself is about four feet high, meaning we can walk at a crouch and then hunker down to sift through boxes. The single space stretches the length and width of the cottage, interrupted only by support pillars.

I do find a box of my grandmother's "pirate booty"—as well as highlander booty, duke booty, and sheikh booty. As I leaf through the moldering paperbacks, I remember the one upstairs and how I'd planned to sneak it onto Gail's nightstand.

I sit there, gazing down at another bare-chested pirate, tears falling on the cover. Then I shove it back into the box and turn to see Josie fifteen feet away. She's reading what seems like a piece of paper.

"Files?" I ask.

She jumps and drops what she'd been holding. Then she holds up an old paperback. "No, just books. Some are falling apart."

"Anything interesting?"

I'm making my way over when her light goes out. She curses, and I hear her smacking at it. Then it comes on, brightening the area enough for me to continue my trek. I join her at the box she's going through, where she holds out the hardcover.

It's an old book titled *Spooky Legends of the Great Lakes*.

"Oh," I say. "That one. Can't remember a word of it, but I read it about ten times as a kid."

She passes it over. "You should take it."

"I will." I tuck the book under my arm. "Anything else interesting?"

"Well, I did find two very tempting boxes of clothing from the seventies."

When I eye her, she says, "I like vintage, okay?"

"No judgment. I just wasn't sure whether that was sarcasm."

"I am never sarcastic about tie-dye and bell-bottoms."

"You can have them if you want. They'd be my grandmother's, and she was about your size."

Josie crawls over and picks up a plastic box. "There. I have my treasure." She peeks over the top. "Unless you see something you want."

"I doubt it."

"Nope, you will. Or I'll find you something. I'll clean everything up, get my mom to help with any repairs, and once you've put in your month here, we are going barhopping, seventies-style. On you, of course, 'cause you'll be loaded."

I laugh softly. "I will be, and we will definitely go out and celebrate. I will even wear bell-bottoms, just for you. Now let's finish looking through this stuff."

Finding nothing else in the crawl space, we retreat upstairs with our treasures, me holding the book on Great Lake legends and Josie with her box of vintage clothes.

As we circle to the front of my grandparents' cottage, Josie tells me the story of her last bar night and the guy she'd picked up.

"So I'm leaving his place afterward, and I see this photo of two little kids, and I'm like, are these yours? Nieces? Nephews? And he says, oh, those are my grandkids."

I snort a laugh. "Underestimated his age, I take it?"

"Hey, it was dark. At the bar *and* at his place. Also there'd been drinking. So he was a little—lot—older than I thought. No big deal. Then I see a photo of his grandchildren's father and . . ." She glances at me. "I dated him in high school."

I start choking on my laugh. "Seriously?"

"Seriously. He was, like, my first boyfriend. Which means I'd also known his dad . . . the guy I just slept with."

"Did he know who you were?"

"I was *not* going to ask. I got out of there so fast. From now on, I'm taking my big-ass flashlight with me so I can get a good look at any guy I go home with. Also, pro tip? Always check the family photos before you hop into bed."

I'm laughing. Then I spot the pickup outside my cottage, Sheriff Smits standing beside it, and everything rushes back, and shame courses through me.

My aunt has been missing for less than a day, and I'm already finding things to laugh about.

If Smits sees anything untoward, he gives no sign of it, only taking off his hat in a way that has my stomach dropping. I pick up the pace and soon I'm running toward him.

"You found her," I say as I stop short in front of him.

He looks startled. Then he seems to realize what he'd done, taking off his hat, the way cops in movies often do before delivering bad news. He quickly puts it back on.

"No," he says. "I'm sorry. We haven't found anything."

He doesn't ask where we were or what we have in our hands. Josie puts the plastic storage box down by the porch, and I set the book on top.

"I just wanted to update you," Smits says. "I know it's hard on families when they don't hear anything, but mostly, that's because we have nothing to tell."

"Okay." I wipe sweaty hands on my jean shorts. "So . . . nothing?"

He shakes his head. "We've checked the lakeshore. I wanted to get a diver out, but there's a strong current, and it's stirring up the bottom too much to see."

"Do you think that current had anything to do with Gail disappearing?"

"I hope not. But I've notified departments all along the lake. They've scouted the shoreline and taken out boats."

"And the sonar?"

He makes a face. "We used it, of course, but it's tricky."

"Because you'd be searching for a body, and even that's tough to find at the bottom, before it bloats and rises."

He glances up sharply in surprise.

"I looked it up when you said you were using sonar," I say.

He nods. Then he squints into the setting sun. "I wish I had more to tell you."

"I understand."

The sounds of tires on the dirt road has us all looking south. Ben's old pickup appears, rolling along. It passes us, and stops about fifty feet away, close to the shore.

As we watch, Ben gets out. He doesn't even acknowledge us. Just takes a tent bag from the pickup bed and tosses it down near my bonfire spot.

"What the hell do you think you're doing?" Smits calls.

"Setting up camp."

"Should have done that last night. Little late now."

I see Ben's jaw tense, but he only starts unzipping the tent bag.

"You don't need to do that, Ben," Josie calls as she heads toward him. "I'll stay with Sam."

"No one needs to stay with Sam," I say.

"Yeah." Ben meets my gaze. "Someone does."

I flinch at that look. I'd thought he meant he was making sure I was safe tonight. But he didn't say that, did he?

Keeping an eye on me. Ensuring I don't test that exception Ms. Jimenez mentioned? Fire a few shots from Gail's gun and claim I narrowly avoided death?

"I will stay," Josie says firmly.

Her father shifts, his gaze cutting to her in a way that says he understands, as her boss, but as her father, he really doesn't want her here.

I agree.

I don't know what happened last night. My brain has been working overtime to shut down every wild imagining. But I do know I don't want Josie here. I don't want anyone here. I've already endangered Gail, might have gotten her—

I take a deep breath. "I'll be fine."

"I'm staying," Ben says. "You saw a man in the shed. Someone has been leaving mutilated dead animals on your doorstep. And now your aunt's disappearance is just a tragic accident? Can someone tell me why it's the damned caretaker—not the local cops—who has a problem with that explanation?"

"Of course we're concerned," Josie snaps. "Why do you think I'm staying? For a girls' night in?"

He meets her gaze. "Yeah, kinda."

She rocks forward, but he raises his hand. "I'm not insulting you, Smits. I'm saying you and Sam are obviously chummy, and that might relax your guard. I don't have that problem. Also, if someone targeted Sam and her aunt, they might see a twenty-year-old girl—even a cop—as another potential victim."

"I'm twenty-*three*, asshole."

"Already? Huh." He shakes out the pop-up tent. "Point still stands. You really want your daughter here, Sheriff?"

Smits clears his throat. "I would advise you to come home, Josie, and let Ben handle the night shift so you can put in the day shift tomorrow."

"I really don't need—" I begin.

Smits continues, speaking to me now. "I have expressed some concerns about Mr. Vandergriff, but I want to assure you, Sam, that they are not the sort of concerns that would affect him staying the night."

Ben mutters under his breath and then says, "That's his roundabout way of saying that whatever horrible crimes I've committed, they don't include stalking, molesting, or assaulting women."

"No physical violence of any kind," Smits says. "Nor any actions against women." He turns to Josie. "Would you have any concerns about Ben staying here?"

"Of course not," she says. "But I also think I should do it."

"Then maybe you two can switch shifts tomorrow. For now, you've had a long day and Mr. Vandergriff has not. He will stay. You will come home and rest."

Eighteen

So I have Ben Vandergriff camping in my yard. Maybe I should have the guts to refuse, but I don't have the strength. Also, if I insist, Josie will stay. I don't have any cause to reject Ben. Even the sheriff—who obviously dislikes him—has no issue with him staying.

Whatever Austin did to me, I've never gotten a hint of those vibes from his brother. Ben's just here making sure I don't cheat and, honestly, if I think it through, that's probably for the best. Ms. Jimenez is correct that I don't want the will challenged. If anything goes wrong, I'd rather have Ben on board as a hostile witness to grudgingly admit that I didn't fake a threat.

It's just past ten when I walk back outside. Ben's in his tent. I head for the beach and barely make it five steps past his tent before he's calling, "Where do you think you're going?"

I look back to see him standing there. "I won't get close to the water. I'm just . . . looking."

"Come back. Now."

I turn, crossing my arms against a chill breeze. "I'm not five, Ben. I won't get close enough to get pulled in by an undertow."

"There's no fucking—" He bites it off. "Come back."

I peer at him through the darkness. "What do you think happened?"

"I have no damned idea, but you shouldn't be here."

I turn toward the beach and keep walking.

He's in my path so fast I jump. He backs up, keeping a respectful distance. "What are you doing, Sam?"

"Trying to figure out what happened."

"You shouldn't be here."

"I will only go—"

"I mean you shouldn't be *here*. On this property. Not when something has obviously happened to your aunt, and it isn't a damn undertow. Whatever bullshit game your grandfather is playing, it should not require you staying under those circumstances."

Does he mean I should be able to leave *and* get my inheritance? That was what he suggested earlier, though I figured I'd misunderstood. Now, though, I realize it's not that improbable. As long as I'm here, his life is on hold "caretaking" both the property and me. As long as I'm here, he needs to put up with the sheriff's shit. As long as I'm here, he has to face me and all the reminders of his brother's death.

"I'm sorry," I say. "I know this is difficult for you, and it's not fair."

"I'm not—" He throws up his hands in frustration. "Whatever. You know what? Let's fix this, Sam. Offer me a payout again."

"What?"

"Offer me a cut of whatever you make off this place."

"I . . . don't understand."

"What's not to understand? Offer me money, Sam."

I glare at him. "If you're trying to make a point by turning me down—" I stop as a chill runs through me. Our voices are rising, and I swear I feel the wind pick up. Just like last night, when I argued with Gail.

I'm being silly. I know I am. But my gut whispers that I shouldn't argue with Ben. Not here.

"Fine," I say. "If I get the proceeds of this place, you get . . . I don't know. A million dollars?"

"Too high."

"Too—?" *Do not argue.* "How much then?"

"A hundred grand."

"Okay, if I get through this and inherit the property, I promise you, Benjamin Vandergriff, one hundred thousand dollars for your help."

"I accept."

I blink. "You . . . ?"

His gaze fixes on me. "You didn't really mean it?"

"Sure, I did. But . . . Okay. Yes. Good. It's settled."

"It is, and now you don't need to suspect that I'm trying to sabotage you. You don't need to question why I'd help you get that money. It's a payday for me, and I could really use one."

"Uh . . . okay."

"If you insist on walking the beach tonight, I'm going with you. But I would rather be in my tent, reading, if it's all the same to you."

"Reading what?" I ask.

"Porn."

"Liar."

His brows rise.

"No one reads porn anymore," I say. "It's all online."

"I'm old-fashioned that way." He makes shooing motions toward the cottage.

"Fine. I'll go back in."

"And stay in."

"Yes, yes," I say, already walking away.

"Good night, Samantha."

"Good night, Benjamin."

I wake to the sound of hoofbeats, and I want to scream. I do not for one second forget what's happened with Gail, and that sound mocks me, a cruel throwback to my childhood here, when the only thing I had to worry about was a phantom horseman without a head, and even then, it'd been more thrilling than chilling.

I punch my pillow and slam my head back down onto it.

I'm lying there, on my back, glaring at the wood-paneled ceiling, when the pounding of hooves comes again.

I sit up and blink hard, feeling something familiar in my eyes. Yep, apparently, I forgot to remove my contacts.

I jump out of bed and stalk into the living room. I'm not putting up with this shit. I don't care what everyone else thinks, I know I saw someone in the shed, and I know someone left those mutilated animals on my step. A very human someone who is now playing a prank by making the sound of horse hooves.

A witness sleeps thirty feet from my front door, and I'm damn well going to make sure he witnesses *this*. Ben can confirm the sound of hoofbeats, proving someone is taunting me with old stories from my childhood, mistakenly believing the sound will frighten me.

It's my cousin, Caleb. I declare that with the certainty that can only come at two in the morning and will probably evaporate with the rising sun. But in this moment, I am furious with myself for not pursuing this lead. Sheriff Smits raised the possibility, and I should have mentioned it to Gail, because it makes the most sense.

Caleb could have been the person in the shed. He's the right size. He could have had someone "lock" him in there so he magically appeared. Caleb might have known about the small animals Austin left for me. He certainly knew about me "hearing" the headless horseman—he'd mocked me mercilessly.

This is all Caleb's doing, trying to frighten me away from claiming my inheritance, and I am glad of it. Fucking delighted, in fact, because that means Gail is fine.

Caleb would never kill our aunt. Not even if it meant he'd inherit this entire property, and right now, he isn't entitled to any of it if I lose. No, this is about making sure I don't get the money, and to that end, I would not put it past him to kidnap Gail.

He sees her go out to look at those bioluminescent lake lights, and he pounces on an opportunity. Take her captive, making sure she doesn't see him, erasing his own footprints from their scuffle and then holding her somewhere just long enough for me to flee the property. Surely, I'll be gone by nightfall. Except I'm not, and he can't keep her forever. So now, in desperation, he's staging the damned headless horseman.

I march to the front window just in time to see something big disappear into the trees. I'm striding to the door when I spot Josie's massive flashlight, which makes me remember Gail's gun. The thought of grabbing the gun flits through my mind, but I'm angry and stalking out into the dark. The last thing I want is to—in my sleep-addled rage—point the gun at Caleb and risk it firing. The flashlight will do.

Outside, I stride straight to the tent and plant myself at the door.

"Ben?"

I need to say it again before a muffled "Mmph?" sounds from within.

"I need you out here."

A sleep-stuffed "Wha . . . ?"

"Something is out here. I need you."

I don't wait for him to dress. I can still hear the clomp of those fake hoofbeats. So I say, "Catch up," and take off at a jog.

When I reach the beach, my rage spikes even higher as I see the hoofprints in the sand. They're right along the water's edge, the surf lapping at them, filling them.

I take a deep breath and force satisfaction to temper my anger. Caleb didn't get away with this. I'm onto him, and he will pay. That one-third of my grandfather's house he gets? It's going to Gail after what he put her through with this fucking stunt.

I'm following the hoofprints when I realize I need evidence. Luckily, I brought my phone. I take it out and snap shots of the prints before the surf erases them. Then a sound comes from somewhere up ahead. I go still, gripping the massive flashlight.

My cousin is there, maybe fifty feet away, moving along the edge of the water. It's a moonless night, and all I can make out is a figure heading in the other direction. In the silence, the distant splish-splash reaches me as he walks in the surf.

I grip the flashlight. Do I shine the beam on him? Or should I sneak along and find out where he's going?

I squint at the figure. It's Caleb. It must be. But something about it . . .

No, it has to be Caleb.

But it's so tall. I can see the boulders and trees along the shore, and the figure seems at least seven feet tall, maybe eight. It's also not human shaped. More . . . animal, with what looks like . . .

Four legs.

I see four long and slender legs moving through the surf.

I blink hard and look behind me. There's no sign of Ben.

Because I didn't actually wake him up. I didn't actually wake him up because I'm not here. I'm in the cottage, dreaming. Or I'm here, sleepwalking.

Seeing a horse walking along the water's edge. A horse with a rider.

I take a slow step back.

No, if it's not real, I don't need to run. I can get a better look.

The creature is at least fifty feet away now, tramping along the water's edge.

I take a deep breath, turn on the flashlight, and lift the powerful beam to land squarely on—

I swallow.

It's a horse and rider but . . .

The horse is green, covered in lake weeds. Huge chunks of flesh have rotted away to the bone, and what remains is pitted, flaps of green skin and horse hair hanging in tatters, as if it's decomposing. Like the monstrous Austin I dreamed the other night.

And there's a rider. A rider with tattered clothing and rotted flesh and . . .

No head.

The rider has no head.

Of course he doesn't, a voice screams in my head, giddy with maniacal laughter. *Because he's not real. He's a figment of your imagination, mingling the headless horseman and the drowned dead.*

Still, the flashlight beam wavers, my hands shaking, and the horse stops. It turns to look at me, and I see white bone and huge dark eyes. The rider turns too, and he lifts a rotting head by the hair and turns it to look back at me with glowing eyes. Then, even from this distance, I swear those eyes blink.

I turn and run.

I don't think. I can't form coherent thought. I run, heart jammed into my throat, blood pounding so hard I am sure I will never hear the horse when it overtakes me and drags me into the lake.

I am going to die. Die, just like—

"Sam?" a garbled voice says, somewhere beside me.

I don't know how I hear that. I don't even know how I decipher the word as my name. But, still unable to process thought, I react on instinct and stop.

I stand there, heart cycloning in my chest, sucking up air and thought, until I can do nothing but shake, looking around wildly.

The horseman is gone.

He's not chasing me. He's disappeared—

No, there he is . . . walking into the water.

He's still where I saw him, but he's turned toward the lake, and the horse is walking into it, the rider holding his head aloft, eyes glowing, like a macabre lantern lighting his path, as the horse sinks deeper and deeper, until both disappear.

"Sam?"

That garbled voice again, the one that stopped me.

I spin, trying to find it.

There, in the water. Out directly across from me.

Something is walking out of the water.

Some*one* is walking out.

I back up slowly. I go to lift the flashlight, but instead, I lift my phone. My finger fumbles to hit the light, and I snap a picture instead, the flash illuminating—

Gail.

My aunt.

Walking out of the water.

"Oh God," I say, and I run toward her. "Gail!"

She keeps coming, slowly, hunched as if dragged down by her drenched clothing. Her skin is so white it's bluish gray. I keep running, trying to run, slogging through the cold lake water. She moves at the same pace, slow and relentless.

"Help," she says, the word as garbled as my name, as if her lips are frozen from the water. I'm no more than ten feet from her when I stop dead, heart launching into my throat.

One of her eyes is missing.

It's *missing*.

The other eye is filmed over. Her skin sags, and there's a gash in her shoulder where I can see through to the bone.

"Sam," she says again. "Help."

She reaches for me, and finger bones poke through her skin, the tips gone, as if nibbled by fish and—

I turn and run for the beach. I splash through the water, hot tears running down my face, my vision blurred as I run for the shore. My foot hits the sand and I veer left, still running blindly.

"Sam? Sam!"

This is a new voice. Not Gail. Not my aunt. I don't know who it is. I don't know where it's coming from. I just run, tear-blinded, until I bash into something. I flail, pushing and scratching as arms fold around me.

"Sam! It's me. It's Ben."

Hands grab my shoulders. Warm hands, hot through my nightshirt. When I try to wrench away again, he scoops me up, holding me tight.

Nineteen

I'm not sure how Ben gets me back to the cottage. I'm not even sure what I do. Fight? Lie there like a limp rag? The next thing I know, he's depositing me on the sofa, and I bolt upright, clawing at the air.

"Gail!" I say. "I saw . . . I saw . . ."

All I see are his dark eyes above me as they widen. "Your aunt? You saw her? Where? I'll—"

"No!" I grab his shirt. "Drowned. She's dead. Drowned."

"Fuck." His eyes shut for a second. Then he takes hold of my upper arms, holding me, his grip so warm I want to melt into it. "Okay. You saw her body. I'll look after this. Just tell me where—"

I shake my head, damp hair whipping my face. "She's alive. Dead, but alive. Walking. Dead. Out of the water. Drowned. The drowned dead."

An exhale that almost sounds like relief, and my brain spins wildly. Relief? Why is he relieved? My aunt is a monster. The living dead. She's—

"It's okay," he says, as that heat envelops me in a tight but quick hug. "You had a nightmare."

"No, no, no! You don't understand. She was dead. Dead! Drowned! Coming out of the water. Coming for me. And the horseman. The—the headless horseman. Drowned. The rider. The horse. Drowned and rotting, just like—"

Somehow, despite my hysteria, I have the presence of mind to clamp my mouth shut before I say more.

Before I say Austin's name.

I gulp deep breaths, and Ben pats one of my hands. The touch is more awkward now, as if his own moment of panic has passed.

"You had a nightmare," he says. "You were sleepwalking and—"

"No!" I say, gaze flying up to his. "I thought it was a nightmare, but I was awake. You were there. I woke you. So I was *awake*. I saw my aunt. Drowned. Dead. The horseman—the horse." My breathing picks up, words tumbling out, hysteria spiking. "Dead. Everything dead and still moving and—"

"Sam?"

"I saw them. Saw her. Her eye was gone and her fingertips and—"

Something appears in front of my face. I didn't even notice him leave but now he's holding out a shot glass of amber liquid that smells of rye whiskey.

"Drink this," he says.

I shake my head, tears spilling, heart racing.

"I do not want to take you to the hospital," he says. "*You* do not want that either. But I will do what I have to do. Now drink it or—"

I slam the shot. It burns, and I gasp, tears spilling out as I cough.

He thumps me on the back. "Just breathe."

I do, and as my heart rate slows, I start to shake, part from cold and part from shame.

"Sleepwalking," I slur. "I used to do that."

"Okay. Good. Well, not good, but at least you have an explanation."

I nod.

"Yes, you came to get me," he continues. "By the time I got outside, you were gone, and I thought I imagined it. I went back in, and then I heard . . ." He throws up his hands. "You in the water, I guess. Splashing."

"And you didn't see anything else?"

I expect a quick answer, and when I don't get one, I look over sharply.

"I . . . saw a shape," he says. "Something in the water. A dead tree maybe? That must be what you saw, too. Because you weren't completely awake, you mistook it for your aunt."

I nod. "That makes sense. I must be partly conscious when I sleepwalk, or I'd be running into walls and trees." Still holding the empty glass, I pull my legs in and take deep breaths. "Okay. I was only partly awake. I woke up hearing hoofbeats." I glance at him. "I used to do that when I was a kid."

The corner of his mouth quirks. "Your grandfather's Sleepy Hollow stories. I heard about that—he insisted the story was inspired by Washington Irving's trip to Paynes Hollow."

"Yes, so I'd imagine hearing a headless horseman, which is why I thought I saw—" I stop, the shivers starting again, and I force past that image of the dead horse and rider. "I dreamed of one, and I thought it was my cousin, Caleb, trying to spook me. I thought he was behind all this." I pause. "He might actually be. That's another story. But I was half awake and half dreaming. That's why I saw that drowned horse and my . . . my aunt."

I pull my feet in. Ben finds a throw and lays it over my legs, which are bare. I arrange the blanket and focus on tucking it down.

"I remember Caleb." Ben sits on the chair opposite me. "He's about my age, right?"

I nod.

"Does he inherit if you don't?"

I shake my head. "He gets a share of the house and estate. A third, with my uncle and . . ." I swallow. "Gail. But Caleb's not in line for this property and he's upset, obviously. Furious. Is he angry enough to drive me off? Just to be sure I don't win the inheritance jackpot? Maybe. But when I went out, I was even thinking he might have kidnapped Gail to make me leave, which proves I was not in my right mind."

Ben shrugs. "I remember Caleb. My parents made me show him around town once, when I was fifteen. He was an asshole. Tried to score with a couple of older local girls by playing Big Man in Town. Telling them how he was a Payne and the only grandson, and he'd inherit it all." Ben rolls his eyes. "The girls were not impressed." He stretches his legs. "Point is, I could imagine him lurking in the shed, cutting up dead animals, maybe even luring you out by faking hoofbeats. Not sure about kidnapping your aunt, but I wouldn't rule it out. Do you know where he is now?"

"He lives in New York City, but we don't keep in touch. I don't even have his email. Oh, and there were also hoofprints . . ." I trail off. "No, that would be part of the dream, right?" I reach for my phone. "One way to find out. I took photos—or imagined I did."

I look around. "My phone?" I start getting up. "Where's—?"

Ben puts out his hand to stop me and rises to retrieve it. "You were clutching that in one hand and a badass flashlight in the other. I made sure they both came back with you."

He hands me the phone, and my eyes well as I look up at him. "Thank you. For everything."

It's the wrong thing to say, but I have to. Otherwise, I'm the ungrateful bitch treating him like an employee who'd damned well better do his job. Treating him like my grandfather did. Like Sheriff Smits does.

As expected, his face screws up, sloughing off the gratitude. "I'm just protecting my ass. If you walk into the lake, I lose my ticket out of here. And Smits would probably find a way to charge me for murder."

I unlock my phone, but when I try to hit buttons, my fingers are still numb. I blow into one hand and pass over the phone. "Can you check? Last photo. It's either a hoofprint in the sand or Josie stuffing a whole tart into her mouth."

He shakes his head and takes it. "Glad to see you two getting along. She needs that. It's tough for her, being the last one left."

"Uh, you're still here."

"I mean she's the last *kid* left." He catches my eye and sighs, "Yes, I know she's not actually a kid, but she's still young, lives at home, all her friends gone. Last photo is . . ." He blinks down at the camera. "What the hell?"

"Is it a hoofprint?" With the blanket clutched around my legs, I scoot over and lean to see what he's looking at. "If there really are prints, then someone is making those hoof noises, someone who knew I used to hear them. That'd have to be Cal—"

I stop, unable to quite make out what I'm seeing. "What is that?"

"Not Josie. And not hoofprints, though I did see them in earlier shots." He starts to turn the photo my way and then changes his mind, angling it so I can't see it. "Did you take a photo of anything else, Sam?"

"I . . ." I think hard. Then I swallow. "When I . . . dreamed I saw my aunt . . . drowned, I wasn't sure what I was seeing and went to shine the cell-phone light on it, but I hit the camera instead." I stand, feeling the blanket slide away and not caring. "Is that what I got a picture of? Whatever I mistook for her?"

I reach for the phone. He pulls it out of my reach.

"Ben," I say. "That is my phone."

He keeps a grip on it.

"Ben . . ."

With obvious reluctance, he turns the screen around. I look at it and then fall back onto the couch, struggling for breath. On the screen is . . .

Gail.

The figure is blurred, out of focus and off to the side of the shot, but it's clearly a woman, with gray-blue skin, her drenched hair and clothing sticking to her body. One eye is a dark hole.

My hands fly to my own eyes, palms pressing against them. "Still dreaming. Still asleep. I'm still asleep. I'm—"

Fingers take my wrists gently. "It's okay, Sam."

"Okay?" My voice rises. "Okay? You see that, right? That is my aunt."

"It's blurry and off-center—"

"But it looks like her. Dead. Drowned. Walking out of the lake."

"Yes," he says slowly. "It looks like her. She looks drowned. But I think that's what she's supposed to look like." He rises. "I need to call Smits."

"What?" I stare up at him.

"I'm calling the sheriff. We need to sort this out."

By the time Sheriff Smits arrives, I've calmed down enough to understand what Ben meant.

It looks like her. She looks drowned. But I think that's what she's supposed to look like.

Faked. That's what he means.

Of course that's what he means. Of course that's what it is. What other explanation is there?

Smits has come alone. This wasn't something he was waking Josie or Danny for. He's frowning at the photo, awkwardly pinching the screen to get a better view.

"Do you have a laptop here, Sam?" Ben murmurs. "Mine's at home."

"Oh, right. Yes." I scramble to find it. When I bring it back and open it, a medical journal paper pops up on the screen.

"So you went to med school after all?" Ben says. "Guess I should be calling you doctor."

"What?" I follow his gaze to the article and give a sharp laugh that sounds more bitter than I'd like. "No, that's my idea of bedtime reading. I didn't get past my undergrad."

"She got into med school," Smits says from across the room. "But there wasn't enough money for tuition. With her mom's condition and all."

I must look confused, because Smits shrugs. "Your mom told Liz. I just didn't want anyone here thinking you couldn't get in."

"Anyone here . . ." Ben mutters, shaking his head.

I ignore them and ask Smits for my phone. Then I put the photo on my laptop, where I can blow it up. Even with that, the figure is unfocused.

"It looks like Gail," I say. "But it can't be."

"You thought it was, though," Smits says. "You were ten, fifteen feet away, and you believed it was her."

"But it wasn't." My voice is firm. "It's someone dressed to look like her. It was night, and I didn't get the flashlight up in time, and I made a mistake."

There's a long silence before Smits says, "What do you know of your aunt's financial situation?"

I look over sharply. "What does that have to do with anything?"

"This looks like her, Sam. Enough like her that I need to ask."

"She doesn't inherit this place if I fail. In fact, if I fail, she's promised me money from her own inheritance, for my mother's care. Not that I'd take it."

I thud onto the sofa, outrage spiking through me.

"I have to investigate, Sam," Smits says softly. "Your aunt is missing. There's no sign of what happened except footprints by the water, but I'm really not convinced that 'undertow' is our answer."

"It's not," Ben says.

"Thank you, Mr. Marine Biologist."

"That would be a limnologist."

"A what?"

"Person who specializes in the science of freshwater lakes."

I take a deep breath. "You can feel free to investigate the possibility that my aunt faked her disappearance and is now appearing out of the water, looking like the drowned dead, to scare me off. Knock yourself out, Sheriff. But that isn't her in that photo."

"Did she say anything to you?" That's Ben, earning him an "*Et tu, Brutus?*" glower from me. He lifts his hands. "I'm trying to figure this out. Just like you."

"She said my name. Her voice was garbled, which could be proof it wasn't really her. She reached for me and asked for my help."

"Okay, so earlier, you thought Caleb might be behind this. That he temporarily took Gail captive to scare you into leaving. What if that *was* your aunt, in makeup that he made her wear. He threatened her, and she was trying to convey that to you by asking for help."

"Sure," Smits says. "She's going to play along with her evil nephew's scheme rather than just say 'Help, Caleb is making me do this.'"

Ben glares at him. "I'm spitballing, okay? We have no idea what he could be holding over her. For all we know, he was there somewhere, with a rifle aimed at her. Or at Sam."

"I will investigate all possibilities," Smits says. "I have no idea what is happening right now, but I will find out. Until then, don't go out at night, Sam."

"But if we think it's just Caleb—"

"No matter what," he says, holding my gaze. "If you think you see your aunt, you send Ben to investigate. You do not go outside."

"Is that safe for Ben?"

Ben opens his mouth, but Smits cuts in. "Fine. Mr. Vandergriff? If you see or hear anything—or Sam reports something—you will call me and get inside with Sam. Understood?"

I brace for a sarcastic reply, but Ben only says, "Understood."

After that, Smits surveys the scene. I need to go out to show him the spots—and there are still a couple of hoofprints visible—but once he knows where to look, he sends me back inside with Ben to watch over me.

I retreat to my room after that. I'm not tired, but my brain is spinning, and I want to be alone.

Talking to Ben and Sheriff Smits, I felt as if I had everything figured out. Yes, I saw someone who looked drowned—hence the photo. Maybe it was Gail under duress. Maybe it was a stranger. But there was a logical explanation either way.

There. Sorted. My terrifying experience may not have been a nightmare, but I didn't actually see my aunt's drowned corpse rising from Lake Ontario. Because of course I didn't.

But what about the headless horseman?

The sound could have been faked. The hoofprints could have been faked. But I saw an actual horse and rider.

A dead horse and rider.

A drowned horse and headless rider.

That had to be more fakery, right?

Extremely elaborate fakery.

Even without our grandfather's inheritance, Caleb has money. Uncle Mark runs some kind of boring but profitable business, where Caleb works. He could hire actors with movie-quality costumes to pull this off.

I have seen nothing I can't explain.

Except Austin.

I shake that off. *There's* the sleepwalking nightmare. I have zero proof that I saw Austin, unlike the photo and hoofprints.

That part did not happen, and the rest is Caleb.

There. Everything neatly tied in a bow.

So why does my gut scream for me to get out of here as fast as I can? Screams that it makes no sense that I saw my aunt in a "costume" matching the one I "dreamed" for Austin. Screams that my aunt isn't an unwilling actor in my cousin's drama of cruelty. That she's dead. Drowned. Dragged into the lake by—

By what? A headless horseman?

Stop this.

Just stop.

There's an explanation for it all, and Gail is fine.

She's fine.

Twenty

If asked, I'd have said there was no chance of me falling asleep after all that. But while I toss and turn, working it through, eventually the world goes dark and, the next thing I know, I'm waking to the sun blasting through my window, my bedside clock telling me it's past noon.

I stumble into the living room to find Josie on the sofa, typing on her laptop. I wait for her to finish, but she must hear me and turns.

"Hey," she says.

"Hey."

"I figured you could use the sleep, so I let myself in." She shuts the laptop. "There's no news on your aunt. I knew that'd be your first question."

I nod and look around, still groggy.

"Let me get you a tea," she says, rising. "It's just the two of us. Dad is off doing cop stuff. Ben is off doing . . . Ben stuff."

I nod again, struggling to focus.

"Sit," she says. "Mom sent sausage rolls for breakfast. We can plan our day afterward. For now, let's get some food and caffeine into you."

I slide into a chair and let her fuss, too brain-numb to object.

* * *

I thought I'd snap out of it with that hot food and caffeine. I don't. My mood only sags, and I can't even rouse myself enough to feel guilty about Josie being left on babysitting duty.

I don't think. I don't feel. I just exist, in some numb bubble.

Naturally, Josie tries to help. Do I want to go for a walk? Build a midday fire and toast marshmallows? Talk? Whatever I need, she's there. I appreciate that, but mostly, I just don't want the obligation of having to be roused from this grief-laden funk. In the end, I say I have to work, and she lets me do that while working on her own laptop.

The afternoon passes. Sheriff Smits arrives with dinner and a non-update. No sign of Gail. No word on Caleb. He's been unable to contact my cousin or uncle or aunt, but also, no one in town has seen them. While he's asked people to be on the lookout for any strangers, it's still late summer in a lakeside town. At least a quarter of the population are strangers.

Ben arrives at some point. He doesn't check in. Just parks his pickup and disappears. I glance out to see him trudging into the forest. Doing "Ben stuff," I guess. Neither Josie nor her father seems surprised—or even annoyed—that he doesn't make contact. He's there, which means he's on Sam duty, and after dropping off dinner and that non-update, Smits leaves with Josie, both promising to see me in the morning.

Once I'm alone, I relax for the first time all day. And apparently relaxing means crying. I don't need to worry about Ben walking in to check on me. He'll do "Ben stuff" until nightfall and retreat to his tent, and I appreciate that because it means I'm free to grieve without anyone telling me that it's okay, that we don't know what happened to Gail, that she might be fine.

Last night, I told myself the same thing.

I had an explanation, and she was fine.

That's a lie. I know it is. She's dead, drowned, and whatever I saw last night wasn't her, but in some ways, it feels as if my fears manifested into that blurry photo. As if I projected that fear so strongly it burned the image onto a picture.

I know that isn't possible, but it's what I feel.

Gail is gone.

My aunt. My friend. The only family I had left.

Of course, as soon as I think that, guilt reminds me that my mother is alive, which launches into a fresh round of grief for the twilight nothingness that is our relationship these days, where I only catch glimpses of the mother I knew, and the rest feels like trying to provide the best end-of-life care I can. As if she's already in hospice.

I've told the nurses a bit about my situation this month. Not the truth, which is too bizarre and would sound like the flimsiest of excuses. I said that I had the chance to go away for a month and earn enough to cover her care, which is true, even if at least one of them nervously asked whether I was doing anything "extreme." I think her mind went to sex work. Which in the end, is not far off. I am selling myself for money—selling my sanity and my peace of mind.

And maybe selling my aunt. What if she's dead because she came—

Can't think of that.

I'd asked the nurses to text me if Mom is in good enough shape for a video call. I haven't heard back. In other words, at no time in the past four days has she been lucid enough to recognize me.

I can't deal with that tonight either. The grief will pull me under and drown me. Instead, I pick up that book I grabbed from the basement. I'd been seeing it on the counter all afternoon, feeling the tug of it but knowing I couldn't read it in front of Josie. She'd have leapt on the chance to have a little fun, immersing ourselves in superstitious old stories, and right now, that is not what I want.

So what *do* I want? I ask that as I settle on the sofa. Answers? Do I expect to open the moldy cover and find an entry on "Headless man riding a drowned horse"?

No. But I'm pulled to it nonetheless.

The book is self-published. I recognize that now. As a child, I wouldn't have known or understood the difference. In small towns like this, there are always self-published—or small-press—books in the general store. Local interest by local writers. This one seems to have been published in the sixties, and a quick internet check shows it's long out of print, with one copy available on eBay for a few hundred dollars.

Just because it's local interest and self-published doesn't mean it's the work of an amateur. The writer is a long-dead professor and local historian with an interest in folklore and a string of journal publications to her name. But a book like this wouldn't have a wide appeal. It's stories told by those living around the lakes, passing on legends from their families. Worse, it specifically omits the one topic that would make it marketable: ghosts. No haunted ships or forlorn white ladies. Also, the language is far too scholarly to appeal to a wide audience, and I'm shocked that I even managed to read it as a kid.

I flip through stories of lake serpents, deadly fogs, and sunken ships. Then I hit one that stops me.

The book is divided into two sections. The first is legends specific to the lake region. They're tethered to things that early settlers experienced living near massive freshwater lakes, surrounded by wilderness and indigenous people. Some of them are obviously ways to explain their unique environment, while others seem like skewed interpretations of native lore, like the Seneca's lake serpent, Gaasyendietha. The second section relates stories that white settlers brought with them. The folklore of their homelands transposed to this new world. That's where I stop. At a chapter about water horses.

Water-horse folklore is popular in the British Isles and parts of Europe, which is where most of the local white settlers came from. The one I'm familiar with is the Celtic kelpie. I remember it as a horse that lured children to the water. They'd climb on its back, get stuck there, and be drowned. With my adult science-leaning brain, I recognize the myth as an explanation for water-related accidents. A child drowns, and no one wants to admit the adults weren't paying attention, so they dream up monsters that lured the children in. If adults are the victims, then it relieves the drowned of responsibility. They didn't do anything as foolish as go swimming alone. They were lured in by something otherworldly.

As I read, old memories surface, memories of poring over this chapter, fascinated by it. I might have only remembered kelpies, but the other names now ring with familiarity. The Welsh *ceffyl dwr*. The Norwegian *bäckahästen*. The Icelandic *nykur*.

My grandfather had mentioned the *nykur*. Something about its connection to the headless horseman legend. In my memory, it was a fairy horse that blurred with the Wild Hunt, but here it seems to be a form of water horse, like the kelpie.

A bit of online research doesn't get me far. It confirms the *nykur* as water-horse folklore, but there's not much more. Wikipedia includes it on a page with humanoid water creatures called nixie, which includes a Dutch form known as *nikker* or *nekker*.

I divert to the Wild Hunt, which again, I only know in the vaguest terms. It's more British Isles and northern European folklore, which does include horses, but mostly as steeds in a hunting party, where the riders collect the souls of the dead.

I set the book down and rub my temples. What am I looking for here? A legend that will explain what I saw? That's the *opposite* of finding a scientific answer. Am I looking to figure out what Caleb—or whoever is responsible—might be imitating? What difference would that make?

I put the book aside. It's barely past seven, still full light and safe to go out.

The danger only comes at night.

Like my grandfather said.

More temple rubbing as I banish the thoughts. The point is that it's full light, and I don't need to stay indoors.

I want to talk to Ben. No, I just want to talk to someone, and not about water horses and wild hunts or even my aunt's disappearance. I want distraction from that, and Ben is sure to provide it, if only by grumbling that entertaining me isn't his job.

I head to his tent first. "Ben?"

No answer.

"Benjamin?"

If he's inside and choosing to be unsociable, using his full name should get a snort and tell me where he is. It's quiet. I peer around. He arrived a few hours ago, and the joke of Ben doing "Ben stuff" doesn't really explain his continued invisibility.

What *does* Ben do here? According to him, he keeps my cottage clean and in good repair, which isn't necessary with me here. He also clears the lane of debris, but that's only necessary after a storm. He's supposed to do regular sweeps of the property, but that was done thoroughly after Gail disappeared.

So what the hell else is he doing out there now?

Ben stuff.

I shake my head and peer around. My gaze settles on the road, and I remember the hole in the shed that he said he was going to fix. That would take some time, and I wouldn't hear him working on it, unlike if he was wielding a chain saw or weed cutter.

I head to the shed, but there's no sign of him. I circle the building, and I'm about to leave when I see the lock is open.

Latched but unlocked.

A shiver runs through me.

I've been trying to solve this mystery since the day I arrived. How could someone have been in the shed when it was latched?

Walking over, I say "Ben?" but there's no answer. I remove the padlock. Then I open the shed and call again, "Ben?"

No answer.

I step inside and pull the door mostly shut. Then I reach through the gap to try putting the lock back on. I can . . . if I just hang it on the outer hasp. When I found it, though, the latch was shut, the padlock holding it closed.

Is it possible to do that so the person inside can still get out?

I spend ten minutes trying to accomplish it. Shut the door with just enough of a gap to get my fingers out and put the lock back on.

Every time I try it, the lock ends up on the ground, fumbled by my contortions. Sweat drips down my brow. I open the door wide to let in the evening breeze. Then I take out my phone, turn on the light, and look around the shed.

Have I missed anything? A spot where someone could access the shed, bypassing the lock?

Part of me whispers "What does it matter?" but I know the answer. Gail thought I imagined someone in the shed.

Imagined it? Or lied about it?

I know I didn't lie. I also know I was not mistaken. Except those aren't the only two explanations, and it's the third one that keeps me out here, checking everything, desperation rising as cold fear seeps in.

I thought I saw lights on the water. I thought I saw Austin's drowned body coming from the lake. I thought I saw some zombified version of the water-horse lore with a headless rider.

Were they sleeping hallucinations? Waking nightmares? The man in the shed doesn't seem to have been either, so maybe the explanation for all of them is that . . .

I'm losing my mind.

The stress of my mother's condition and my financial situation and my grandfather's will and even the recent death of my cat, and then coming here, reawakening all the feelings I've suppressed about this place. Could that be the impetus for a mental breakdown?

If I can prove that there was a man in here—despite the door seeming latched—then that will also prove I'm not having a breakdown. Of course, that's bullshit logic, but I cling to it. Just prove this one impossible thing that I saw actually is possible and—

My light hits something in the corner. The same corner where Gail found the hatchet and bloodied gloves. Those are gone—and I haven't seen them since—but now there's something else in their place. A pile of clothing.

I grab a rake and poke at the pile. It's soaking wet. There are denim shorts and a tank top and—

This is my clothing.

It's what I wore the day before yesterday.

I lift the shorts on the end of the rake. They're whole, no signs of damage, but they're drenched, as if they'd been dropped into a bucket of water and balled up here with my shirt.

Why are my shorts and tank out here? And why are they wet?

I lift the shorts higher. Something is caught on them. I shine my light to see a lake weed tangled in the belt loops, and my breath catches.

I wore this clothing the day before last. I was wearing it the night Gail died.

The night she left marks on the sand, as if dragged into the water.

I drop the rake, and it thumps to the dirt floor as I back away.

I hear Gail again, in this shed, showing me the hatchet and bloodied gloves, telling me she believed I'd cut up the fox. Everything in me had been horrified by the thought. How could she think I had done that?

But now here, in the same place, is my wet clothing, after Gail has disappeared, after it seems she was dragged into the lake.

No, after *I* thought she was dragged in. That's how I interpreted the marks in the sand. No one else saw them and thought that same thing. That was me. All me.

My mind goes back to that night. To hiding in my room, pretending to sleep, not wanting to go out and face my aunt after our fight.

When had I taken off my clothing?

I don't remember.

Oh God, I don't remember.

Twenty-One

The morning I discovered my aunt missing, hearing the slap of the cottage front door, I'd gone running out in my nightshirt. I don't remember putting it on. I don't remember taking off my shorts and tank top.

Was Gail right?

Did I cut up that rabbit? That fox? Did I stage those horrible tableaus?

Did I kill my aunt?

I race from the shed, my chest ready to explode. I can't draw breath, but I keep running, branches scraping my face, feet moving of their own accord. When I finally see where I am, I stop short.

My old tree fort. A simple platform of wood nestled in three forks of an old oak, with steps nailed into the trunk.

Time shivers, and I'm twelve, staring up at that platform, at the dismembered squirrel pieces hanging from it. My gorge rises, and I turn away, whimpering as I clutch my stomach.

Then I see him.

Austin Vandergriff. Standing there, smirking at me.

"Nice artwork," he says. "A little creepy, but that's you, isn't it, Sam? A little creepy."

"You—you did this."

His eyes widen. "Me? No." He steps closer, and I shrink back, hitting the tree. "*You* did this, Sam, and if you tell anyone, that's what I'll say. I saw you chopping up the squirrel with your hatchet."

I boomerang back to the present, scrubbing my hands over my face. I didn't kill that squirrel. I did not, for one second, believe I had. The smirk on Austin's face told me who'd done it.

It'd been a threat. Not just the promise to claim I'd done it, but the squirrel itself. Do as he said . . . or else.

I'd taken that threat seriously. I'd been a child, with no coping mechanisms for anything like what I endured with Austin. The only thing I could think to do was to get through the summer.

Until I couldn't.

Until I broke and told someone what was happening to me and—

I rub my face harder. Don't think of that. Focus on the present.

Did I chop up a dead rabbit and fox? No.

Did I drag my aunt into the lake? Absolutely not.

I'd been a mess that night, and it's no wonder I don't remember taking off my shirt and shorts. Hell, I don't consciously remember getting changed last night either. It's an automatic part of going to bed.

Gail was wrong. I'm not responsible for any of this. I can't be.

Someone is framing me.

How easy would it be to bloody that hatchet and gloves? I'd left them outside. Equally easy to take my clothing from the hamper and do the same. Gail had been the one to lock the cottage door—I keep forgetting, as if this place makes me a child again, expecting someone else to do that.

But why put the wet clothes in the shed? Who was likely to see them? Not Sheriff Smits. Ben?

Or me.

The most likely person to find that hatchet and gloves and wet clothing was me. I've been the one going to and fro, checking out the shed, getting the hatchet, in there once or twice a day.

Someone wants me to think I'm losing my mind, that I dismembered those animals, that maybe I even drowned my aunt. Someone with access to the—

"What the hell are you doing out here?"

I wheel, see Ben striding through the forest and back up, slamming into the tree trunk, just as I had all those years ago with his brother.

Ben stops short. "Sam?"

"Where have you been?"

His face screws up, as if he doesn't understand the question.

"Where have you been?" I repeat, fighting to keep my voice steady. "You got here hours ago and then vanished."

"I'm dealing with a problem."

"What problem?"

"Caretaking. Which is my job. What's up with you?"

He peers at me and takes another step. Then he must see my expression. He stops, hands up, palms out.

"Okay," he says slowly. "I'm not coming any closer. What's wrong, Sam?"

"Someone's trying to scare me off the property."

"Uh, yeah." He eases back. "That's what I've been saying to anyone who will listen. Someone very clearly wants you—" He stops. "You think it's me? Didn't we resolve this last night? If you stay, I get a big payout. Therefore I can't be the one trying to make you leave."

I shake my head. "Money isn't everything. You blame me. For what happened to Austin. You think I had something to do with it."

He watches me long enough to make me squirm. Then he shoves his hands in his pockets.

"I don't blame you, Sam. If I've given that impression, I apologize. I could have happily gone my entire life without seeing you again." His hands rise. "Not because you had anything to do with Austin's death, but because you're a reminder, okay? If Austin hadn't liked you and kept coming here . . ."

He trails off and exhales. "That wasn't your fault."

The back of my neck prickles.

But what if it was my fault?

What if my father—

No. He wouldn't.

But he did, didn't he? He killed Austin after I told him—

"Sam?"

I wrap my arms around myself. "I didn't do anything to Austin."

Another exhale. "I know. Look, I'm a mess, okay? Everyone knows it, and I don't even bother pretending otherwise. What happened back then . . ." He sucks in breath. "He wasn't supposed to come here."

I don't answer.

Ben rubs the back of his neck and shifts his weight. "I don't know what happened between you two. You had a fight or something? Doesn't matter. But Austin wasn't supposed to go to your place. He was grounded, and I was in charge of him while our parents went out for the evening, and I was a stupid sixteen-year-old who didn't want to look after his little brother, so I wasn't paying attention."

I try to follow what he's saying. My memories of that week are jumbled, the timelines wobbly.

Everything had started the day before the annual town-founders bonfire. I'd refused to go, which exploded into a family drama, my grandfather shouting that everyone expected us there and Dad shouting for him to back the hell off me.

I'd run into the forest, and Dad came after me, and I broke down and confessed that Austin had given me until the bonfire to agree to be his girlfriend, and if I didn't, he said he was going to "accidentally" swing a burning marshmallow into my face. I told him everything. The threats, the dead animals, the pictures, all of it. Dad said he'd handle it, and then Austin was dead and—

But that's not how it happened. Ben's confession fills in a piece I'd forgotten. Dad had gone to speak to the Vandergriffs. Then he said I didn't need to worry about Austin coming by anymore.

He'd spoken to the Vandergriffs and told them enough for them to ground Austin, and to forbid him from ever coming here again.

Ben was supposed to watch him, but he didn't, and Austin came that night and . . .

Dad killed him?

That makes no sense.

It's never made sense. That was the problem.

Could I see my father as a child killer? Of course not, but people don't exactly walk around with "murderer" tattooed on their forehead.

When they're caught, everyone says they can't believe it. So while I can't picture my father as a man driven by inner demons, it is the explanation that makes the most sense.

Tell myself that I didn't really know him. He was evil. End of story.

But what about the other explanation? The one I've been suppressing for fourteen years? That this *was* my fault. I told my father about Austin, and he confronted him, and something went wrong and Austin ended up dead, my father frantically burying the body.

That explanation makes everything in me shrink, trying to hide under a blanket of guilt and recriminations.

If that's what happened, it was my fault. My fault for not handling things better. Forget the logic that says I didn't kill Austin and I actually *did* handle it properly, by telling my father.

But if Dad went to the Vandergriffs and told them to keep Austin away from me, and Austin came back and my father killed him, that's not an accident. That's not blind rage. Killing Austin under those circumstances makes no sense.

I'm missing something.

No, I've forgotten something.

Suppressed it.

I realize Ben is watching me. And then I realize that he's just made a huge confession, and I didn't respond, lost in my own memories.

"I . . . I don't remember what happened," I say because it's all I can think to say. "Between Austin and me."

He shakes his head. "I wasn't asking. Like I said, it doesn't matter. The point is that I fucked up and my brother died. Your father killed him and then your grandfather—" He bites off the words with a sharp shake of his head. "Your grandfather was his usual asshole self, and I should have refused the job, whatever the cost."

"You couldn't," I say, my voice barely above a whisper. "Because of your father. I get that. It's—it's why I'm here, too."

"For your mother." He runs a hand through his hair. "So that's our story, then. Letting your grandfather manipulate us because others will suffer if we refuse. But I have no stake in chasing you off, Sam. I'm angry for a whole lotta reasons that are tangentially linked to you, but I'm not your grandfather. I know who I'm angry with, and I'm not going to punish someone connected to that anger because I can't punish the actual source. Your grandfather's problem was with your dad, but he couldn't confront *him,* so he took it out on you and he took it out on me. I wouldn't do that to you. Whatever is happening, I swear it isn't me."

"Then what have you been doing out here?"

He throws up his hands. "Back to that? Fine. I was trying to handle a potential issue without alarming you. Someone has set up camp in the west field."

"What?"

"There's a tent and what looks like bicycle tracks. The campers aren't there, but I've been keeping an eye on it so I can tell them to move on. And before you wonder whether it could be your cousin or whoever is doing all this, I very highly doubt it. They aren't exactly hiding their campsite. It's in the middle of a damn field."

"Can I see?"

Another hand toss, clearly exasperated. "Fine. Whatever. Come on."

Twenty-Two

Ben takes me along a path. The western field is the most common place for campers. We used to camp there ourselves when we had an extended family gathering. It's a big open meadow, flat and perfect for pitching tents.

Before we even get there, the smell of smoke tells us the campers have returned. We come through the forest to see a small pop-up tent. A touring bike with saddlebags is parked beside it.

"I'll handle this," Ben says.

He strides forward, and his gait says he's about to blast the trespasser, but when he calls, "Hello!" it sounds like a friendly hail.

The campfire is on the other side of the tent, and it takes a moment before a man appears. He's maybe in his late forties, with graying dark hair, lean and tanned in the way of long-distance cyclists.

"This spot's taken," the man says.

I look around. The "spot" is several acres of open land. Even if it were in a park, I'm not sure how he'd justify claiming it all for his personal campsite.

"You are correct, sir," Ben says, his tone still friendly, but now ringing with false joviality. "This spot—this three-hundred-acre spot—is taken by the person who owns it. You are camping on private property. I'm sure you saw the signs."

The man only crosses his arms, jaw setting. He saw them. He just doesn't give a shit. I remember back when my family did allow people to camp on the grounds. Most were happily appreciative, but every now and then you'd get the ones who expected to use the facilities at our cottages. Because clearly, if you're letting strangers stay for free, you owe them free showers.

Ben continues, his too-friendly tone edging deeper into sarcasm. "Perhaps, sir, you passed through the town on your way? Stopped for supplies? Paynes Hollow is the name. This here is Ms. Payne. The landowner."

The man only snorts. "And she called her boyfriend to scare me off?"

"No, her caretaker—me—noticed your tent and has been waiting for you to return to it."

A second snort. "So she called her goon then. Of course. Little rich girl isn't going to get her hands dirty. Use the local yahoos for that." He straightens. "I assert my sovereign right, as a descendant of the original settlers, to camp wherever I like."

"Your sovereign right?" I say.

Ben lifts a hand to stop me. "Understandable. I'm sure Ms. Payne will recognize the hereditary land rights of the original settlers. I only need to see your tribal ID card."

The man scowls. "I don't mean *that* kind of settler."

"You aren't local? That's fine. Ms. Payne will recognize any tribal card, and happily allow you to camp—"

"Stop your bullshit. You know exactly what I was saying. I have the right to be here, and I do not recognize the authority of any rich little girl whose great-great-great-granddaddy bought this land."

Ben frowns. "And yet you assert your own right based on some equally distant relative?" He shakes his head. "Never mind. The answer is no. Pack your shit and get on your rusty steed, cowboy."

"My bike isn't rusty."

I bite my cheek at the guy's obvious indignation, but I stop smiling when he stalks toward Ben. I jump between them. I don't think about what I'm doing—just that I need to defuse the situation. Ben barely gets out a sound of warning before the guy slams his hand into my shoulder so hard I fall on my ass.

"What the hell?" Ben says, lunging forward.

"Oh come on," the guy says. "That was a pratfall. I barely touched her."

As the wind whispers around us, Ben helps me up and then turns on the man. "You knocked her down. For trying to stop you from taking a swing at her employee. Pack your stuff. Now."

"Or what? You'll pack it for me? Lay one finger on my gear, and you'll regret it. I'm a lawyer."

Ben stares and then he starts to laugh. "Of course you are."

"I am."

"That wasn't sarcasm, asshole. I believe it. I'm also pretty sure that if I ask for your ABA card, you're as likely to pull that out as a tribal ID card."

The man's jaw sets.

"Good guess, huh? A lawyer, but not the practicing sort, or you'd be too embarrassed to even try that sovereign-right shit. Now if you've humiliated yourself enough for one day, it's time to go."

The man steps toward Ben, who doesn't even tense.

"You want to hit me, too?" Ben says. "Go ahead. I won't even hit back."

The guy's eyes narrow.

"Have you wondered how I knew you were here?" Ben waves at the forest. "Smile, you're on camera. It's a really good one, too. Rich people, huh? Always protecting their private property with high-tech toys. Right now, it has footage of you striking Ms. Payne, unprovoked. The angle is . . ." Ben squints that way. "Exactly right. Excellent. It'll be up to her whether she wants to press charges or not. But if you hit me, I will definitely press them. I need all the money I can get. You might not be a practicing lawyer, but you know what an easy case that will be. Guy trespasses on private property. Is politely asked to leave. Knocks down the young woman who owns it and then hits her employee, who doesn't even strike back. Maybe you can try out your sovereign-right defense."

The man steps right up to Ben, who lifts his hands.

"Note for the camera that I am unarmed and in a position of surrender, making no attempt to defend myself against this trespasser on my employer's property."

The man stomps his foot an inch from Ben, as if to startle him. When Ben arches an eyebrow, the man's scowl is truly worthy of a toddler throwing a tantrum.

"Fucking piece of shit land anyway," the man says. "Can't even see the lake from here."

"Most of the lakefront land around here is privately owned," Ben says, "but if you drive about twenty minutes west, there's a state park with some very nice lakeside sites. Decently priced for small tents, too."

"Fuck off," the man spits.

"Have a nice evening!" Ben calls, waving for me to start walking and falling in behind me. "If you aren't gone in twenty minutes, I'll be calling the sheriff, who is a close personal friend of mine. Drinking buddy, in fact."

There are no cameras on the property. That's what Ben had said earlier, and I know that hasn't changed, considering Ben had been watching for the guy to return to his campsite. Ben confirms the bluff as he shows me to a spot where he can watch the field without being seen. The cyclist fumes for a few minutes and then stomps off to look for the nonexistent camera. He's obviously watching the time, though, and twenty-three minutes later, he's packed and gone. He certainly wasn't giving in to "the man" by leaving *within* twenty minutes, but neither was he sticking around to talk to the cops.

"You do know a bit about the law," I say as I follow Ben back to the cottages. "Like you told Ms. Jimenez."

He snorts. "Doesn't take a law degree to recognize guys like that."

"Failed lawyers?"

"Started the degree but couldn't finish. Or finished, but couldn't pass the bar. Or passed the bar but couldn't hack the job. Dime a dozen. Like I said, I've taken a few courses. Saw plenty of them, sometimes as teachers. Talk like they're a fucking lawyer, but say shit that proves they aren't."

We continue on, me tramping after Ben, nearly jogging to keep up.

"You want to sue him?" he says. "Charge him?"

"No."

"Figured that. Just thought I should ask instead of being a total dick who ignores the fact you got knocked down."

"I'm fine."

"And you'd say that even if you weren't, so I didn't bother asking earlier."

I roll my eyes and hop-step over a fallen branch. "About cameras. That'd be a good idea. A really good one."

"Yep."

I chew the inside of my cheek. "I, uh, really am a bit short on funds."

"Dead broke from what I hear."

I tense. "What?"

"Sorry. I misstated. Dead broke means you have no money. You're in debt. That's worse."

My eyes narrow as my hackles rise. "My financial situation is none of your business."

"Well, the person who told me thought it was. They figured if I knew how bad off you are, I'd stop being an asshole to you. Their mistake. I'm an equal-opportunity asshole."

I shake my head. "My point is that I don't have a ton of spare cash for cameras, but some cash was left in the cottage. I used most of it to pay my mom's bills, but I have a few hundred left. Would that be enough?"

"Not for a decent system. Doesn't matter anyway. It won't work."

"We could try," I say, trying not to grind my teeth.

"Already did." He takes another step, and then sighs, as if realizing I'm not going to drop this, which means he needs to say more than a line or two to shut me up.

"Seven years ago," he says, "I was out here, on my rounds, cleaning up trash from picnickers, checking the cottage for damage, and I thought, what the hell am I doing? Cameras could handle this. So I contacted your grandfather. It was one of the rare times he bothered to reply. He said they wouldn't work out here. I was young, naive, felt a little sorry for the old guy who didn't understand modern technology, so I explained how they *would* work. He sent back one line: Why the hell would I be paying you if I could monitor the property that way?"

"Charming."

"Always. Two more years pass, and an old school buddy of mine goes into home security. I ask him to demo a system for me. A cheap one. Not that I'm trying to avoid doing my rounds, but because I'd rather avoid cleaning up shit from campers and vandals. He comes out. Sets it up. Doesn't work. Can't get a remote signal. There's cell service, obviously, but it's not connecting, no matter what he does. Some technical shit about the cell signal here. Long story short, I can set up game cameras and download the photos, but the only thing that's good for is blurry pictures of deer."

"Okay."

He glances back at me for the first time since we left the camper. "You are free to try yourself. Don't take my word for it."

"No, I figured there was a reason we don't have security cameras."

"Yep." He resumes walking. "And it's not my incompetence."

"I never said it was, Ben." I take a few more steps. "How much are trail cams?"

He sighs.

"I'll look it up," I say. "I don't know whether I can get deliveries out here, but I'm sure Josie would let me send them to her."

"I already put up three. You want more? A hundred bucks a pop."

I don't say anything. I do not even make a noise, but he throws up his hands as if I won't shut up about it.

"I installed them today, okay? That's part of what I was doing. After you got that photo at the lake, it made me think there might be a point in trail cams. Get shots of anyone snooping around. One is aimed at the beach. One at the steps of your cottage. One over by the shed."

My heart picks up. "There's one by the shed?"

"Yeah."

"Can I see the pictures?"

He shrugs. "Sure. I need to download them manually, but I'll show any to you tomorrow."

"Can I see them now?"

He peers back at me.

"Please?" I ask.

I wait for him to ask for an explanation. He only shrugs. "You're the boss."

Twenty-Three

The trail cams only snap shots when movement is detected. The one by the shed has taken two since Ben set it up. A picture of me entering the shed and one of me leaving. They're from early this evening, when I went inside and found my wet clothing.

Ben shuts down the phone app, muttering. "I need to get this to my truck, charge it up."

"It's at fifty percent."

"Yeah, and I don't let it go below that while I need to be monitoring your ankle bracelet. If my phone dies, the app alerts your grandfather's lawyer that I'm not doing my job. It'd also be an excuse for your uncle and cousin to say you could have left the property."

"Okay. But the camera, what time did you set it up?"

When Ben doesn't answer, I look over at him. We're in the cottage living room, and he's paused by that book of Great Lake legends.

"This yours?" he says.

"My grandfather's. I rescued it from the crawl space. I used to read it as a kid."

He nods, but his gaze seems distant.

"Ben?" I say. "When did you set up the shed cam?"

"That was the first one. I put it up earlier today."

So whoever put my wet clothing in the shed did it before then. I'd been hoping it would catch some stranger sneaking in with my lake-drenched clothes. But there are only those two shots of me, nothing in my hands.

I peer outside. "It's getting dark."

"Yeah, yeah. I'm going. You're the one who wanted the photos, Samantha."

"That wasn't a hint, Benjamin. If I wanted to kick you out, I'd kick you out."

He snorts. "You absolutely would not."

"I—"

"If I hadn't been here, would you have told that camper to leave? Or politely asked him to be gone by morning, despite the fact that someone has been trying to drive you off and may have kidnapped your aunt, and it could be that guy impersonating a camper."

"Do you think he was a fake?"

"No. I'm making a point. Protect yourself, okay? Ask for cameras. Buy more if you want them. Demand strangers get off your land. Tell me to leave your cottage because it's past dark."

"That's not—"

"And get out your aunt's gun, for God's sake. You have it. Use it."

"On you?"

"Sure. If I attack you in the night, you absolutely *should* shoot me. You have my permission to do so. Now get some sleep."

I do sleep. Again, I'm not sure how, and even when I do drift off, my mind lashes me for the insensitivity of falling asleep while my aunt is missing.

I've spent the last two days silencing the voice that screams that I'm not doing enough. I should forget this stupid inheritance and take her car and . . .

What? Check her apartment in case she went home and failed to tell me?

Canvass the residents of Paynes Hollow, who already know she's missing and have been on the lookout?

Drive up and down the back roads in case she's lying alongside one?

Forget leaving. I should be out there walking the property every daylight hour, in case she's lying in a thicket, injured. I should be out on the lake, in case . . . I don't know. She washed up alive on a sandbar somewhere?

I know I can't do more than I have. I know I need to leave this to the authorities, whom I trust. This must be how every person who has a loved one disappear feels. Guilty over not searching twenty-four hours a day. Guilty over sleeping, eating, laughing.

I know someone who did have a loved one vanish. He's outside in a tent. It'd taken nearly two days for Austin to be found, the same amount of time Gail has been missing. I could talk to Ben, reassure myself that what I feel is normal or get tips on how to deal with it.

Yeah, I could do that . . . if it were anyone except Ben Vandergriff, who will neither answer my questions nor appreciate me asking.

The only thing I can do is reassure and comfort myself, which works reasonably well . . . until I'm asleep. Then I dream that my aunt is half drowned and washed up less than a mile along the beach. That she went for a walk at night, was hit by a car, and is lying unconscious in a ditch. That she was kidnapped by Caleb, who forced her to play the drowned dead last night. That she had been kidnapped by the cyclist-camper, who'd had her in his tent the whole time we were out there arguing with him. Or that she'd been kidnapped by Ben and is apparently in *his* tent, thirty feet away. And each time I find her, it is by accident, me having a fun time at the cottage and stumbling over her as she gasps her last breaths.

Then comes the last segment, where I'm the one who kidnapped her. Where I'm holding her hostage in the shed, and then I take the hatchet and I step toward her, and she knows what is coming, and she screams a bloodcurdling shriek that has me rocketing out of bed, hands to my ears, vomit in my mouth as I gag.

And yet the screams keep going.

Distant, horrible human screams.

I hover there, sour bile dripping before I slowly wipe it away. And the screams continue.

I'm still asleep. I'd only dreamed that I woke up—

Banging sounds on the front door.

"Sam!" Ben shouts. "Samantha!"

I turn slowly in that direction. The dream lingers, hazy, and I can't focus. Ben curses and then the front door slaps open.

"Sam!"

Footsteps pound. My bedroom door swings open, and Ben is silhouetted there for a heartbeat before he jumps back.

"Jesus!" he says, retreating fast until he's out of sight. "I'm sorry. I didn't mean—I thought—Someone's screaming, and I thought . . ."

He thought it was me. That much penetrates as my brain turns on, but it's still sluggish, and I can only make out bits of what he's babbling in the next room. Something about a key. That he still had the cottage key. That he should have returned it to me.

Then, "You heard the scream, right?" he says.

I rub my face and croak, "Yes."

So it wasn't a dream. Unless this is.

"Am I dreaming?" I ask.

"What?"

His disembodied hand reaches around the doorway and flicks on the light, fumbling a bit, as if he's trying to do it without looking into my room.

"I'm decent," I say.

He edges into the frame. "Are you okay? You seem . . . You took something. To sleep. Of course you did. Dumb question."

He's babbling still, which means he really doesn't sound like himself.

I shake my head. "I didn't take anything. Just . . . having nightmares." I fold the comforter over the soiled part where I threw up and hope he can't smell it. "That sound. I thought it was part of my dream." I blink. "Fox, right? That was a fox screaming?"

"Oh." He rocks back. "Maybe? Fuck." He rubs his face. "Okay. Maybe? I guess so? That makes sense, doesn't it?"

"*Was* it a fox?"

He doesn't answer.

I stand up. "Ben?"

"Hell if I know." He's awake enough to sound more like himself. "I woke up to it. Thought it was you, and when you didn't answer the door I remembered I still had the key on my ring." He pulls the ring from his pocket, finds the cottage key, and yanks it off. "I shouldn't have this."

"Ben, I don't care if you have the key. I don't care if you came in here to check on me, in case I was the one out there screaming. Good. Great. Thank you. But *was that a fox*? I remember hearing one as a kid but—"

I press my palms to my eyes. "My aunt is missing. Last seen on this property. We just heard screams. And we're standing here debating whether it was a fox. Fuck!"

I stride to the door, squeeze past him, and yank on my sneakers.

"Sam . . ."

I spin. "Yes, it was probably a fox. But I just woke up from a dream where I kept finding my aunt too late because I didn't look. Well, except for the last one where I was the one holding her captive and about to chop her up with the hatchet, which apparently explained the screaming."

"What?" His face screws up and then he shakes it off. "Never mind. Okay. You're right about it probably being a fox. But—"

I'm already out the door. He clatters out after me, but by then, I'm off the porch, staring out at the water.

"Ben?" I say.

"I see that," he says as he comes up beside me. "Your lights."

"So I'm not imagining them."

"No."

"Unless I'm imagining being awake."

He ignores that and strides past me. I catch the back of his T-shirt, and he spins, hands flying up. I quickly let go.

"Sorry, sorry," I say.

"It's fine."

"Just . . ." I chew my lip as I look toward the lights, and I want to tell him to stay here. Wait for me. Don't go near the water. Let me do it. I'll be fine.

Does that make sense?

Does any of this make sense?

Maybe I really am losing it.

"I'm getting my phone," he says. "Come with me."

I do, and once he has it, he says, "Stay close."

"You, too."

A sound between a snort and a gruff laugh, as if to say he's hardly worried about himself. But he should be. My gut says he should be. My gut also says that I can't trust him to be. I can trust him to worry about me but not about himself.

That makes *no* sense.

He doesn't give a shit about me.

Maybe not, but he gives even less of a shit about himself.

Where the hell did that come from?

"Sam?" he says, squinting at me. "If you took something to help you sleep, just say so. I'd understand."

I shake my head. "I didn't. I'm just a little . . . off-balance. Things are happening and . . . and—" I blurt the rest before I realize what I'm saying. "I think I might be responsible."

I have no idea what I expect him to say to that, but he only looks out at the water. "Did you put lights out there?"

"No."

"Then come on."

Twenty-Four

I go back inside to put in my contacts first. I'm no longer taking any chances that what I see is the result of poor eyesight. Then we walk to stand on the lakefront, and all I want to do is drag Ben away from the water. I can't look at the lights. I can barely force myself to glance at them.

"Weird," he says as he snaps pictures. "When you mentioned it, I pictured lots of lights. Maybe reflections? But there's only a few. You thought it was something bioluminescent?"

I force myself to nod as my brain screams to get him away from the water.

"Could be," he continues. "But I've lived near the lake my whole life, and I've never seen this. It's like there's something under the surface."

Before I know it, he's walking into the surf.

I lunge. "No!"

He glances back.

"Please," I say. "Don't go in. Not at night."

"Not . . . ?"

"Maybe I am losing it. I think I am. Just please, please, please stay out of the water. Out of the water and out of the woods. At least at night."

He tilts his head, and I see myself in his eyes and shrink.

"I'm not making sense," I mumble. "I know that."

"Just tell me what you're thinking."

"I—I don't even know. Just . . . my grandfather always said to stay out of the woods and the lake at night. So did my parents."

"Stay out of the lake and the woods at night," he says slowly. "That's what they told you?"

I flail my arms. "It's basic safety. I know that. I'm freaked out over being back here and my aunt going missing, and I'm seeing things and overreacting."

"I won't go in the water," he says. "But whatever we heard seemed to come from the forest."

I swallow. "So we need to go in there."

"We'll get Josie's big flashlight. And your aunt's gun. If there's any chance—"

His head jerks up. He stares at something down the beach.

"Sam?" he says. "What am I seeing?"

I squint in the overcast night. Then I suck in a breath. There's a shape on the beach. A heap that looks like a human form. As if someone washed up on the sand.

I take off at a run, even as Ben yells behind me. His fingers graze my side, but I'm already out of reach. With every step, any doubt that the heap is a human form evaporates. A bare arm extends upward toward the water. A leg is askew, twisted as if broken.

And then there is a noise. The rasp of breath, and the fluttering of that extended hand.

It is a person, and they are alive.

It must be Gail. She's alive. Badly injured. There's blood and twisted limbs and obvious pain in that labored breathing, but she is—

I'm close enough to see the leg now. A muscular leg covered in dark hair. Then the head, with equally dark hair and tanned skin.

I'm seeing a man.

I stop short. Ben knocks into me, and then, before I know it, I'm behind him.

"Fuck," he says. "It's the guy. The cyclist. The camper."

He fumbles to pull out his phone.

"I'm calling for help!" he shouts to the man. "Just hang tight. I'm—"

Ben stops short and sucks in breath. Then he backpedals, his arms out to keep me back.

Something moves up ahead, right on the edge of the forest. I can't see what it is. Just a huge dark shape against the trees. Then there's a *clomp-clomp*, the sort of noise that you wouldn't expect to recognize, but you do. The sound of a horse's front hooves lifting and lowering in impatience.

I tear my gaze away and look down at the sand. Hoofprints. All around the dying man are hoofprints.

Ben stands frozen. He still has his phone in hand, and I pry it from his fingers. Then I turn on the flashlight. It illuminates the figure at the edge of the forest.

The horse. The rider. The rider's severed head, outthrust in his hand, turned toward the lake.

"What the hell?" Ben's voice comes high, words nearly unintelligible. "What the hell is that?"

"The horseman," I say, and my voice is horribly calm. "The headless horseman."

The rider's arm moves, turning the head our way. I grab Ben and yank him back, seized by the impulse to get him behind me. But the head only looks our way for a moment, and then the arm moves, and it is gazing out at the lake.

"I'm dreaming," Ben says. "You thought you were, but it's me. Right? It's me. *Right?*"

Something moves to our right, and we both jump. It's a light under the water, another behind it. Then the light goes out and something dark begins to rise from the lake.

The figure of a man. A tall man. Nearly naked, his remaining clothing in tatters, his flesh gray and rotted. Ben gets in front of me, arms out again, backing us up. The figure doesn't look our way. Doesn't seem to notice us. It's advancing on something else, and too late, I realize its goal.

The injured man.

I try to lunge forward, but Ben keeps inching us backward. I want to dart around him, to run to the man before it's too late, but a primitive corner of my brain overrules the impulse. It whispers not to get between the tiger and its prey. Just run. Give thanks that we aren't its target and run.

I still hesitate. I can't help it. If there's any way I could stop that creature from getting to the camper...

Except it's not just that one creature. There's another behind it, bobbing along and then dragging itself out on a body with one missing leg and the other nearly bone. Two other shadowy shapes emerge behind them, and even then I'm trying to figure out a way to save the camper. But the one in front, the tall male figure, charges and falls on the camper, head dropping and ripping into flesh.

The camper only makes a gurgling sound, as if he's barely conscious. Another of the drowned dead falls on him, biting and ripping, but the first knocks the second flying with a backhand, grabs the camper by the hair, and drags him toward the water.

Other dark shapes swarm, taking hold of the camper by whatever body part they can reach as they walk into the lake. And throughout it all, the horseman watches. The horse stands on the shore, the rider holding his head out to the lake.

"Sam?" Ben's voice is ragged. He's backed up until there's only a sliver of space between us. He wants me to retreat—desperately wants me to retreat; I can see that in his wide eyes. But he won't grab me or push me. Nor will he run past me to flee.

I need to get out of here—get both of us out of here. Before those things emerge from the water again. Before more appear. Before the horseman remembers us.

I take one slow backward step and then another. The figures in the water are nearly submerged. Another's head rises above the surface. I don't stay to get a better look. I turn and I run, and I get three strides before I realize Ben isn't behind me.

I wheel to see him still back there, staring at the lake.

"Ben!" I shout.

He breaks from whatever holds him and sprints until he's right behind me, his hands out as if to spur me on. I run as fast as I can, and he's right there on my heels as I pass his tent and then scramble up the cottage steps.

"No!" he shouts, and I turn to see him gesturing at his truck.

He gets the passenger door open first, throwing it wide for me before opening the driver's side. He's inside in a blink, starting the truck, backing out, and then roaring down the drive. I sit there, numb and staring at the rutted road until I see the gates ahead.

Then I shout, "Wait! I can't leave!"

He hits the brakes hard enough that I slam forward against my seat belt. I wait for him to shout at me to forget my damned inheritance. Nothing is worth staying after what we just witnessed. But he only puts the truck in park and leaves it idling there as he breathes.

"You should go," I say softly.

"What happened back there?" he says. "What the *fuck* just happened, Sam?"

I don't answer. We both know what we saw. The only question is how it was possible. What it could have been. And I don't have answers for that.

"Sam?" he says. "You saw that, right? The horseman? Those— those things, coming out of the water. That camper. What they did to him."

"Yes."

He turns, vinyl seat squeaking under him. "That's what you saw, isn't it? Your aunt. The blurry photo. That's what she looked like."

"Yes."

"And the horseman?"

I nod. "I saw him, too. The horse, and the rider holding his head in his hand. Like the legend. Except . . . drowned."

"You saw it when you were young, too."

I shake my head. "Back then, I'd only hear a horse. Everyone thought it was my imagination. Dad gave my grandfather shit for filling my head with those stories. Even I thought it wasn't real. That I was amusing myself by making up stuff."

"Amusing yourself . . ."

I tense and then wrap my arms around myself. "What we just saw . . . Obviously that's different. Like I said, I never saw anything like that until last night. It's just . . . the way my grandfather told the stories, they weren't scary. Even the part about not going in the forest or the lake at night. It wasn't because I'd be hurt. It was just . . ." I shrug. "I don't know how to explain it."

"The horseman didn't come after us," Ben says. "You shone the light right on him. He just looked at us and then looked away. What about last night?"

"The same."

He goes quiet, thinking. I should be doing the same. Working it through. But every time my thoughts slide in that direction, I shrink back.

Don't think about it.

Don't analyze it.

"Those things killed that camper," I whisper. "Or the horseman did. The guy didn't leave the property after all. He just moved to a different camping site. The horseman . . . The screams . . . The hoofprints . . ." I swallow. "We need to call Sheriff Smits."

"Yeah."

I relax, as if I'd half expected him to say no. Don't call the sheriff. The cyclist is dead and gone into the lake. Pretend nothing happened. Because that's better than explaining what we saw.

"What are we going to tell him?" I say.

"What we saw. The . . . things from the lake. Like your aunt in the photo. They dragged him in."

"And the horseman?"

He goes quiet. "Did you get a photo?"

I shake my head. "So we don't mention the horse. That's my advice. We say we thought we saw a shape, maybe a horse, and the hoofprints might be there, but we don't say . . . exactly what we saw. The drowned horse. The headless rider."

"Yeah."

I exhale, relieved.

"If we go too far, he'll think we're high on something," Ben says. "Or he'll think I'm high and snuck you some. I did stuff when I was a kid. Experimenting." He pauses. "A bit of selling. That was years ago. I haven't so much as smoked a joint in a decade, but that won't matter."

"He'll say the horseman was a drug-induced hallucination."

"Fuck, even with those things from the lake, he might say that."

Ben bangs back against the headrest and closes his eyes. "Zombies coming out of the lake."

"The drowned dead. But we have the photo."

He exhales a slow breath. "Calling in Smits is probably a bad idea, but I don't know what else to do. A man is dead."

"And if anyone comes looking for him, we don't want to need to lie about him being here."

"Yeah. Agreed." He rubs the back of his neck. "I'm going to call Smits, but while we're waiting, I need to ask you about something."

Twenty-Five

Sheriff Smits is on his way, and even without the phone on speaker, I know he's not happy about it. Ben said we believe a would-be camper was dragged out into the lake, and Smits clearly seems to think this is Ben being an asshole.

Maybe it would have helped if I'd called while Ben was driving headlong through the dark, both of us caught in the wild panic of watching a man die at the hands—and teeth—of the drowned dead. By the time Ben placed that call, we were both calm. Too calm? In shock? Or just relieved that we were still alive? Even now, when I'm sitting in the truck, what happened feels like a nightmare I've woken from, feeling unsettled but also detached.

Just a nightmare.

Except it wasn't, and I don't think either of us knows how to deal with that.

"Earlier, you said things were happening," Ben says, "and you thought you might be responsible."

My stomach clenches, and I look out the truck window.

"Sam?" he says, his voice low. "I'm not asking you to confess anything. Trust me, I'm the last person you want for your Father Confessor. But I think you're really mixed up right now, and after what happened—a man *died* in front of us—you don't want to take responsibility in front of a cop. In fact, I'm going to very, very strongly advise against it."

My lips twist in a humorless smile. "Practicing law without a license?"

He snorts. "Don't need a law degree to know that's a really bad idea. Tell me what you think you did so I can tell you you're wrong."

"What if I'm not?" I say, looking out again.

"Well, then I'll be the first person to tell you that, too."

I lean my cheek against the cool window, unable to look his way. "My aunt found the hatchet in the shed, along with my gardening gloves. Both had blood on them."

"Okay . . ."

"The animals."

Silence. "Your aunt thought *you* carved up those animals?"

I swallow hard. "I didn't. At least, if I did, I don't remember it. But what if I wasn't fully conscious. Sleepwalking. Or in a . . . a fugue state."

"While killing small animals, chopping them up, and making creepy serial-killer art with their body parts?"

"They could have already been dead."

He thumps back into the headrest again and groans.

"Not the point, I know," I say.

"Have you ever been tempted to do something like that?"

"What?" I recoil. *"No."*

"Then why would you, even subconsciously, be doing it?"

I look out the window again and my voice drops. "My father."

"What about him?"

That has me glancing over, eyes narrowing. "You know what. He murdered your brother. Gail was obviously concerned I could have some of that in me."

"Uh, isn't she his sister? *Full* sister? That means she shares more DNA with a confessed killer than you do. She also shares whatever fucked-up childhood your grandfather inflicted on them. She actually thought you did that? I barely know you, and I'm sure you didn't, just by the way you're reacting."

I blurt, "My wet clothing is in the shed. Right now."

His face screws up.

"The clothing I wore the night my aunt disappeared," I say. "I found it tonight in the shed. Drenched in lake water and covered in weeds."

"And . . ."

"Gail drowned, Ben," I snap. "She was pulled into the lake and drowned. I saw the drag marks, and I know what happened. In my gut, I know, and maybe that's why."

"Because *you* dragged your aunt into the lake and drowned her?"

"Yes."

He sighs, so deeply that I scowl. Do I really believe, in my heart, that I did these things? No. But for some perverse reason, I don't want him dismissing the possibility so quickly. I want to be taken seriously—not about having done it but about being genuinely scared that I might be losing my mind.

"That's why you wanted to see the camera shots," he says.

"Yes."

"Anything in them?"

"No, but that just means my clothing was there before you set up the camera. I don't remember taking it off, and now it's in the shed, in the exact spot where the hatchet was, and the hatchet is missing and . . ." I twist my hands together and mumble, "What if I did it? What if I've just . . snapped?"

"Do you want an answer to that? Not my opinion, but proof, one way or the other."

My scowl turns to a hard glare. "Of course."

"Maybe there's a faint chance you did cut up the animals, like you said, in some kind of fugue state. Buried psychopathy from your father, surfacing under stress. That must be what your aunt figured. Not that you did it on purpose but that, as you say, you snapped. I'm not a shrink. Your aunt was one, right?"

"A social worker."

"Whatever. The question is, if you killed her, would you want to know that for sure?"

I meet his gaze. "Yes."

He takes out his phone and unlocks it, flipping through apps.

I twist to face him. "You have other cameras?"

"No, I have exactly the ones I told you about. But I have something else. Your ankle monitor."

I shake my head. "That won't help. I didn't necessarily cross the boundary even if I dragged my aunt into the lake."

"I never said it only tracked you crossing the boundary." He taps his phone. "I didn't want to freak you out by letting you know I can find you wherever you go. I told the lawyer I just wanted to get alerts, but she insisted I have the full app."

"So it's a GPS tracker?"

"Yeah. I don't look at it even when I might wonder where you are. But it doesn't just track. It records." He finds what he's looking for and grunts. "Here's the history from the first night you were here, when you found the rabbit in the morning."

I'm not sure what exactly I'm looking at. It's just squiggles and then a flat line and then more squiggles.

"You seemed to get up just after midnight, but you didn't leave the cottage. Then you returned to bed until morning. The following night, you got up again, after one. This time it looks like you went out to the lake."

I shiver as the memory slides back.

"Sam?"

"The first night I heard hoofbeats and saw the lights out the window, but I didn't leave the cabin. The second night, I heard hoofbeats again and went down to the lake where I saw . . ." *Your brother. Austin. Dead.* I swallow and instead I say, "I saw one of those drowned people. I ran back to the house, and I told myself I imagined it. That I was sleepwalking or something."

"Well, you went out for about fifteen minutes." He zooms in on a map that shows my trail. "Straight to the water's edge, walked around a bit, came back inside. That's it. In two nights, you made one brief trip outside to the beach. You were not out killing and chopping up small animals." He meets my gaze. "Or finding dead animals and chopping up the bodies."

"Okay. But what about—"

"Here's two nights ago, when your aunt disappeared." He holds up his phone. "You went to your room and didn't leave until around five, which is exactly the story you gave." He frowns at the screen and taps something. "This says you were in bed by five at night?"

"That was after my aunt confronted me about the hatchet. I holed up in my room."

"Then we have an accurate record of three nights when you did not leave the house for long enough to cut up dead animals . . . or drown your aunt." He looks at me. "We saw a man dragged into the lake, Sam. You didn't do it tonight and, if it happened to your aunt, which I really hope it didn't, you didn't do that either. Those creatures did. So I do not want to hear you blurt to Smits that you might have—" His chin jerks up as lights appear down the road. "Speak of the devil. Okay, I'm going to turn the truck around and lead him in."

When we get out of the vehicles, Ben takes charge. He tells Smits what happened, starting with the encounter in the field, where the camper agreed to leave. Then he skips forward to hearing a scream and coming to check on me. Of course, in this version, it sounds as if the camper only half-heartedly grumbled before leaving and Ben just came to the cottage door and knocked after hearing a scream. He doesn't say that specifically—he's very careful not to lie—but he slants the narrative with the expertise of someone who has dealt with law enforcement before.

Ben is correct to do it like that. The camper is dead, and unless necessary, we are not admitting that the man argued with Ben and pushed me down. Nor do we want to sound as if we were in an absolute panic after the screams, Ben bursting into the cottage to find me.

From there, Ben does mention the lights, confirming that he also witnessed them. Then we saw a crumpled form on the beach, thought it was Gail and ran toward it, only to see the camper, who seemed badly injured. There was a figure farther down, at the edge of the woods. Before we could get a look at it, more figures emerged from the water and dragged the injured man in.

"People came out of the water and hauled him in?" Smits says, his gaze on me, as if I'm the one who will clearly tell him he's mishearing.

"They were . . ." I take a deep breath. "They looked like my aunt in that photo. Like they'd drowned."

Smits looks at Ben. At me. Steps back and rubs his forehead before rocking forward again.

"They looked *drowned*," Smits says.

"Dead," I say. "Dead and drowned."

"So you saw people dressed up like zombies, dragging a man into the water to scare you."

I check in with Ben, only to find him doing the same to me. We exchange a look. Then I answer, slowly, giving Ben room to cut in. "We don't know what we saw."

"Well, you sure as hell didn't see actual zombies," Smits snaps. He inhales and rubs a hand over his face with a long sigh. "Okay. I know you're freaked out, Sam. Someone is going to a lot of trouble to scare you."

"Yeah," Ben mutters. "Murdering a camper. I'd say that's a 'lot of trouble,' all right."

Smits shakes his head. "No one was murdered, Mr. Vandergriff. That camper was obviously in on it. They staged this whole thing to frighten Sam. She wakes hearing a scream, runs out and sees that scene play out. That camper made sure you saw him earlier—it wouldn't work as well if you just saw some random person being dragged off. Instead, it's an innocent camper you'd spoken to earlier."

"That's what you think happened?" Ben says.

"No, I think zombies came out of the water and killed that camper. Get your head out of your ass, Vandergriff. I know Sam is going through a really rough time with her aunt missing, but if *you* think you saw zombies, then maybe you need to come down to my office for a little test." He locks gazes with Ben. "For old times' sake."

"When we go back to the cottage," Ben says, his voice even, "I will find a bottle and pee in it for you, Sheriff. I've been clean for years. Whatever we saw, we are reporting what appeared to be a murder, and you damn well better take that seriously enough to at least walk the property with us looking for that fellow's gear."

Smits turns toward the forest. Am I imagining it or does he blanch? Don't go in the forest at night.

"Fine," Smits says. "We will drive over to the campsite where you saw him. The west field?"

"Yes, but the cyclist left that spot. He must have set up camp somewhere else on the property. There are a few decent places I know of." Ben pauses for a beat. "Can't drive to them, though. We'll need to walk. There's a path through the forest—"

"We'll drive to the west field," Smits says. "There are a few other spots we can see from the road. If you want to keep searching after that, be my guest. But this is the second night in a row I've been called out here, and I really need to get some sleep."

In the west field, Smits finds signs that the camper had been there earlier—peg holes and campfire remains—but the man's gear is gone. Smits checks a couple more places he can see from the road, and maybe he really does just consider this a wild-goose chase, but it seems clear to me that he really doesn't want to go in the forest.

An hour later, Ben and I are back in the cottage. Smits is gone, and I'm trying to wrap my head around what just happened.

We saw a man die tonight. Ben and I have zero doubt of that. And yet here we are, in the cottage, the sheriff gone, the investigation apparently over, as if we'd hallucinated everything.

The problem is that I can see Smits's point. Even Ben can, given the fact that he didn't push the matter.

On the surface, Smits's "it was all an act" explanation makes sense. Especially when the alternative is "the drowned dead dragged a man into the lake while a headless horseman watched."

I'm sitting on the sofa, my knees drawn in. Ben is slumped on the recliner. At least thirty minutes have passed, and neither of us has spoken.

"We did see what we thought we saw, right?" I whisper finally. "There's no way that was actors."

"It wasn't."

I chew my lip. "We shouldn't have called him."

Ben stretches his legs. "Yeah, we should have. The point was that we reported what we saw. I didn't expect him to believe us. And I sure as hell don't expect him to solve it."

"That's on us," I say. "To figure out what happened."

"It is."

This is where we should start talking. Sharing ideas. Comparing notes. But we only lapse back into silence, both falling into our thoughts as the night envelops us.

I fall asleep on the sofa, and when I wake, Ben is gone. I bolt up, my breath coming fast as I scramble to my feet, imagining him being dragged into the lake—

He's right on the other side of the window. There's a chair, but he's leaning on the railing, staring out at the lake.

I push open the screen door. "Coffee?"

He nods without turning.

I hesitate and then say, "You don't need to stay. In fact, it's safer for you if you don't."

"I'm fine."

I prop the screen door open. "Ben?"

He grunts and keeps looking toward the beach.

"We saw a man dragged into the lake last night," I say. "And maybe you don't want to bring it up, but we both know that—" My throat closes, and I force myself to keep going. "We know that's what happened to my aunt. The photo . . ."

I can't finish. I swallow hard and say, "It happens at night."

"Seems so."

"You're here *at night*."

"It's not night now."

"So you'll leave by dark?"

Silence. Then, "We shouldn't argue about this. *That's* not safe."

I swallow again. "Gail and that camper both fought with me. That's what you're thinking."

"I saw him last night," he says, his gaze on the water, voice hollow.

"My brother. Austin. He was one of those—those things, coming out of the water."

I flinch, my stomach tightening, but Ben's still looking forward and doesn't see my reaction, only continues with, "He was still a thirteen-year-old boy. Still dead. But that's not possible."

When I don't answer, he peers over. "You saw him last night, too."

I pause, wanting to offer comfort in lies. Then I say, "It was the night my tracker shows me going out. I saw the lights, like I said. But what the tracker doesn't show . . ." I wrap my arms around me. "I didn't walk back to the cottage. I ran."

"Because you saw him."

I nod. "That's another reason I thought I was losing my mind. Not just seeing the drowned dead. Seeing Austin. He didn't drown. My dad . . ." Another hard swallow. "My father killed him and then he was buried. He's not in the lake. So it must be a trick. Maybe . . ." I look at him. "Maybe that's it. Like Gail. It's not her. It's some creature imitating her to lure me in. Same as Austin."

"Looking like Austin to lure you in. To lure me in. Yeah, that makes sense, I guess."

He looks back at the lake, forearms on the railing as he bends down. I'm about to head inside when he glances over. "You wouldn't happen to have a smoke, would you?"

"Cigarette? No. You smoke?"

"Not since I was a kid. But today?" He looks at the lake again. "I could really use one."

"My aunt Ellen is a smoker," I say. "There might be some in their cottage, if you don't mind fourteen-year-old cigarettes."

He snorts and says, "I'll pass," but his gaze still flicks in that direction as if considering it.

"You could go to town and grab a pack," I say.

He doesn't even answer that. Again, I'm starting to retreat when he speaks, not looking over. "You read that old book you brought from the crawl space?"

"Yes."

"I took a look last night. You saw the parts on the water horses?"

"Yes."

He turns, his hip resting against the railing. "And you weren't going to mention it?"

"How? It's not like I read a chapter in a marine-biology text that explains seahorses. Water horses are myth. Legend. Folklore."

"Yeah, it's folklore found in a whole lotta places. All roughly the same. As if people were all talking about the same rare animal."

"We didn't see a rare animal, Ben. Rotting animals are *dead* animals."

He straightens. "Actually—"

"Yes, there are parasites that can cause flesh decomposition in living creatures. So can infection. I'm a wannabe doctor, remember?"

"So you do still want to be a doctor?"

"No, I love being a lab tech, making minimum wage with an undergrad degree. It's awesome. The point is that there is no natural explanation for what we saw."

"Then maybe there's an unnatural one."

When I pull a face, he says, "You believe Smits then. That it's someone in a costume."

"No. If you saw what I did, then we both know that was no one in a costume."

"You're going in circles, Sam. What we saw has no natural explanation, and we definitely saw it. Yet it can't be something supernatural?"

"I never said that. I grimaced, because I'm uncomfortable with the idea, but yes, I think we saw some kind of water horse. A cross between those and the drowned dead. With a rider. A headless rider that is . . ." I let out a breath. "I don't even want to go there."

"Because your grandfather insisted 'Sleepy Hollow' was based on a local legend, and he might actually be right? He's allowed to be right. Doesn't make him less of an asshole." Ben steps away from the railing. "If we're accepting that we saw something impossible, then I have something to show you."

He walks past me and down the steps, leaving me to follow.

Twenty-Six

We're at the shed. When Ben goes inside, I tense, hesitating. Then I slip in after him. He has his cell-phone light on.

"The clothing is over there," I say, pointing.

He barely glances that way and only grunts as he walks toward the hole in the foundation.

"I'd like you to check it out," I say. "Confirm what I saw."

He makes a noise of obvious annoyance but heads over and lifts my discarded tank top on the end of a spade. "Yep, it's wet. Yep, it's been conveniently festooned with lake weed. Can't confirm it's yours, but it looks like the sort of thing you wear. Cutoffs and tank tops. Cottage girl circa 1990."

"Hey!" I say.

"It's a timeless fashion. Also, those weeds mean it's a setup. How the hell are there weeds on your shirt after you walk into the lake—presumably dragging your aunt no further than necessary? And why are they still there after you've removed your clothing? They could be tangled in your sandals, yes. Caught on your arm or leg, yes. Still wrapped around your tank-top strap after you remove it? No."

"So someone's framing me?"

"Uh, yeah, Samantha. Keep up. My money is on your cousin, who seems to have inherited your grandfather's asshole genes."

"But we don't think Caleb staged the drowned dead and horseman."

"Just because he didn't do it *all* doesn't mean he didn't do *any*. The drowned dead—as you call them—are not going into your hamper to take out your clothing. If Caleb keeps going, though, you won't need to worry about him. Those dead things really don't like anyone targeting you. They're like zombie guard dogs—" He stops and says, gruffly, "I shouldn't be flippant."

"But you think that's what they're doing?"

He doesn't answer. He heads to that hole and grabs a spade resting against the wall. "I said I wouldn't fix this because your grandfather refused to comp me. That's half a lie. I was worried about some critter making a nest inside and your grandfather blaming me for the damage. So I tried finding a way to block the hole as cheaply as I could. Instead, I discovered why the foundation was crumbling."

I wait for him to go on, and then say, "Okay. Am I supposed to guess?"

"No, that was a dramatic pause."

I roll my eyes. "Fine. Tell me, Ben, why was the foundation crumbling?"

"Because there's a secret compartment in it."

"Huh?"

He starts digging in lieu of an answer. It takes a few minutes before he has the spot cleared, maybe six inches below the surface. There's a box—a metal box—inlaid in the concrete, which has crumbled around it.

"I . . . don't understand," I say.

"Don't ask me. It's your messed-up family." He stops abruptly.

"Fuck."

"In order to collect my multimillion-dollar inheritance, I'm sentenced to a month in the place where my father murdered a child. 'Messed up' is the nicest way to describe my family."

"It's not that." He leans on the spade. "Your family has owned this property for hundreds of years."

"Yep."

"They built this shed and laid the foundation maybe a hundred years ago."

"That's the story. The current shed is newer—my grandfather and my father replaced it before I was born. But the foundation predates both of them."

"Then so does this compartment and what's in it. But it's still your family. Your history. I wasn't thinking about that. I made up my mind to show you and just plowed forward. I've been avoiding it because I didn't want to seem crazy, when I should have been avoiding it because it's your family history. I don't know if it's true or not, Sam, but it's messed up."

"I believe we've already established that my family is the very definition of messed up."

I keep my tone light, but there's a buzzing in my head that says I should stop now, that I don't want to see what's in that box.

"Please tell me it's colonial witchcraft," I say. "My distant female ancestors breaking free of their Puritan shackles to dance naked around a fire and copulate with the devil."

When he doesn't answer, I say, "I'm kidding. Unless that's what it is, in which case, it's nonsense. Nothing wrong with a little pagan nature worship—and consensual sex orgies—but witchcraft and devil worship are bullshit, like the Satanic Panic when my parents were teens."

He wipes the back of his hand over his sweaty brow. "I don't quite know what it is. Weird and creepy stuff that seemed like silly hocus-pocus fantasies until . . . until last night."

I crouch at the hole. The cavity in it was obviously created at the same time as the original foundation. We've been referring to it as concrete, but that's because neither of us is a builder. It's a solid stonework foundation. Concrete? Mortar? I don't know. But whatever it is, whoever built it included a cavity to fit that metal box. In the last decade or so, the material around it has started to crumble, leading to the hole, and the box is no longer firmly fixed in place. I can slide the whole thing out, which I do. I set it on the dirt floor of the shed as Ben shines his cell-phone light on it.

The box isn't much taller or wider than a standard sheet of paper.

It's maybe three inches deep and obviously very old. There's a keyed lock in one end, but that's broken and looks as if it has been for years. When I pull on the lock, a drawer slides out. In it is a book wrapped in . . .

I look up at Ben.

"It was like that when I found it," he says.

The book is in a freezer bag. A modern plastic freezer bag with a zippered seal.

"So it hasn't been in here, untouched, for a hundred years," I say.

"No."

I unseal the bag and slide out the book. Despite the modern waterproof wrapper, the book is old enough that I'm hesitant to even touch it.

I carefully open the leather cover to see yellowed pages, handwritten like a journal, with ink so faded that Ben needs to give me his phone. Even then, I can barely read the writing. It's cursive, which I didn't take in school, but I did spend a summer learning for fun. This isn't like the cursive I know, though. It's closer to calligraphy, and I struggle to make out a few words, only to realize they're in an older form of English.

Colonial English, with unfamiliar words and spellings. I flip through a few pages, skimming and trying to make sense of what seems incomprehensible. Then I hit a word that stops me cold.

Nekker.

I point at it. "I saw this in the other book, too. Nekker. Nix. Nixie. The drowned dead."

"Yeah."

I look up at him. "Yeah?"

He lifts one shoulder. "I saw it in there, too. Until then, I just figured it was made-up nonsense."

"It's not. It's another branch of water-creature mythology. I've seen the word before in video games. But this . . ." I squint down at it. "I can't make heads or tails of it. Are they reporting what they saw here? In the lake?"

"Bring it inside. You need better lighting and the internet for deciphering. It's slow going, and I didn't get far. Just far enough to . . ."

Another one-shouldered shrug. "Far enough to decide it was delusional superstitious nonsense. Until last night."

I slide the book back into the bag, and we leave the shed.

At the sound of a car, I hand the book wordlessly to Ben, who tucks it into his waistband, his shirt pulled down over it. We head to the drive, expecting to see Sheriff Smits. Instead, Josie is climbing out of her compact car.

She's facing east, the rising sun obviously hiding our expressions, because she grins and holds up a takeout bag.

"Breakfast from the diner," she says. "I skipped their coffee. It's shit, as Ben can confirm. You two are up bright and early. Quiet night, I hope?"

I glance at Ben, who says nothing.

"You . . . haven't spoken to your dad this morning?" I say as I walk over.

She stops, her smile fading. "Uh, no. Is something wrong? I . . . Well, I wasn't at home last night. Dad and I had a bit of a blowup."

"Everything okay?"

She shrugs, her expression guarded. "Okay enough. Living under the same roof, Dad and I butt heads. In the offseason, I cottage-sit, but in the summer, I'm stuck back home. No rental vacancies in my price range. And then they wonder why all the young people move out." She trails off. "Well, that was fast. We lost Ben already."

I glance over my shoulder to see his retreating back.

"Off to do Ben stuff," I say. "No need to say anything first."

She rolls her eyes. "Right? Social niceties are really not his thing. Let's get this breakfast inside, and you can tell me what happened last night."

Twenty-Seven

Goddamn Ben Vandergriff. He knows I need to tell Josie some version of what's happened, and yet he's wandered off before we can discuss *what* we're going to tell her.

Once in the cottage, I find my phone and text him.

> Me: Thanks

An answer comes a few seconds later. It's a thumbs-up.

"Jerk," I mutter under my breath.

> Me: I need guidance here
> Me: What do I tell her?

> Ben: Your call

I resist the urge to type back a finger emoji of my own and roll my shoulders, sloughing off my irritation.

> Me: So everything then? You're fine with me telling Josie everything?

>Ben: Your call

I was being sarcastic. I'm sure he doesn't want me to tell her everything. I'm about to text back when he beats me to it.

>Ben: I'm fine with you telling her everything or telling her nothing
>Ben: I'm not worried she'll run back to Daddy with the whole story
>Ben: It really is your call. An outsider view might help us see stuff we're missing. But if you're worried about scaring her off, that's your call, too

I deflate. Fine. He's not being a jerk. He didn't abandon me to a hard choice. He left me to make my own decision.

And that decision is . . . ?

I'm not sure. He's right on both counts. We could use a third party who wasn't here and can poke holes in our bizarre story. But I'm also reluctant to scare off an ally . . . and a potential friend.

"We had to call your dad out last night," I say as I plug in the kettle for tea. "Something happened."

"You're both okay?" She sees the answer in my nod and quickly says, "Is it something about your aunt?"

I shake my head. "Yesterday evening, shortly after you left, Ben and I had a run-in with a cyclist trying to camp on the property. Words were exchanged. The guy left—or seemed to. Then we woke up to screams."

She's in the middle of calmly adding milk to her coffee and pulls back so fast she sloshes it.

I continue, "Ben came and got me. We headed out. We saw something on the beach to the west. It was the camper. Badly wounded. Lying on the shore. We were running over when something came out of the water and dragged him in."

She's still. Utterly still, milk carton in hand, her gaze on mine, searching my face as if awaiting the punch line to a very unfunny joke.

I hold out my phone. "I don't think you saw this photo." It's the blurry one of Gail coming out of the water.

"What the hell?" She recoils, and her gaze flies to mine. "My dad said you got a photo of someone dressed up to look like your aunt, to scare you. That is not . . ." She swallows. "That does not look like an actor. It looks like your aunt. Except . . ."

"Dead," I say. "Drowned. That's what the figures last night looked like. They hauled the camper out into the lake."

Josie's still staring at me, still waiting for the punch line, her expression shuttered with the look of someone who fears she's being mocked. The little girl hanging out with the older kids who tell her wild stories and then laugh when she believes them.

She finally says, "You told my father that you saw zombies drag a man into the lake and he . . . what? Is there an investigation? There can't be. He'd have called me. So what did he do? Does he think you're pranking him? That Ben's playing some elaborate hoax?"

"He thinks *someone's* playing one. On me. That it's all part of scaring me into forfeiting my inheritance. My cousin or maybe my uncle. They hired the camper and staged the whole thing."

"Is that possible? Given what you saw?"

My eyes prickle, and it takes me a moment to recognize the sensation. Tears. Not tears of grief or frustration or confusion. Tears of gratitude for that simple question.

Josie doesn't jump on her father's interpretation. She doesn't even pause to consider her own interpretation. She asks me. What did I see?

That tells me where I want to go with this.

"No," I say. "Same with Ben. Neither of us can fit what we saw into that narrative, as much as it makes sense."

"But my father wasn't there. He didn't see it with his own eyes."

"Didn't see it, hear it, smell it, feel it. Ben and I were freaked out, but neither of us looks back and thinks we saw something staged. I would love to believe that. I don't even know how to wrap my head around anything else. But . . ."

I swallow and lift the photo again. "This is my aunt. Of course I'd rather believe she staged it herself, out of jealousy. I'd rather discover she's alive and betrayed me. But I know what I saw. She's dead. Someone—some*thing*—dragged her into the lake. And now it happened to this camper."

"Who my dad believes is part of the stunt. An actor."

"He's your father, and you two are having some friction. I don't want to add to that."

"You're not. My father is the sheriff. My boss. If he decides no one actually died here, I can't overrule him. But someone disappeared last night, and that's going to come out eventually. He'll need to investigate then."

Will he?

That feels disloyal, as if I'm accusing Craig Smits of something. I'm not. I have no doubt that when relatives come looking for that cyclist, Smits will investigate. But will he believe we told the truth that the guy was dragged into the lake? Or will he stick to his own interpretation and find a way to fit that?

I remember those memories that resurfaced a few days ago. The ones about people that disappeared and everyone shrugged it off.

Not our problem.

It happens.

Can't prove they disappeared here anyway.

"Sam?" Josie says. "You're thinking something."

I choose my words with care. "You're right. Eventually someone will report that cyclist missing."

She nods. "Whichever department it's reported to will ask all regional law-enforcement agencies whether they saw him. It could take a while, so you'll need to make sure my dad takes down all the particulars. He's not necessarily going to hear next month that a guy went missing and think of the camper you reported seeing dragged into the lake."

"Because it happens. People go missing. It's cottage country. It's not the middle of the Alaskan wilderness, but people are passing through all summer, biking, hiking, camping. Sometimes they're reported missing."

I expect a quick and easy reply. Yes, people disappear. Instead, she wraps her hands around her coffee cup.

"Josie?"

"People do go missing," she says slowly. "Like you said, it's cottage country. Lots of people pass through, many doing sports with a risk factor. But some people think too many who've vanished had connections to Paynes Hollow. That what they have in common is that they were known to be here, specifically."

"The Bermuda Triangle of Upstate New York," I murmur.

Her head jerks up. "You heard that podcast episode?"

"My grandfather sent it to me a few weeks before he died. Apropos of nothing in particular. He did that sometimes. He'd send things that, in his mind, exonerated my father. Once it was an article on a serial killer operating in Syracuse around the same time. Once it was some weird junk-science piece on chemical-induced psychopathy from factories along the Great Lakes. I read enough of this podcast to get the gist. People have disappeared in the region, all linked to Paynes Hollow. As if that's how Austin Vandergriff died, and my father was, I don't know, just burying a boy he found dead from mysterious causes."

"Except it's true. Not about Austin, of course. But I talked to the woman who did the podcast while she was researching it last year." She pauses. "Don't tell my dad. Please."

"I wouldn't."

"I didn't give her anything. I didn't *know* anything. But we talked, and I got curious. So I went digging on my own. She had a point. Over the years, more than half of the people who disappeared within a hundred-mile radius had some connection to Paynes Hollow."

"Like what?"

She shrugs. "Passing through, mostly. This was often their last known stop. They popped into the general store for supplies or someone in town reported speaking to them. Most were traveling solo, though there were a few couples and in those cases, they both vanished."

"How many are we talking?"

"Maybe three dozen. That seems like a lot, but they're scattered over a century or more. On that kind of timeline, it doesn't seem so strange, especially when they were just passing through, which makes it difficult to say they disappeared *here*. Sure, maybe they were last seen shopping locally, but that only means they had enough supplies that they could have been in Ohio or Vermont when they disappeared."

She leans forward and continues, "When you're talking a hundred years, a serial killer is out of the question. That's why I never mentioned it to my dad. It'd need to be, like, a father and son and grandson. A killer family. I sure wasn't taking *that* theory to my dad."

A killer family.

I think of that book tucked into Ben's waistband. What exactly is in there? Something he wasn't sure I should read.

"So what are you thinking now?" I say as neutrally as I can.

"I have no idea," Josie says. "Except that you and Ben watched lake zombies drag a guy into the water, presumably killing him. A lone camper. And if my father didn't take the particulars from you and he gets a report weeks from now of some random camper disappearing somewhere in the upstate area, he'd never think to connect the two. Maybe you found the answer."

"The drowned dead."

Her cheeks flush. "I should be glad Ben wandered off before this conversation or he really would think I'm a little kid, blaming zombies for missing people."

"He wouldn't," I say. "That's what we're already working through. We just hadn't extrapolated into anything larger. What can you tell me about these stories? I could listen to the whole podcast, but I'd rather hear it from you."

She nods. "I have my notes on the cloud. Let me pull them up."

Twenty-Eight

Josie shares her research with me. It's what she already summed up, people disappearing who were last seen in this area. Only, in her research, they come to life as individuals. Two brothers who'd arrived seeking work during the Depression and disappeared, the story being that they fought, one killed the other and then fled. A woman on her own in the 1940s, who had "clearly" walked into the lake and drowned herself after failing to find a husband. A honeymooning couple in the fifties, who'd pitched a tent outside town and the woman woke to find her new husband missing, everyone whispering that he'd run off. The stories seem to trickle off after that, with only three until the late nineties. Then five disappearances in twenty years, ending a decade ago.

I need to talk to Ben. There are things I still haven't told Josie, starting with the headless horseman and ending with the book Ben found. He might say it's my call, but I'm at the point where I need a second opinion, whether he wants to give it or not.

Finding him is easy enough. He's out by the lake, staring into the water.

"I'm fine," he says without turning as I approach.

"Because it's daylight?"

He grunts and keeps staring out. Then he shakes it off and turns. "Because I'll see them coming."

"You're thinking about Austin."

His gaze darts back to the water, telling me he doesn't want to discuss it. Neither do I. It's too fraught a subject on too many levels. I only asked because I want to acknowledge his pain and confusion, in case he needs to talk.

I tell him what I've shared with Josie. Then I tell him about the missing people.

"Huh," he says when I finish.

"'Huh'? That's all you have to say?"

"Yep."

When I glare, he says, "What else do you want me to say, Sam? That all these missing people were dragged into the lake? To prove it, we'd need to dig up photos of each person and compare them to the creatures we saw."

"We could do that."

"And then what? Tell Sheriff Smits? Does knowing who they are help us stop them? Or put them to rest? Or whatever the hell they need? Does naming them even mean that's who we're seeing? We've already speculated that they might take on the appearance of someone who died."

I shove my hands in my pockets. "Okay."

He sighs and drags a hand through his hair. "I'm not trying to be a jerk, Sam. You and Josie came up with a theory that's interesting in a theoretical way. But practically, it doesn't help us."

"So what does?" I shake my head. "Never mind. That's not why I'm here anyway. I didn't tell Josie about the horseman. Should I do that?"

"Sure. Why not?"

"And the book?"

He hesitates. Then he shakes his head. "You need to read it first."

"To make that determination?"

"Yeah."

"Can't you just tell me what it says?"

He exhales a slow breath and runs his hand through his hair again.

"You want me to figure it out for myself," I say.

"I'll guide you through it." He looks out at the water. "Before sundown."

Silence falls, and we both stand there, staring at the water before I whisper, "What are we doing, Ben?"

"I have no fucking idea."

More silent staring as my thoughts and stomach roil. Finally, I say, my voice low, "I should leave, shouldn't I? After what we saw, I should give up. I don't know what's happening, but it's getting worse every night, and I'm not going to last a month."

"Physically?" He shoves his hands into his pockets. "I think you'll be okay."

My stomach tightens. While the horseman hadn't paid any attention to me, I keep thinking of Austin coming out of the water, the hate in his eyes.

Ben continues, "But even if you're not a target, you survive at what cost? First your aunt and then last night, while someone's trying to make you think you're responsible for everything . . ."

"So I should give up. Leave."

He turns to me. "What's stopping you? I don't think it's the money. You need it badly. I get that. Not millions, but you can't opt for less and leave early. That's why you came, but is it why you're staying?"

I wrap my arms around my chest and look out at the sun-dappled waves before saying, "No."

"Is it to beat your grandfather? Win his game?"

"I came for the money. When things started going wrong, I didn't want to be scared off by a couple of dead animals. Then Gail . . ." My voice catches, and it's a hoarse whisper when I say, "I wanted her to leave. I *insisted* she leave. But even then, I didn't really think she was in danger. I should have pushed harder." My arms tighten. "No, I should have left myself. She'd have come with me."

"When something like that happens, we always think back on the things we wished we'd done differently. But we only feel guilty because things went wrong. Otherwise, we'd never have thought twice about it. Like not keeping an eye on my little brother when my parents told me he was grounded. How many times had I done that and nothing happened? I never once felt guilty."

He hunches his shoulders in. "Not to interject myself in this. I'm just saying I get it. As the person who screwed up, no amount of justification is going to make me feel better, so I know that saying this isn't your fault won't help as much as it should, but . . ." He meets my gaze. "It's not your fault."

When I don't answer, he says, "If Gail had a near miss and you begged her to stay anyway, yeah, you'd have a reason to feel guilty. Not with this."

"But now that Gail and that camper have been killed, and I'm still not leaving? Letting you and Josie stay here?"

"Josie will be gone by nightfall. I'm staying even if you leave."

"Why?"

"That was my question to you. Why are you staying, Sam? Not for the money. Not even to prove something to your dead grandfather. So why?"

Long silence, as we both look out over the water.

"Because I have to know," I murmur finally. "I feel as if this is connected to me. If my leaving would stop anyone else from dying, I'd go. But I need to know what's happening and maybe, once I do, I'll make an informed decision to leave. Otherwise, in a year or two, when my mother's in some crappy home and I'm in an even crappier apartment, working sixty hours a week at a crappy job, I'll be convinced I made a mistake. That I let my cousin or uncle scare me off. My aunt suffered some horrible tragedy, maybe connected to the staging, and I dishonored her memory by quitting before I knew what happened."

"Yes."

That's all he says, and then we stand there, looking out, until I say, "Will *you* leave if you're in danger?"

"If you come with me."

I nod. "Okay."

He looks over. "You mean that?"

"I don't have a death wish, Ben. If I think you're in danger, I'll go if it means you'll go. But will you do me one favor? Stop wandering off. Yes, it's daytime and you're entitled to your privacy, but what if we're wrong about everything? What if something happens to you because I didn't have the guts to ask you to stay close?"

"I didn't 'wander off' today, Sam. I went looking for that guy's camping stuff. Then I realized I probably shouldn't be out there alone, so I came back. But I take your point. No one should be here alone." He looks back at the cabin. "Even Josie shouldn't be in the cottage alone. But that loops us back to the book question."

"It does."

"I'm going to tell her to leave."

He strides off, and I hurry along after him.

"You can't do that," I say.

"Why? Because it's rude? That's why I'm the one doing it."

Before I can catch up, he's at the cottage door, swinging it open and stepping inside.

"Sam and I need to do a few things," he says. "It's best if you aren't part of that. But it's also best if no one is alone here. So you need to leave for a while. Come back with lunch. Also smokes. I really need a cigarette."

Her brows shoot up. "Uh . . ."

"Your dad is the sheriff. Your boss is the sheriff. It makes things complicated. If it's something Sam and I can share, we will."

"So lunch and cigarettes?"

"Yeah."

She puts out her hand. He sighs, but slaps a twenty in it.

"Big spender," she says. "For that you get cigarettes and you can reheat your breakfast."

I take a couple twenties from the leftover cash in the envelope, but she shakes her head.

"This one's on me," she says with a smile and then leaves.

Josie is gone. Ben and I are in the kitchen, with the book on the table, me on one chair while he straddles another backward. I've plugged in a lamp so I can see the pages better, and I have my phone to look up words I don't recognize.

I start at the beginning. The first entry is actually a preface, explaining that this is a translation from the original Dutch. As a surname, Payne is often associated with the British Isles, but my Payne ancestors originated in France and ended up in the Netherlands, and that's where they were when they immigrated with a wave of Dutch settlers coming to New York State.

At the time the journal was translated, the Paynes had been in America for several generations and they spoke English. The writer translated it because it was—as she said—a work of vital importance that could not be lost.

For the first dozen or so pages, the book seems like a standard journal, mostly interesting for the family history. I already knew a bit of that. The Paynes came to America in the mid-eighteenth century. That's long after the *Mayflower*, but it's right at the start of when Europeans began colonizing upstate New York.

When I was little, my grandfather always made it sound like the typical pilgrim narrative. My ancestors came over and found vacant land and worked hard to turn it into what is now Paynes Hollow. At that age, while I certainly knew there'd been people in America before the Europeans, the reality never fully penetrated, because the indigenous people played no role in my grandfather's stories. It was as if this particular region were just empty land.

Now, reading those early pages, my skin crawls with the reality. My many-times-great-grandmother gushes about the lake and the land and the bounty, and marvels at their luck "finding" this piece and "claiming" it for their own, and when she does mention the native people, it's as if they're in the same category as the wolves and the bears. Invaders on the land my family "owns" by right of their land claims.

That's a horror story in itself, but it's not the purpose of the journal, and what seems like a typical pioneer story quickly turns into something else.

Whenever people immigrate, they bring their own traditions and culture. In this area, many of the colonists were Dutch. They brought with them games like ninepins and ice hockey, foods like waffles and doughnuts. My ancestors also brought something else.

As I read, the old language smooths out, my eyes skimming over unfamiliar words and turns of phrase and modernizing them.

Before we left the old country, my husband's mother taught us how to create nekkers, to ensure our prosperity in this new land. The process cannot be rushed, particularly as it might take years to complete the first step. The good fortune we brought with us eventually ran out, and all we could do was wait. Wait for tragedy to strike our family.

It finally happened last month, when we received word that my husband's youngest brother, Bram, perished in the war for independence. He died in the most horrible way, his head nearly cleaved from his body by a British soldier. Given the state of his remains, the army wished to bury him, but we claimed membership in a religious community that required an appropriate burial, and they allowed my husband and his brothers to retrieve Bram's remains.

By the time the body arrived, the poor boy's head was no longer attached to his neck, and we fretted over how that would affect the ritual. Yet there was no way to swiftly consult with the elders, and we dared not miss this opportunity. We followed the ritual and killed Bram's horse and then arranged them both in the lake bottom, the horse pinning Bram's body and head beneath it.

Next we had to perform the binding. I have left instructions for it in these pages. The person bound must be a Payne, sharing blood with Bram. It is best if the person is young, so that the binding might last as long as possible, yet it is unwise to bind a baby who may not survive infancy. As my husband is the first son, it was decided that our eldest—Elsie—would be bound. We performed the ritual and then we waited.

It took thirty days, long enough that we began to worry that the condition of Bram's body meant he could not serve as the seed. Our distress grew so great that once, when my husband had drunk too much, he questioned whether Elsie was his child! But then it happened, exactly as it should. A light appeared under the water at night and Bram rode out on his horse, his head held in his hand. He did not know us, of course, but he rode right up to our homes, searching for Elsie. When we brought her out, he was satisfied and returned to the lake.

Each night until the lake freezes, Bram emerges to ride through the woods, seeking any source of danger to our family, but mostly to Elsie.

We are all tremendously careful not to discipline the child. That is the one danger of the ritual. Bram will protect us all, but he will also protect Elsie from us. Even a backhanded slap could result in retaliation. My husband says his grandmother always told the story of her uncle, who had been bound to their nekkers. A cousin, in his cups, struck her uncle a blow, and the next day, the cousin was gone. A few days later, he appeared from the lake as a nekker, having been trampled to death by the horseman and dragged into the lake by the nekkers.

When the bound person passes, another may take their place. If there is no suitable replacement, the nekkers will remain dormant until a new bonding. However, if the nekkers lie dormant, the Paynes receive no benefit from them.

The nekkers offer more than protection. Much more. Some of the old stories say that the nekkers offer bargains, wishes granted in return for sacrifices. That is adjacent to the truth, which is that they offer a boon in return for sacrifice—the very specific boon of good fortune.

For as long as the nekkers are pleased, the Paynes will enjoy fortune. Their crops will grow. Their children will be healthy. Their fish nets will be full. It will never be so much that others notice and grow suspicious. It will simply seem as if fortune smiles on them more often than others.

To continue earning their blessings, there must be a Payne bound to the horseman and there must be sacrifices to keep the ranks of the nekkers full because, with the exception of the horseman, they will eventually rot under the waves.

A sacrifice every fifth year is enough. Look for those who travel—trappers and hunters and fishermen and laborers passing through. Take their lives with the ritual detailed in this book and then leave them by the water's edge for the nekkers to claim. Do this every fifth year, and your fortune will remain strong. This fortune will also extend to anyone who aids you in this, such as a trusted servant. It is advisable to cultivate such a person, who can do the deed in return for the reward, and who could also be given to the authorities if the need arises.

The book continues from there, but I have to take a break, rubbing my eyes and struggling to process what I've read.

Finally, I look over at Ben, who's been helping me through.

"You wanted me to read this for myself," I say. "So there's no question that you're misinterpreting."

"Yeah."

"How the hell would you misinterpret, Ben? This isn't in code. It's not even vague. It clearly spells out a ritual that explains the horseman *and* the drowned dead *and* the missing people."

"I didn't want you to think I was making it up. Better if you read it for yourself."

I push back my chair. "So you found this book back when you were trying to fix the wall."

"Yeah."

"And?" I tap the book. "You read it and shoved it back into that compartment? Forgot about it?"

"Nah. I decided to tell Sheriff Smits that the Paynes murdered my brother as part of a ritual where they're creating lake zombies to bless them with good fortune. Because that's a thing that happens in the real world."

He shakes his head. "What would *you* have thought, Sam? If you read this after hearing hoofbeats and seeing lights under the water? Would you have jumped on this as the explanation?"

I lean back. "Fine. You're right. I would have thought I'd overheard a family story that was making me hallucinate hoofbeats and lights. Or, at most, my ancestors were delusional murderers, killing strangers because they believed it brought them luck."

We go quiet again. On the surface, this seems to answer all our questions. But even if it does—and I'm not completely sure of that—it doesn't fix anything. It doesn't bring my aunt back. It only means . . .

I'm not even sure of what it means. I do know one thing, though.

"I want to tell Josie," I say.

Ben doesn't answer. Just taps his fingers on the table.

"You disagree?" I say.

"No, I'm just . . ." He stretches his legs under the table. "I don't know."

"If you don't trust her—"

"It isn't that. It's that I'm not sure what she can do with this. Not sure what any of us can do with it."

"That's why I want to tell her. Get an outside view. Someone who didn't see what we did and can look at this"—I tap the book—"from that perspective."

He nods slowly.

Twenty-Nine

When Josie returns, Ben takes his cigarettes onto the deck without a word. I figure he just needs to smoke one, so I eat lunch with Josie. I didn't think I was hungry until I took a bite, and then my body remembered that it hadn't eaten since yesterday. I might not be in the mood for food, but my brain needs the nourishment.

We finish, and Ben is still on the deck.

I excuse myself and slip out to find he isn't even smoking. The unopened pack is on his knee as he stares out at the lake.

"Ben?" I say gently.

He yanks his gaze from the water. "Yeah?"

"It's time to tell Josie."

He grunts and makes no move to get up.

"Are you . . . helping with that?"

"You need help? I figured that's what you were already doing."

"I could use some backup."

He exhales and fingers the cigarette package. Then he jerks his chin, which I interpret as a motion for me to move closer.

"If you need help, I will," he says. "But it'll be better coming from you."

"Why? You and Josie get along."

"Yeah, but. . . ." He exhales again. "It's a small-town thing. She's always going to be a little kid to me, and I'm always going to be an older kid to her. She's careful around me, like she doesn't want to embarrass herself. A weird dynamic, but we're used to it. With this, if I'm there, she's going to censure her reaction and try to gauge mine. She's more relaxed around you."

I nod, leave him to his lake-gazing and his not-smoking, and head inside.

I start by telling Josie how I'd hear hoofbeats as a kid and my grandfather played along, and that I've been hearing them now and seeing prints in the sand. Then I tell her about seeing the horseman.

"Did you tell my father about this?" she asks.

I shake my head.

"Why not? A headless horseman isn't something someone can stage."

"Isn't it? It's an obvious setup. My grandfather always said the horseman was from here, and I used to think I heard it. My cousin would know about both."

"Okay but . . ." She shifts in her seat. "*Could* it be staged? Elaborately? Not to dismiss what you two saw . . ."

"But a staged monster half hidden in shadows makes a lot more sense than an actual monster?"

Her cheeks flush. "Yeah. Sorry."

"Don't apologize. That's why we're telling you. We want someone to say we're exhausted and not thinking straight. So that's the whole story. Then there's this . . ."

I pull over the book and explain where Ben found it and what it seems to be. Then I read Josie those few pages about the horseman and the nekker. She sits back, clearly processing. Then she says, "I have questions."

"Good," I say. "Are you okay with me calling Ben in? Or would you rather talk to me alone?"

"Bring him in."

Ben might have said he didn't want to interfere with Josie processing the book, but I think that was at least fifty percent bullshit. He's the one who's uncomfortable. He wanted to sit outside so he didn't see the local deputy—who has always defended him against the sheriff—peering at him for signs of duplicity or drug use, wondering whether her dad had been right all along.

Now when I call him in, he drags his feet and slumps into a chair.

"How do we know this book is real?" Josie asks.

Ben's shoulders tense. "That I didn't write it, since I'm the one who found it?"

"I never said that, Ben. If someone wrote it recently, it's a ridiculous amount of work to go through." She hefts the book in one hand. "Anyone who's been in a library knows this is really old. It's not a school project where you scuff up a leather binding and smoke the pages to look yellowed."

"But what if someone faked it a hundred years ago," I say. "Like making a time capsule, except what you put in it is a prank. A false journal about Dutch folk magic, imagining someone in the future reading it and thinking it's real."

Josie leans forward. "Exactly. Is the folklore real? Have you looked it up?"

"Nekkers are a regional variation of something also known as a nix. It's common Western folklore. The horseman is a variation on the kelpie, and there's an Icelandic form directly connected to the nix lore. What they describe doesn't match anything I've found elsewhere but . . ." I shrug. "It's folklore. There are as many variations as there are storytellers who use it."

"Okay, what if one of your ancestors pulled a prank using Dutch folklore? Or someone who hated your ancestors wrote this to accuse them of witchcraft? When were the Salem witch trials?"

"Late seventeenth century. Before the Paynes arrived in America."

Ben shakes his head. "I understand where you're going, Josie, but logically, it doesn't make sense."

She flushes, but he doesn't seem to notice. I glare at him—wasn't he the one worried about embarrassing her?

He continues, "What Sam and I saw last night seems to be explained by the book. That only works as a setup if the book is new.

How would someone stage last night based on a book they couldn't have read?"

"Because maybe they *did* read it," she says. "Read it, put it back, and staged it."

"And then we would just find it today?"

"But you didn't 'just happen' to find it today, Ben. You found it a while ago. I'm not saying you set this up—"

"No," he says. "Sam needs to work through all the possibilities, and that one actually makes sense. I find this book, which gives me the idea for the staging. Not sure how I'd afford something that elaborate, but forget that part. What do I stand to gain by scaring Sam off?"

"Revenge," she says simply.

"Because her dad killed my brother. That has nothing to do with Sam, but okay, sure, let's roll with that." He turns to me. "You need to explore that possibility, Sam. Don't ignore it because you feel bad suspecting me. But also . . . are we still sure your dad killed Austin?"

I jerk back. Of course I've been thinking it. But if I start down that road, aren't I as deluded and desperate as my grandfather? My therapist kept me from even peeking in that direction.

Accept what he did.

Deal with what he did.

When I don't answer, Ben's voice drops. "I didn't connect the dots when I read the book, but after last night? You said you don't want to fight with me. Why is that?"

I glance toward the window. An image flashes back, my hand bleeding at the gate, blood seeping into the ground, the memory of my hand bleeding in the forest when I was young and I couldn't remember how I cut it.

"Because you saw the truth before reading this book," he says. "You sensed the connection, and now this book confirmed it. Someone— your grandfather, I presume—bonded you to these creatures. They protect you. You argued with your aunt. Was there any physical violence?"

"She grabbed me, and I fell," I whisper.

"And then that camper fought with us and pushed you down." He taps the book. "Physical violence against the bonded one brings the horseman, even if the one committing the violence is another Payne."

I squeeze my hands into fists. Josie reaches over to lay her fingers on my arm.

Ben continues, "Your aunt didn't know. She was raised in a family where you didn't discipline kids with corporal punishment, which is normal enough. It's probably what your mom was told, too. Not that she'd have spanked you otherwise, but it'd have been made very clear that wasn't done in the Payne family."

I look up, meeting his eyes. "You think my father knew."

He pulls back, as if at the mention of my dad. "I don't know. But I'm guessing there's a reason he might be really quick to bury a kid he found dead on the property." He looks at me. "Do you know how Austin died?"

I shake my head. I'd never wanted to know.

"I was told he'd been beaten," Ben says. "Badly beaten, with broken bones. You know what that also sounds like?" He taps the book. "Trampled by a horse. Like the camper on the beach."

"So what are you saying?" I ask. "That the horseman killed Austin when he disappeared, and then my dad found the body, knew what happened, and buried him. Only I caught him and he panicked and . . ."

"Shot himself," Josie whispers. "Oh, Sam."

I straighten fast. "We don't know that's what happened."

"But it fits," Ben says. "Your dad came to my house and told my parents that Austin wasn't welcome on your property."

"Protecting him," Josie says. "Your dad knew what would have happened." She looks at me. "Austin hurt you, didn't he? He must have, for the horseman to go after him."

A memory flashes. I'm in the forest, running. It's getting dark and I shouldn't be here, but I need to get away. Someone is right behind me, and I have to get away. I trip, and he falls onto my back, hands going around my throat, choking me, telling me this is all my fault, he's in trouble and it's my fault, he's grounded and it's my fault. The wind is rising, and the sound of hoofbeats distracts him. I bite his hand as hard as I can. He curses and pulls away. I scramble out from under him and run.

Him.

Someone.

I know why that was, even if my memory wants to haze over it.

Austin.

When I don't answer, Ben says, "By mistake. Like your aunt. You guys were having a spat, and he showed up and you argued. He grabbed your arm or something like that. You guys were . . ." He shrugs. "Having a little tween romance, and you broke up or whatever. That's why you didn't want him around. The horseman misinterpreted."

"A little tween romance?" Josie says. "What the hell, Ben?"

I fight against folding in on myself, and I open my mouth, but nothing comes out.

"You know what I mean," Ben says. "Austin had a crush. Maybe Sam reciprocated, maybe she didn't, but the point—"

"Crush? Romance?" Josie sputters. "Seriously. What the *hell*, Ben. Is that what you tell yourself? How your family rewrote this?"

I want to tell her to stop, please stop, but I can't speak, I can't move.

"Austin *stalked* Sam," she says. "Even I saw that. He wouldn't leave her alone, and when she wasn't interested, he . . ." She swallows and looks at me. "I didn't know about the rest, Sam, not until I saw the police file. I just thought he was pestering you, and I tried to run interference, making sure he wasn't alone with you, but I was a kid. I didn't really understand what was happening. I'm sorry."

"Sam?"

I can feel Ben's gaze on me, but I don't look up.

"Is that true, Sam?" Ben says. "It's not, right? I don't know what the sheriff put in his report, but I saw that carving on the tree, with you and the flowers—"

"Knife," I say. "That's a knife."

He shakes his head. "You're holding flowers. Austin carved you—"

"He carved me with a knife through my heart, Ben," I say, anger welling. "He *told* me what it was."

"But—"

"But what? I'm lying?" I push back from the table. "Making it up to justify what happened? Maybe you want to see your brother's other artwork. His other carvings. They're a whole lot clearer. How about the one with me hanging from a noose? Or the one of me chopped into pieces and—" I slap my hands to my mouth as I see his expression.

"I didn't mean—" I begin.

Then I scramble up and run from the cottage.

Thirty

I'm on the driveway, tucked between Ben's pickup and Josie's car. I'm struggling for breath, half doubled over, and when I hear footsteps, I want them to be Josie's but they're too heavy and slow.

"Go," I croak. "Please. I don't want to fight with you. We can't."

Silence. Then, "I'm not fighting, Sam. I'm apologizing. I shouldn't have questioned you when you told me what . . . what that carving was."

My shoulders hunch in. "Maybe I misheard him. Maybe—"

"Stop," he says, his voice low. "You didn't mishear, and you aren't lying about the other carvings. You don't want to fight with me, but I'm not fighting. If you want me to keep my memories of my little brother intact . . ."

He exhales. "Fuck."

"I'm sorry."

"No, I'm sorry, because I'm an asshole. I kept talking about how Austin had a crush and how you two were friends, and that was a shitty thing to do, especially because I was saying it for me. If I said that, and you didn't correct me, then my suspicions were wrong and my brother wasn't a baby sociopath who terrorized you."

I turn, slowly, still not looking at him. When I finally do lift my gaze, he's staring out at the lake.

"I saw what he was," he says. "My parents saw it. They pretended they didn't, and if I said anything . . ." He rubs his mouth. "I learned not to say anything. Otherwise, I was being paranoid and jealous."

"Jealous of Austin?" I say.

"When I was a kid, I was a straight-A student, responsible as hell," he says, glancing over with a twisted smile. "Hard to believe now, huh? Then I hit my teens and acted out. Typical teen shit. Smoking weed, skipping school, don't-give-a-shit attitude. My parents forgot the good kid I'd been, and suddenly I was demon spawn and Austin was their new angel, and if I said I caught him torturing a wounded squirrel, I was the lying monster. Then he died, and we all got stuck in our places. He's the dead angel, and I'm still—"

He rubs his mouth. "This isn't about me. Back then, I *did* worry about Austin's interest in you. I talked to him, and he blew me off. I didn't see anything—I'd have stopped him if I did—but I didn't look too hard either. When our parents said he was banned from your property, I laid into him. Told him if you weren't interested, he needed to back the fuck off. We had a big fight, and he stormed off to his room, and I thought I'd won."

He shoves his hands into his pockets. "I was too much of a dumbass to realized he'd climbed out the window, and I didn't check on him because I was done with his shit. Sat on the porch, listened to tunes, smoked a joint and told myself I had it under control."

"I'm sorry."

"Because I'm an asshole?" He shakes his head and then lowers his voice. "Those animals you found this week. They reminded you of something he'd done, didn't they."

I tense.

"I'll take that as a yes," he says. "You don't need to confirm or deny. I'd caught him with small animals. You think he's responsible this time, too. Whatever he is, however he got out there in the lake, he did it. Cut up the rabbit and the fox. Maybe even tried to frame you. Like when I caught him with the squirrel, and he told our parents that I did it."

"I didn't think . . . Not consciously . . . I don't know." I wrap my arms around myself. "But what we saw can't be Austin. He's buried, right?"

"I saw the casket lowered, so I don't know how he'd get out, short of some zombie-movie scenario where he dug his way out. That sounds ridiculous but—"

Gravel crunches. Ben peers over. When Sheriff Smits's truck appears, Ben curses.

"Just what we need," he mutters.

"I'll get rid of him."

"And I'll just try to keep my mouth shut."

Smits ambles out of the truck as Josie exits the cottage. She stops and nods. He tips his hat but doesn't speak to her.

"Can I help you, Sheriff?" I say.

He studies my expression and then shakes his head. "You're not happy with me either. Can't say I blame you. Last night, you told me you saw a man die, and I blew you off. Treated you like a kid getting all worked up over nothing."

"It's fine," I say. "You were probably right anyway." I give a small laugh and hope I sell it. "*Probably?* You were certainly right. What else could it have been? Actual drowned dead killing a cyclist?" From behind Smits's shoulder, Ben gives me a look to say I'm *over*selling it.

Smits laughs obligingly. "Well, it still bothers me that I dismissed it so quickly. I've been looking on the wire for anything about a missing cyclist. Nothing yet, but if there's a chance a lone traveler really is missing, it'll take a while for it to be reported."

"Okay . . ."

"I'm certain there's a very simple explanation, and it probably involves your cousin. But still, what if this guy got caught up in your cousin's plan and was actually injured? Accidentally drowned? What happens when someone comes looking for him? I can't lie. I'd need to admit it was reported, but I dismissed it."

"I'm happy to retract it." *Anything to get you moving on, Sheriff.*

"I'd never do that. If it's bothering me, that's a sign I haven't done my job properly." He looks at Ben. "I'll get a boat out, maybe the one with sonar. Meanwhile, you and I are going to do what we should have done last night, Mr. Vandergriff. Take a better look around for any sign this was an actual camper—bike, gear, whatever."

"We've looked," I blurt, ignoring Ben's side-eye. At Smits's steady gaze, I realize that my lie implicates all of us—me, Ben, and Josie. "I mean . . ."

"Sam and I took a quick look," Ben says. "But if you want to search more, go for it. I'm a little busy—"

"Protecting Sam? You seem to have done a one-eighty on that, boy. You finally realized she's coming into a bit of cash, huh? Decided to go all white knight?"

Ben tenses and opens his mouth, but Josie cuts him off as she walks over. "I'll go with you, sir."

Smits flinches at the "sir" but shakes his head. "I'd like you to stay with Sam. I'm concerned about what's happening out here, and I trust *you* to look after her."

He waves to Ben. "Come on, cowboy. I'll have you back by suppertime."

I don't want Ben going into the forest, but no one else argues, and I decide I'm overreacting. It's hours from nightfall, and he'll be with Smits. The sheriff might not like him, but he's not going to run off and let Ben fend for himself if . . .

If what? The horseman makes a daytime appearance to kill Ben for briefly disagreeing with me? Yeah, that didn't even qualify as an argument, and I've already gotten the strong sense Ben doesn't like physical contact, so he's barely touched me.

As long as it's daylight, we're fine.

And after daylight? Once night falls? Ben thinks I'm safe, since I seem to be bonded to the nekkers, but I keep seeing Austin, the hate in his eyes.

I shiver and push the thought down. I just want Ben here to help us plan for when it's *not* daylight.

After Ben and Smits leave, Josie and I comb through the journal looking for ideas on how to get rid of the nekkers.

"Do you *want* to get rid of them?" Josie asks finally.

My brows shoot up.

She flushes. "Sorry. That was insensitive, with your aunt and all. Obviously you don't want to worry about the horseman trampling anyone who shoves you. But this part"—she flips pages—"suggests the nekkers can be controlled by the bonded one."

"Maybe, but I don't understand any of it. Can you?"

"No, but . . ." She glances at me, almost sidelong, unsure. "What if you could control them, Sam? If they were no danger, but you could reap the rewards?"

I stare at her, and she flushes again, glancing away. "I just thought it wouldn't be such a bad thing. Fortune and safety. Maybe a little luck for your mom."

"At the cost of a life every five years?"

Her eyes widen. "Oh, no. I didn't mean *that*. But the life has already been paid, by that camper, and you didn't have anything to do with it. Maybe you could reap the benefits until the next sacrifice was due and then stop. Put them to rest."

"Okay, that makes more sense. But whoever wrote the journal couldn't figure out how to control them either—how to keep them from coming out and hurting people. She just transcribed what her mother-in-law told her, in case someone else could do it. Also, what proof do we have that the nekkers actually confer good fortune?"

I push my seat back. "We know the protection part works, but fortune? Isn't that why people keep doing magical rituals like this—they tell themselves it worked? Obviously the Paynes got rich. Was that the nekkers or because they were the colonial equivalent of cutthroat industrialists?"

I tap the book. "I don't think the nekkers did anything. My ancestors weren't nice people who just happened to make a lot of money. My grandfather was an asshole from a long line of assholes, and by the time it got down to him, the money was already drying up. The bulk of his wealth is here, in land that's been in the family for centuries."

She squirms. "Okay, when you put it like that . . ."

I squeeze her forearm. "It's tempting. I get it. What if this good fortune could heal my mother? Help me earn the money for her care, instead of inheriting it from a grandfather I hated? If I knew it could do that?" I shake my head. "Probably better that I don't, or I'd be tempted—"

Footsteps sound on the steps, and we bolt upright. Josie slaps the book shut and tucks it off to the side as her father walks in.

"Please tell me you've seen our Mr. Vandergriff," he says, taking off his hat.

"Ben?" I say, rising.

"Damn lazy bastard wandered off again. Said he thought he saw something. I waited a few minutes, and when I called out, he didn't answer. So I went after him, and he was gone."

My skin prickles, dread creeping through me. "You said he saw something?"

Smits holds out his hand. "Not like that, Sam. He didn't walk away and get grabbed by your cousin or whatever. He's just being his usual contrary self. We had words. He didn't like what I had to say. He stewed about it for a few minutes, and then off he goes, muttering that he thinks he saw something. I figured he needed a moment to cool down. Apparently not."

I grab my phone. "I'll call him."

"You can try. When I did, he answered and hung up on me. Didn't say a word. Just hung up." He shakes his head. "I know that boy went through a lot, but there is no excuse for him to keep acting like a sullen teenager."

We all got stuck in our places.

Smits admits he said something that pissed Ben off, so I can see Ben not answering his call. But he'll answer mine.

His phone rings straight to voicemail.

I chew my fingernail, staring down at the screen. Then I text. It doesn't even show that it's been delivered.

"Can I ask what you two fought about?" I say carefully.

"Wasn't a fight." Smits slumps onto a kitchen chair. "Earlier, you heard me tell him I don't much like how he's suddenly worried about you. It's not his style. When we were out there alone, I was a little blunter. Said he'd damn well better not be expecting a big payout if you get through this."

I wince.

"Well, I mean it," Smits says. "The only person who should benefit is you, and that's not just because you deserve the money. It's for your own safety. No one else should have a stake in whether you stay. If they do, you can't trust they'll tell you to leave when you should."

Fair point. I can also see why Ben would have reacted. Because he *is* getting a payout.

Am I naive if I think that's not the only reason he's sticking around?

My sense is that Ben needed that money as an excuse. He couldn't admit he needed answers about Austin. He sure as hell couldn't admit he cares what happens to me. Is that immature? Yes, but Ben Vandergriff is a very damaged person who hasn't properly processed his trauma. And I say that as someone who can squeeze into the same boat with him. I thought I'd overcome it. I hadn't. Neither has he, and his is a lot more guilt-layered than I realized.

But he promised me he wouldn't take off again, and now he's not answering my call or my text.

Am I overthinking this? It's not as if Ben is an old friend. He might be someone who can make a promise like that, only to forget it when he's in a mood. God knows, he can get in a mood.

Smits lowers his voice. "If you're worried, Sam, we can go look for him."

I peer out the front window. It's only five. Hours of light left.

"I'd like that," I say. "I take it you didn't find any trace of the camper?"

"No, but there's a lot of ground to cover. How about you and I do that while also looking for Ben?"

I nod. "Thank you."

"I'll join you," Josie says. "Three sets of eyes are better than two."

"'Fraid not, hon. I need you back in town." He lifts his phone to show her something. "Got another report of someone lurking around the kids' camp. I need you to take a look."

She shakes her head. "It's not a pedo, Dad. It's the same thing it was last time—a parent checking on their kid by lurking in the forest."

"We don't get to choose which reports we follow up on. That's why I came here to look for this camper. It's why Sam and I are going to hunt for Ben. And it's why you need to check this out."

She huffs but says, "I'll do that and come straight back."

"Your mother's making dinner for you and Sam. She'll have that ready at seven thirty."

"Fine, fine. I'll check the kids' camp and pick up dinner."

Thirty-One

Josie is gone, and Sheriff Smits is getting a glass of water before we go. I've called Ben again and left another message. I'm sending him a new text when Smits says, "What's this?"

I glance up to see him lifting the old journal. Josie had shoved it aside, but we hadn't exactly hidden it.

I hold my breath as Smits flips through a few pages, but his expression stays somewhere between distracted disinterest and mild curiosity.

"We found it in one of the crawl spaces," I say. "It seems to be a journal from one of my ancestors. I was showing it to Josie. Neither of us can make heads or tails of it. I think it was translated from Dutch, and it's not a good translation."

Smits nods in what is obviously a show of polite interest. He's already put the book down and is finishing his water. He sets the glass in the sink. Then he looks at my bare legs and feet.

"Might want to put on long pants and sneakers," he says. "If we're going to do a proper search, we'll be going off path."

"Good idea."

I head into my room and change. When I come out, he's by the door, leaning against it. As I'm passing the table, I notice the pad of paper where I'd been deciphering the journal with notes. It's sitting right there, opened, where anyone could read it.

I glance at Smits, but he's only checking his phone.

He looks up. "All set?"

I nod and follow him out the door.

I don't think I ever really understood how big our property is until I'm searching it for someone who might be incapacitated and unable to answer my shouts. It's possible to get lost in three hundred acres, but I never have. I know every trail and every landmark and how long it will take to get from point A to point B. To do a complete circuit of the perimeter is a three-hour hike, which I only ever did with my dad, when we'd packed lunch and made a day of it.

Dad always called this our own private park, and that's what it was. Not a huge state park, but more of a recreation area, the kind of place you visit for a night or two and traverse the whole thing easily. But imagine combing that same park—most of it wooded—for one person. We'd looked for Gail, but that had been different. No one really thought she was lost in the forest.

We've been out here for nearly two hours, and I feel as if we've barely made a dent. If Ben stalked off, maybe it had nothing to do with the sheriff's needling. Maybe he just realized the futility of searching all this forest for a camper's gear and . . .

And what?

What would Ben do if he said "screw this"? Go home without a word to anyone? No. If he wanted to leave, he'd tell me. He also wouldn't walk away without his truck. Still, if he realized the futility of the search and was annoyed with Smits for this performative effort, he would indeed walk away.

If he didn't come back to the cottage, he's in trouble.

If he's not answering his phone, something has happened.

So why don't I speak up? Because I haven't worked up the courage to tell Smits that I believe I know Ben better than he does.

Craig Smits was the officer who interviewed me all those years ago.

He was the one who found my father's body. As patient as he has been, I can't help feeling like that little girl trembling as she told her story, half afraid he'd lock her up for fibbing.

I'm intimidated by Sheriff Smits, and I also respect him the way you respect authority figures you knew as a child. You don't shake those old dynamics. I don't want to look foolish in front of him, so I'm not saying what I think.

That Ben is in trouble.

That Ben wouldn't ignore my calls.

What am I afraid Smits would do?

Give me a patronizing pat on the head and tell me everything's fine, don't worry? I can deal with that.

Am I afraid of a pitying look—or mockery—if I suggest Ben gives a damn about me? Again, what does it matter? If I'm wrong, it wouldn't be the first time, but I really don't believe Ben would turn off his phone and—

I look down at my ankle bracelet. I've gotten so used to it that I forget it's there. I remember Ben yesterday, when his phone was running low and he needed to charge it.

If my phone dies, the app alerts your grandfather's lawyer that I'm not doing my job.

I take out my phone. Smits is up ahead, beating the bushes and peering behind them. I look for the lawyer's number and text her.

> Me: Sorry to bother you. Bit worried about Ben. Can't get in touch. Silly question, maybe, but he said you'd know if his phone was off, for the monitoring device

I'm about to pocket the phone when she replies.

> Ms. Jimenez: I was just debating whether to reach out. I received an alert two hours ago. I'm not going to penalize him for letting his phone run dead, but it's been long enough to recharge it. Is everything okay?

> Me: He was looking for something on the property and didn't come back. Can you tell what time his phone went off?

A moment passes. Then she replies:

> Ms. Jimenez: 4:45

I glance over at Smits, but he's disappeared into the bushes, not noticing I'd stopped.

> Me: You said you wouldn't penalize him. What's that mean?

> Ms. Jimenez: According to the will, he needs to have his phone on, ready for alerts, at all times. If it's down more than ten minutes, he loses the money for his father. Obviously, I'm not going to be that much of a stickler. But over two hours is very concerning

> Me: Yes

> Ms. Jimenez: You do realize I also have access, yes? I can see that you are out on the property. The west side. Just over half a mile from the cottage

I frown. I figured she had access, but this sounds like a warning.

> Me: I'm well within the boundary

> Ms. Jimenez: I know. I wanted to be clear that just because Ben's phone is off doesn't mean you aren't being monitored. He receives the alerts, but now that I am aware of the situation, I have turned on my own alerts

> Me: Okay

Silence. I read back through her texts.

> Me: Hold on. Do you think I have something to do with his phone being off?
>
> Ms. Jimenez: I said no such thing. But if you did think that was a way to get a few hours off of the property, it is not. I will see you if you leave, and you would be jeopardizing Ben's reward
>
> Me: I wouldn't do that
>
> Ms. Jimenez: Good. I know he can be difficult, but I think we can agree he has been doing his job

I pocket my phone and rub my face, sloughing off my anger. I've been here despite dead animals being left on my steps, despite my aunt *disappearing*. Now she thinks, what? That I'd steal Ben's phone so I can traipse off to the nearest city for a latte?

"Sam?"

I look up to see Smits on the edge of the bushes, frowning at me, and I realize I haven't moved from where he left me ten minutes ago.

"The lawyer texted me," I say. "I didn't dare ignore her."

"Texting about what?"

I shrug. "Lawyer stuff? She needed some financial details. I didn't mention any of this. Not her concern."

He visibly relaxes, and I don't miss that. I'm already on alert for it, ever since Ms. Jimenez told me what time Ben's phone went off. Ben wasn't just "not answering" his phone earlier. It's been off since before Smits returned to the cottage, saying Ben was missing.

Imagine Ben does stalk off. Smits calls him. Ben's pissy and shuts off his phone. That fits. However, he is never doing that if ten minutes of phone downtime means his family suffers.

Ben did not shut off his phone. Yet it went off shortly after he allegedly walked away to check something. He leaves Smits's sight and is grabbed by a rare daylight nekker . . . who shuts off his phone?

We'd started at the spot where Ben supposedly disappeared. It was at least a ten-minute walk from the water. Even if a nekker grabbed him and dragged him to the lake, it would take time for his phone to become waterlogged and shut down.

That is not what happened. A human being turned off Ben's phone.

I can blame my cousin or whatever mystery person we suspected had been behind this, but after reading that journal, I no longer really harbor "human staging" as a possibility. And if it was, how did someone silently grab Ben with the sheriff close by?

"Sam?"

I jerk from my thoughts.

Don't do that, Sam. Don't let him see you thinking, wondering, questioning.

Because I suspect Smits of hurting Ben? I don't know. Part of me screams that I'm losing my mind, seeing the drowned dead and the headless horseman and believing they're real and my ancestors created them and I'm bound to them. And now I think Sheriff Smits is . . . Doing what? And why?

That inner voice of denial is screaming as loud as it can, but it's such a small voice now, drowned out by the weight of evidence. That objecting voice is pride, the part of me that fears being made a fool of, and it's shrinking with every passing moment, suffocated by the certainty that I do not give a shit whether I make a fool of myself, if the alternative is letting Ben suffer because I didn't have the guts to suspect Craig Smits.

Smits saw the journal. He didn't react, and I took that as a sign he didn't know what it was. Why would I think he might? Did some part of me already suspect he might?

Yes.

He hadn't reacted, and I'd been relieved. He didn't question it either, though. I chalked that up to a lack of interest, but it could just have easily been studied disinterest.

And the notepad. Something about it caught my eye. I'd thought it was just the fact that I'd accidentally left it out.

No, it'd been moved. In my memory, I see myself setting my pen on it and pushing it aside after reading passages to Josie.

My pen hadn't been on the book when I last saw it. That's what caught my attention. The pen was set aside, and the book was angled differently than it sat imprinted in my subconscious.

Smits had advised me to change my clothing, which would require going into my room and shutting the door. Giving him time to see what was on the notepad. To see how much we knew.

Could I be wrong?

Absolutely.

But I can test the theory easily enough.

"It'll be dark soon," I say, peering up.

If my stomach didn't plummet, it might be comical how quickly he checks his watch.

"You're right," he says. "Josie will be back at the cottage shortly. We might want to think about heading in."

"And getting flashlights. Bringing Josie out after we eat."

He shakes his head slowly. "I don't think so, Sam. It gets awfully dark in here at night."

"Dangerous, too."

His head jerks up.

"We could trip," I say. "Especially if we leave the path." I peer around. "But, while it seems to be getting dark, that's mostly just the forest. We still have time, and Josie isn't due back quite yet."

"I still say we ought to head in. We can keep calling for Ben on the way."

"Okay. You're right. It does get dark faster in the forest—" I jerk my head. "Did you hear that?"

"Hear what?"

"It sounded like a moan." I turn to him, my eyes wide and innocent. "What if Ben's hurt?"

Smits eases back, getting comfortable in that way of his. The good ol' boy. The voice of authority. *Well, see here, little miss, you've got nothing to worry about.*

"He's not," Smits says. "I'm going to kick his ass for worrying you like this, but it's just Ben being Ben. Thoughtless and inconsiderate. I'm sorry, hon. I can't tell whether you've developing feelings for the boy, but I really hope not."

Oh, nicely played. There's been nothing romantic between me and Ben, but it's a sure way to make me uncomfortable. Suggest I might be "developing feelings," and I'll back off, not wanting anyone to mistake my concern for *that*.

I smile and shake my head. "I like my guys a lot less moody. But I can still be concerned about him. He—" I look behind me again. "I am definitely hearing something. I'm going to check it out."

I take off at a lope. It's a moment before Smits even calls after me, meaning Ben is not in this direction. But he does call soon enough, and when I ignore him, he comes after me.

"None of this, Sam," he calls as he stalks my way. "It's getting dark. If you're worried, I'll bring search help out tomorrow, but I'm sure by then, Ben will have turned up."

I keep going. When I feign stumbling, his strides turn into a lope. "Sam. It is *too dark*. You're going to get—"

I stumble, arms flying up, timing it for when he's right behind me. I let out a shriek as I fall, and he grabs my arm. I twist, pushing at him, and he backs up fast, eyes widening as he lifts his hands.

"I was just trying to help," he says.

I clutch my shoulder. "You *wrenched* my arm. That *hurt*."

Again, it's almost comical how fast he retreats. Or it would be if it didn't confirm what I suspect.

Craig Smits knows all about the nekkers . . . including who is bonded to them.

Thirty-Two

"Don't want to hurt me, huh?" I say. "I wonder why. And don't say it's because I'm descended from the town founders or any shit like that."

He winces at the profanity. "Sam . . ."

"You have two choices, *Craig*. Well, three. Option three is that you physically stop me and suffer what we both know are the consequences. Option two is that you pretend you don't know what's happened to Ben and I call the lawyer, who was wondering why his phone was off. Apparently, she gets an alert. Also? If Ben's phone is off, he doesn't get money for his father, which means he did not turn off his phone or let the battery die."

Smits tries not to react to that, but I see his wince.

"Option one?" I continue. "Tell me where the fuck Ben is. I don't care about the rest. I want to know where to find Ben."

"It's not what you think."

"Of course it's not. It never is."

Smits eases back. "I know the legend. About the Paynes and the drowned dead. My family has been here nearly as long as yours. People talk. But that's all it is. A legend. After I leafed through that book inside, I realized Ben had shown you that to convince you it was real—after setting it all up to scare you off, make you lose your inheritance. I confronted him. He stalked away. He turned off his phone because he knew the gig was up."

"You've heard the legend."

"Yes, like I said—"

"I want the truth, Sheriff. There is no way you flipped through that book and recognized the story. The writing is faint, the penmanship is hard to decipher, the language is old. Flipping through only told you that we'd found a book you've seen before. My notes told you we'd deciphered it."

"I—"

"You're afraid to hurt me based on a legend you don't believe?" I meet his gaze. "Bull. Shit. You know the legend is true, and you know I'm the focus. Do you know why my aunt died? Because she was trying to restrain me when we fought. She let go, and I fell. That was it. A mistake. So if I attack you, and you justifiably stop me . . . ?"

I step toward him. He backs up.

"Tell me again how you don't believe the legend," I say.

"It's not—It's complicated, Sam, and I think Ben has been messing around, thinking it's just some old story, and it's not. All right? It's not."

He starts to shove his hands into his pockets and then thinks better of it, keeping them where I can see them. "I said the Smitses have been here forever. For generations, my ancestors worked for your family. They . . . assisted them. In return for some of the benefits."

I remember that from the book. The recommendation that the Paynes bring someone local in on the plan. Both to help find victims and as a potential fall guy.

"So your family sacrificed travelers—"

"What? No. Of course not." He takes a breath. "That isn't how it works, Sam. Yes, sacrifices are needed, but no one kills anybody. This is a vacation spot. Swimmers drown. Boaters capsize. Campers stumble over a cliff going to the bathroom at night. Things happen, sometimes to lone travelers who don't have ties to the area. My family helped yours find dead people, who were then given to the lake, to the horseman."

"They fed people to the nekkers, forcing them to rise from the dead *as* nekkers, trapped in their bodies—"

"*No.*" He shifts in frustration. "They might retain a bit of memory temporarily, which is why your aunt called to you. That fades quickly. Their souls pass on, and what's left is the shell, which eventually rots."

"So no one was murdered."

He sighs. "I can't say never, Sam. All I know is that by some point, we were using people who were already dead. It's one of the reasons my family went into law enforcement. We could find those who died in accidents, and sometimes, we could get them to the Payne property before anyone knew. Is that a cruelty to their families? Of course. But it benefited everyone in the community."

No, it benefited his family and mine. I only say, "And Austin Vandergriff?"

Another sigh, deeper, pain written over his features. "I don't know what happened there, Sam. I only found Austin's body after your father . . ." He swallows. "After your dad took his own life. Austin had been trampled. That means it was the horseman, likely protecting you. Later, your mother told me that Austin had been tormenting you. That night he ran off, he was here after dusk and he must have hurt you then, when it was truly dangerous. I presume your father was hiding the body from the search when you found him and he panicked."

"I've seen Austin. Among the dead. After he was allegedly buried."

"He wasn't buried. The horseman killed him, so his body had to be given to the lake. An empty casket went into that hole."

"And the letter my father wrote, taking responsibility and ranting about inner demons?"

"I don't know. I can only guess that was his way of explaining the inexplicable. In his own way, I suppose he did feel responsible."

I fall silent.

"What happened to your aunt was horrible, Sam. A terrible accident. Your grandfather should have warned her, but you know how he was. All that mattered was his firstborn son. Your father knew the secret. *Only* your father. But no one else needs to die. I can teach you how to control the nekkers and harness their power, just like your dad did."

"And Sam's mother?" The question comes from our right, and we both startle as Josie tramps from the forest.

"No, Dad," she says. "I didn't just get back. I was *not* leaving you alone with Sam."

"I would never hurt—"

"You wouldn't dare, apparently. Now, what about Sam's mother?"

Smits's brow creases. "Veronica? Are you asking whether she could benefit if Sam controls the nekkers? Yes. The fortune conferred from the nekkers could help Veronica's health, especially if we brought her here—"

"I mean you said her dad could control them. And her mom?"

"Veronica didn't know anything about—"

"Liar." Josie spits the word with enough venom to make me jump. "I know about you and Veronica Payne, Dad. I found letters you wrote her."

"What?" Smits says as I stand there, staring.

She pulls a page from her back pocket and shakes it. "Should I read it? I found these in the crawl space under Sam's grandfather's cottage. Tucked into a book. I—"

She stops short, turning to me with dawning horror. I barely see it. All I see is Josie in that crawl space, reading something, and when I notice, her light goes out for a moment. Then it comes on, and the page is gone.

She squeezes her eyes shut. "I'm so sorry, Sam. I didn't mean to do it like this. I didn't mean to do it at all. I was going to confront him on my own. That's why I moved out last night. I was working it through, because a lot of it didn't make sense, but now, with all this . . ."

"I don't understand what you're saying." My words come slow, echoing in my ears.

"I . . ."

"Tell me."

She holds the letter awkwardly. "My dad and your mom were having . . ."

"An affair." My voice is hollow. I say that because it's the obvious conclusion, but her relief says she mistook that to mean I already knew or suspected.

"Yes. I found the letters while we were searching. I don't know why they'd be there. In your grandfather's crawl space."

I look at Smits. "He found them, didn't he? My grandfather. You're the one who broke into the cottage looking for them. Did my grandfather blackmail you with them? Or just use them to make sure my mom never dared ask him for a penny?"

His jaw sets, and he looks at Josie. "It was a very long time ago, hon. Your mom and I had some troubles, and I was young and stupid—"

Her bitter laugh cuts him off. "I don't give a damn about the affair. Well, I do, for Mom's sake, but you've always treated her like shit. Just never shitty enough to make her leave. A garden-variety lousy husband."

"Now, Josie—"

"The affair is irrelevant. That's why I didn't confront you or tell Sam. The parts that bothered me were lines like this." She holds up the letter and reads. "*Yes, I know we need to find someone before the end of the summer. I'm on it. Your in-laws leave in a week, and Harris goes back early for class prep. That'd be the ideal opportunity, when they're gone but a few people are still passing through. We have time.*"

My gut goes cold. "That was to my mother?"

Josie glances over and nods. "I'm sorry, Sam. I really am."

"But I had to know." I look at Smits. "You never killed anyone for the sacrifices, right? And it was my father and grandfather who knew about them."

He doesn't look at me. "Josie, hon. Read that again. It was just me talking about getting someone in to do some work around the property. Best timing was when just Sam and her mom were here, but there were still people passing through, looking to take on odd jobs."

"The shed," I whisper.

They both look my way.

I turn to Smits. "You or my mother found the journal when the shed was being rebuilt. Just before I was born. It'd been lost. Someone in my family decided to stop passing along the story of the nekkers.

That's when our fortunes nosedived—and when the local disappearances stopped. You and Mom resurrected the old practice."

He straightens. "All right. Yes. I found the journal. I gave it to your mom. We were . . ."

"Good friends," Josie says sarcastically.

"We were friends, and I knew she liked historical documents. That's what she did, right? A history teacher. She deciphered it and told me, and at first, it was a lark. We were young and goofing around."

"Goofing around with folk magic requiring human sacrifice?" I say.

"It wasn't like that. *At all.* But I remembered a story from my family, about the nekkers. Then you were born and . . ." He exhales. "When it came to your health, Sam, your mother was neurotic. Terrified you'd inherit the gene for early dementia. Her dad had just been diagnosed, and your mom was . . . not in a good place. I agreed to help perform the bonding ritual to make her feel better. But we never killed anyone." He points at the letter. "That says I was going to *find* someone. Not kill them."

"Find a victim," Josie says.

"No, hon. Absolutely not. We did it for you, too. Protecting Sam from that terrible disease but also, if my family could benefit, I wanted that. And it worked. Everything got better for both families. Until Austin died and Sam's dad . . ."

He looks at me. "I hate to say this, Sam, after everything you've been through, but your father wasn't a good person. Part of that magic was about protecting you and your mother from him. From his temper. I told your mom that the horseman trampled Austin, but I'm not completely sure it wasn't your father. I wanted to protect you. You and your mother. From your father, in life and after his death."

And here's where it all breaks down. Oh, his story has been tattered since he started, but with this, it explodes, as he's unable to keep from casting himself as the hero. With this, the lies shine blindingly bright, because I could sooner see my father as a closet serial killer than an abusive father and husband.

That lie scatters the veil I've pulled over my father's memory. The shroud that keeps me from remembering his kindness and his gentleness and his goodness and his love, because if he'd murdered Austin Vandergriff, all my memories had to be wrong. They're not.

I say my mother and I didn't get along after Dad's death, and it was my fault, lashing out, but we'd never been close. She might have done this "for me," but it was my father who'd been the light and warmth in my life . . . as I'd been in his, and when that sun went out, I was left with the cold and distant star of my mother.

Smits is lying. He's constructed a story woven of half-truths and outright lies. But I'm not calling him on it just yet, because I still need something from him.

"Where is Ben?" I ask.

Smits sighs, the sound bone-deep, the put-upon grown-up retaining patience when a child asks for the ridiculous and impossible.

"I don't know, Sam. I already told you—"

"You've told me three versions of the story. He left because you snapped at him. No, he left because you said I'd better not be paying him. No, the real reason he left is because he staged a fake legend . . . which you've just admitted isn't fake at all."

"Answer her question, Dad," Josie says. "Where is Ben?"

"I don't know, hon. He took off—"

She pulls out her gun. I startle and quickly glance over, trying to catch her eye, to tell her no, please don't escalate this, but she won't look my way.

"*Josie*," her father says, sharp but calm, as if she kicked him during a tantrum.

"Where. Is. Ben."

"I don't—"

She swings the gun barrel on him.

"Josie," Smits says, struggling to gentle his voice. "You're upset. I understand that. This is all very confusing—"

"I'm not a fucking child, Dad. Don't talk to me like I'm five."

"Then don't act—" He bites that off. "I'm sorry. I'm not trying to diminish your right to be angry with me—"

Her harsh laugh cuts him off. "Wow. You actually were awake during those family-therapy sessions Mom begged for. Could have sworn you nodded off. Or maybe you just pretended to, being a jerk like always."

"Josie." His tone firms. "I've already admitted that your mom and I had problems. She's never been easy to live with and—"

"Mom?" Josie's voice rises. "Mom is the single most easy person to live with. She's a fucking saint who put up with your shit. Now where the hell is Ben?"

"I don't—"

"Count of five, or I swear I will shoot you."

Every muscle in me tenses. She's shaking, and I want to get her attention, reassure her, get her to lower that gun. But she will not look my way, and I'm afraid that if I speak, it'll only upset her. One more person telling her to calm down when she has every right to be furious.

"Five. Four."

"Josie," Smits says. "I can't tell you what I don't know. Do you want me to lie? Fine. I think he's over there." He waves an arm so dismissively that my anger turns on him.

"Stop patronizing her," I snap. "You did something to Ben. You've already admitted to the rest so—"

"Why not admit to this? Good point. Obviously, if I knew where Ben was, I'd admit—"

"Three."

"I didn't hurt Ben, Josie. I didn't hurt anyone. The only one threatening here is you, honey, and—"

"Two."

He steps toward her. "You aren't going to shoot me, Josie."

Her hands adjust on the gun.

I lunge their way. "Stop. Sheriff, please just—"

"Stay out of this," he snaps. "This is your fault. You already got your aunt killed."

"Sam didn't—" Josie begins.

"Of course she did. You believe this nonsense that she only just found out about the nekkers now? No. That's why she came here. She enlisted Ben Vandergriff—"

"Dad! Stop!"

"I'm just telling you—"

"Stop *lying*." Josie's eyes fill. "Please. If you care about me at all, stop lying. Stop blaming everyone but yourself."

"What did I do? I didn't kill her aunt. Didn't kill that little boy. I'm just the sucker her mother used—"

"Dad, stop!"

"*You* stop, Josie. This is enough. Give me that damned gun."

He lunges, grabbing for it. She swings the gun up. Smits grabs her arm, and she starts to topple backward. I run, screaming for them to stop, just stop. Smits is trying to wrestle the gun from her, and they're in the shadows, and I can't see—

The gun fires.

Smits flies back, hands going up. He starts to fall. Josie tumbles backward, gun still in her hand. Smits hits the ground, hands flying to his chest.

Blood. I see blood.

He's shot.

I run to him, but he's already scrambling up, snarling at me to get the fuck out of his way. There's no bullet hole. Just a splatter of blood, as if the shot grazed him. He stalks over to where Josie fell backward and he reaches down to snatch the gun.

"You're lucky you didn't—" he snaps.

Then he stops.

There's a sound. A low animal sound. Smits drops to his knees and shakes Josie, and her head flops up and—

There's blood on her face.

Not just blood. Torn flesh and gray bits and—

A hole where her eye had been.

Thirty-Three

A whimper bubbles up in me, and I rock there, telling myself I'm wrong, Josie isn't dead.

Not dead? With that wound?

Then I've lost my mind. It snapped when my aunt disappeared, maybe even before that. Yes, this is the answer. Gail was right—I killed those animals and chopped them up, my father's dark side finally bubbling to the surface. The rest has been a fever dream, where I'm wandering around the property alone, scenes playing out in my head, and now I'm imagining Josie is . . .

Josie is dead. She is dead, and I am here, awake, lucid.

"Josie?" My voice comes out as a whimper.

This cannot be happening.

First Gail, who had only tried to help me. Now Josie, who'd done the same. Funny and clever and lonely Josie, making me feel as special as a shy first grader who catches the attention of the most vibrant girl in class.

Josie.

I drop to my knees beside her. I stare at her beautiful face, always so alive, every expression writ large, from her joy to her worry to her fury. Josie, exploding with decades of repressed anger toward her father and hurt, too, because he'd proven to be everything she'd always feared, and she was finally going to stand up to him and make him tell the truth and—

Rage creeps in as my gaze rises to Smits, holding his daughter's hand and saying her name.

Josie. Sweet Josie. His only child. Maybe the one person he'd actually loved. And he'd killed her. As much as he loved her—*adored* her—he still would not back down and just tell her what the hell he did with Ben. He fought knowing she had a loaded gun—

"Get away from my daughter."

Smits is rising, his voice a rasp.

"Get the fuck away from my daughter, you twisted piece of Payne shit."

"What?"

"You and your family. You're all alike. Lording it over us, using us, making us kill people for scraps of what you already have. A little bit of luck, that's all we ever wanted. Enough to get by, while you hoarded the rest for yourselves."

"I had nothing to do—"

"You're a Payne," he spits. He's on his feet now, and I get to mine, very aware of Josie's gun near his feet. "You came back, and I played my role. The Smits role. I looked after you. I let my own daughter come here when she wanted to get to know you. I thought that was good. The next generation. Give you time, and then I'd tell you the truth, and you and Josie would take over, and it would be the way it used to be. Do you know what that makes me?" He lunges toward me. "A goddamn fucking fool!"

I stand my ground, watching the gun, ready to run if he reaches down for it. He doesn't. Even in his grief, he knows better.

"You did this." He jabs a finger at Josie. "As sure as if you pulled the trigger. You are your mother's daughter. Your fucking sainted mother, who screwed me in every way possible. A coldhearted bitch who didn't give a damn about me. Not about you either. She pulled me in by claiming she wanted to protect you, and I got that. I wasn't a dad yet, but Liz and I were trying, and I desperately wanted a child, and when I had one, I knew I'd do anything to protect her. But it was never about you. It was about making sure your mother didn't get sick. She bonded you—her only child—and then took all the benefits. All of them, aimed toward saving her from her family curse." A harsh laugh. "All that work, and she's in a care home at fifty, already losing her mind. Serves her fucking right."

I can't respond. Can't move. My blood runs cold, not at the revelations, but at the certainty that, finally, he is telling the truth. His daughter is dead, and he no longer cares enough to lie.

"You staged those dead animals," I say. "You said my mother told you about Austin tormenting me and you—"

"I didn't do that."

"But you staged the hatchet and bloody gloves. The wet clothing. You wanted leverage, in case I didn't go along with your plan to take over the nekkers."

He only sets his jaw.

"And Austin?" I say, though it's not Austin I care about. It's someone else, and a truth I can see, cold and bright in the dark. "What happened with Austin?"

"Your mother found him, trampled by the horseman. I wanted to drag him into the lake before anyone knew, but she said no, we had to use him for the ritual that night. So I hid his body. Only your dad, out looking for the brat, found him . . . and then you found your dad. I think he knew. Suspected anyway. He had some inkling that your mother was responsible, and he was burying Austin to protect her. You told your mom, who told me to handle it. And she told me how to handle it."

"Kill my father," I whisper. "Make it look like suicide."

"That's the kind of woman who whelped you. She murdered your father and wrote that note and destroyed his memory, and he hadn't done a damn thing to deserve it. He was trying to protect her by burying that brat."

I sway, the earth threatening to open under my feet.

My father was a good man. A decent man. A wonderful father who loved me and absolutely did not kill anyone, and I knew that. In my soul, I'd always known, and I'd betrayed him by letting my mother convince me otherwise.

My grandfather had been right.

I want to scream at that. Scream hysterical laughter. The old bastard had figured it all out. Found the letters. Linked them to those old stories of the horseman, legends passed down as family lore. He'd realized they were true and my mother was at fault and my father died for nothing, and what had he done? Let me be raised by a monster. Let me give up my dream of med school and live in squalor to help a woman who didn't deserve it. Sent me here, to face the truth . . . or die trying.

You fucking horrible bastard. If you could die again, I'd kill you myself.

No, I'd drag his sorry ass here and let the nekkers take him.

I look down at Josie's body, and my rage at my grandfather evaporates.

Josie is dead. Gail is dead.

And Ben?

"Ben," I croak. "What did you do—?"

Smits snarls and lunges, sending me falling back. "Ben Vandergriff? Who the fuck cares what happens to that waste of fucking cells. He let his brother climb out the window and run off, and then it all went to fucking shit. Do you know that, girl? This is all Ben Fucking Vandergriff's fault, because he was a lazy good-for-nothing brat who sat on his porch smoking a joint while his brother escaped. The kid came here, and he hurt you after dark and died for it. Then you found your father burying him, and that was the end. Everything gone to hell. Your mom came back once for another sacrifice, but it was already too late. She wasn't here often enough. The magic had ended—for both of us. I was stuck here as a fucking sheriff, and she lost her fucking mind. Because of Ben Vandergriff."

"You feel guilty," I whisper as it hits me. "You see Ben, how much he's suffered, and you feel guilty."

"Why would I feel guilty?"

You do. Deep in that twisted brain, you feel guilt, and you don't know what to do with it.

He continues, "It's his fault and yours. You were a stuck-up brat who couldn't handle one little boy with a crush. You got scared, and the horseman came, and then you saw your father burying the kid, and it was all over. If Ben had done his job and you hadn't been a snotty brat, everything would have been *fine*. But what happened to Ben? Was he punished? No, he got this cushy caretaking job that I asked for. If I'd gotten it, I could have kept up the magic, but no, your grandfather forbid me to come out here and gave the job to the dumbass teen who let his brother die."

Smits steps toward me. "If it weren't for you and Ben, my luck wouldn't have gone south. My daughter would have had the money to go to a real school and move away to a real job and not be lying . . ." His voice breaks. "Lying in the fucking dirt. Where you should be. Where Ben Vandergriff is going to be."

He smiles, an ugly, teeth-baring thing. "Ben will be reunited with his brother. As soon as the nekkers come for him." He looks up. "As soon as it's full dark."

I turn and run.

"Had enough, little girl?" Smits shouts after me. "Maybe I can't touch you, but I can make damn sure you go to prison for the rest of your life. Killing your aunt, Josie, Ben . . . Guess it runs in the family!"

I'm not fleeing to the cottage. I'm finding Ben. Smits said that the nekkers would take Ben when they came at full dark. That means he isn't dead. Not yet.

Smits has put Ben somewhere to be taken by the nekkers. Not killed by the horseman, because Ben never hurt me. Instead, Smits must be using him as a sacrifice, following the ritual in the book. Ben is out here, on the property, probably near the shore, immobilized and waiting for the nekkers.

Waiting for full dark. Which is coming fast.

I race for the lake and burst out of the trees, hoping to see that it's lighter here. It's not. The sun has fallen below the horizon, and its light is sliding from the world.

"Ben!" I shout.

If Smits left him awake, he would have gagged him, but if Ben hears me, he can make a sound. A muffled cry. A kick against driftwood. Something. Anything.

I run blindly along the shore, knowing I need to slow down and search properly, but I can't. The sun is gone. The moon is out. Ben is here, somewhere, about to suffer the same fate as the others, dragged into the lake to become a nekker, like his brother.

He didn't do anything, I want to rage. He has done nothing except suffer for what happened all those years ago, with Austin, and he did not deserve that either.

He is blameless. But so was Josie. So was Gail. So was my father.

So was everyone dragged into the lake. All those people that Smits killed for my mother.

He also murdered my father. On my mother's orders.

I can't process any of that. Focus on finding Ben. Get to Ben before—

A shape rises from the water, less than a hundred feet away. A figure, a little shorter than me, huge eyes fixed on me as he bears down.

Austin.

Thirty-Four

I backpedal. Austin keeps coming, and I want to turn and run, but Ben is here somewhere, and if I run, Austin and the other nekkers will kill him.

"Austin," I say, and my voice wavers and cracks.

Austin left those animals for me. I might have accused Smits, but he'd had no reason to lie when he denied it, and my gut says it was Austin.

Smits said the nekkers' souls—consciousness—were gone. Was that a lie? Either way, something remained, enough for Austin to lay out those dead animals for me.

Enough for him to attack me?

He keeps coming, and I inch back. Then I stop myself.

No more running. Not from Austin. I did the right thing to run as a child, but I am not a child now.

I reach down and scoop up the biggest rock I can fit in my hand. Then I wait.

Austin continues his relentless trudge my way. His gaze never wavers from my face. He sees his target. He has always seen his target, and I don't know what I did to deserve being it.

Nothing. I did nothing. I was a child. I didn't "lead him on." I didn't even want to be his friend, something inside me always wary around him. Others—my mother, my grandparents, Austin's parents—pushed me to be nice to him. Was that why he targeted me? Because I'd shown him some attention? Or had they pushed me to be nice to him because he'd already targeted me, and oh how cute, Austin has a crush on Sam?

What matters is that I did nothing to deserve the hell he put me through, and now I stand there with that rock, ready to do what I wished I could have done fourteen years ago. Drive him away. Hurt him, if I need to.

I feel terrible that he died because he hurt me, but I didn't *make* him hurt me. I did everything I could to stop him from hurting me, and my father did, too, and yet Austin would not stay away, and he died for it, and I will not take responsibility for that. Or for whatever I need to do to protect myself now.

He stops in front of me, and it is so strange, looking down at him. He'd been growing fast at thirteen, towering over me. Now I look down and I see a boy. Nothing but a boy.

His gaze lifts to mine, the hate blazing. My hands tighten around the rock. But he just stands there, glaring, and even as hatred pulses from him, it's empty and unfocused. As if he knows he hates me . . . but doesn't know why. Doesn't know what to do with that.

When he moves toward me again, I take a deep breath and stand my ground. Is he a threat? He doesn't *feel* like one anymore. Just a lost and angry little boy, needing a target for his rage and seeing me and . . . somehow no longer able to connect the two. Whatever remains of Austin in there, it's not enough for him to understand why he hates me.

Then a sound comes from behind him. Some noise I can't make out. Austin stills and slowly turns as another object emerges from the water.

A head, lifted by a hand, as if its eyes can still see. Then the man—Bram—and his horse, rising, the headless horseman walking from the lake.

That noise comes again. From Bram? From the horse? I can't tell, but it must be a sign to Austin, a warning, because Austin grunts and steps away and then just . . . shuffles off.

I stare out at the horseman, ready to flee. Then I remember I have nothing to fear from Bram. Nor does Ben.

I race toward the horse and its rider, and Bram holds out his head to see me as he slows the horse. I run until the horse has fully emerged from the lake, Bram's head still turned toward me.

"I need help!" I say. "Please. Can you do that?"

The head stares. Up close, it is little more than pocked flesh over bone. Huge glowing eyes, a hole for a nose, a hole for a mouth. Like a jack-o'-lantern, I think, a hysterical laugh bubbling up. The headless horseman and his jack-o'-lantern head.

"Can you help me?" I say. "Can you hear me?"

No reaction. We stare at each other. Then, at a sound farther down, Bram swings his head that way.

The lake is almost still, only the faintest ripple in the water... except for one spot, farther down, where ripples are growing, and the crown of a head emerges.

A nekker.

I race past the horseman and down the shore, frantically looking for Ben.

"Stop," a voice calls.

My head jerks up, and I follow the voice to see Smits in the moonlight. He's dragging Ben's bound and unconscious body toward the lake.

When I take another step, he says, in that same calm voice, "Stop, Sam. Look behind you."

I glance over my shoulder to see Bram there, his horse sloshing through the water as he trails behind me. Bram holds his head out toward Smits.

"He's staying close," Smits says. "Protecting you."

"Yes, which means you'd damned well better drop Ben and—"

"No."

"The horseman—"

"—will kill me if I touch you. He'll trample me. Which means he will also trample Ben, and since you'll be here, caught in the fray, you won't escape either. The horseman might protect you, but that horse is a mindless beast that will not understand it's trampling you, too."

I open my mouth to say I'm willing to take that chance. Then I shut it. Whether I'm in danger or not, Ben is.

I watch the nekkers—four dark shapes standing motionless in the water. They're watching. Drawn in, but having no reason to come closer. Not yet.

"Watch and learn," Smits says. "If you have any of your mother in you, you know this is the time to think about saving your own hide, Sam. Let me give Ben to the lake." His gaze meets mine across the twenty feet between us. "Prove that you have her blood. That you can do this. Show me that, despite everything that's happened, it's in my best interests to let you take your mother's place."

Let him sacrifice Ben, he means. Smits envisioned Josie and me as the next generation of Smitses and Paynes, working together. Josie is gone but if I play my cards right, maybe we can still make this work. That's what he's telling me.

He starts the incantation. If asked an hour ago whether I'd remember the words from the book, I'd have said no. But as he speaks, they roll from my subconscious. An invocation to the water and the power there, to the nekkers, asking them to accept this sacrifice.

At first, Smits is watching me, but when I don't move, he turns toward the nekkers, voice rising as he calls them, and they begin to wade closer.

The one in front is the man I saw last night. The one I'm now certain is the figure I'd seen in the shed, drawn there by my return. I kept trying to figure out how someone entered with the door latched—because it was a some*thing* not a some*one*.

Then comes a woman I don't recognize. Austin falls in behind her, and he looks my way, pocked lips curling as if in a hiss. Another one appears, and my stomach clenches. It's the camper, who stops there, looking about as if confused, not knowing why he felt the need to come to the shore. Two more nekkers follow, their attention on Smits and Ben. On the caller and the sacrifice.

"Wait!" I shout.

Austin turns my way, and my gut freezes. But the man in front turns toward me, too, and something cold and wet brushes my arm as the horse moves up beside me. The nekkers all stop, attention turning to Bram, to their leader.

"I am the bonded one," I say. And stifling my revulsion, I lay a hand on the horse's cold, slimy flank. "I am a Payne. This man is nothing."

Do they understand me? I doubt it, but nor do they move. Huge liquid eyes and empty sockets turn my way.

I am the bonded one. I am a Payne. Whether they understand my words or not, they understand my truth.

"Sam," Smits warns. "You're going to upset them. Confuse them. The horseman can't protect you if they—"

"I call you, creatures of the water, guardians of the lake," my voice rings out in the invocation, and they all turn my way.

"Let me do this," I say to Smits, my voice low. "It will be stronger if I do the sacrifice."

Smits rocks, uncertain but not interrupting.

I continue the invocation and the dedication, saying the same words he had. Then as I near the end, passing where I'd cut him off, I turn his way.

"I bring you this offering, children of the lake," I say. "This man, for you to devour and claim as your own."

Smits lifts Ben by the collar.

"I give you this man," I say. "Yours, in return for your favor. This I offer to you, my guardians, my protectors."

The nekkers draw closer. Smits holds out Ben for them, and then lets go. Ben's limp body drops face down into the water.

"All yours," Smits calls, waving at Ben.

I watch Ben there, his nose and mouth under the water, unable to breathe. Smits walks away as the nekkers close in.

One step. Two steps. Three—

I run for Ben. Smits hears me and whirls, but I'm already there, yanking Ben by the collar, getting his head from the water.

"Sam," Smits snaps as the nekkers stop. "You've already given him to them. Don't interfere. You'll get hurt. It's too late to save him."

"I didn't give him to them." I struggle to hold Ben up out of the water. "I gave *you*." I wave at Smits. "There. That is the one I gave you."

Smits only rolls his eyes. "It's too late. You—"

"—said I was giving them a man. That's you." I start dragging Ben toward shore, angled away from Smits. I wave at the sheriff. "Him. That's your target. Take—"

Smits charges, snarling. He doesn't get within a yard of me before the horse gallops into his path.

"I didn't touch her!" Smits says. "I never laid a finger on her."

The horse stays where it is, Bram holding out his head to watch Smits. The sheriff is yelling something at me, furious, feeling safe if he stays where he is. He doesn't see the legless nekker pulling itself through the water. He doesn't see the others, turned his way, beginning to move. His focus is on the horse and rider. As long as he doesn't touch me, he's safe.

Except, with the horse between us, the nekkers understand. I am holding Ben. Protecting Ben. And Bram is protecting me. Which means the sacrifice . . .

The legless nekker wraps one hand around Smits's ankle. The sheriff jumps. It's barely a startle, as if lake weeds touched him. Even when he sees the nekker, he only yanks his leg free and backs up.

"Not *me!*" he shouts. "Him!" He gestures at Ben.

The legless nekker keeps pulling itself along, slowly but inexorably pursuing Smits as the sheriff backs up. And that's all Smits does. Backs up. Focused on this broken creature, no threat to him, easily escapable. But the others are coming his way, too, and he doesn't see them until the tall nekker is nearly on him. Then Smits's head jerks up and . . .

Do I see recognition flash in his eyes? His lips form a word he doesn't utter, and his gaze locks on the man, as if he recognizes him.

"One of yours?" I call. "A traveler you just happened to find dead? Only he wasn't dead, was he?"

The nekker keeps tramping toward the sheriff. Smits backs up faster, half trips over a piece of driftwood and then whirls to run. The nekker lunges. He catches Smits by the back of the shirt, but the sheriff yanks free and gets two running steps before the legless nekker catches his foot.

Smits pitches face-first in the water. The tall nekker falls on him, biting his shoulder. Smits screams and punches and kicks, but the others swarm over him.

I want to look away.

I do not look away. I set them on Smits, and whatever he has done, I must watch what *I* have done. Understand what I have done and will never do again.

The nekkers rip into him, taking mouthfuls of flesh, blood spraying, Smits screaming. They don't tear him apart. They don't devour him. They only bite and rip and taste. And then, as the sheriff screams and thrashes, the tall nekker grabs Smits by the hair and drags him into the lake and the others follow, ready to catch Smits if he escapes.

He does not escape.

The nekker walks deeper into the lake, dragging Smits, until the water closes over both of them.

I still stand there, watching, in case Smits comes back, in case I need to defend Ben.

Silence falls. Something moves beside me, clammy flesh touching my bare arm, and I look to see the horse there, Bram holding his head to look out at the lake. Guarding me and watching.

I grab Ben under the armpits and haul him farther onto the beach. I'm dropping beside him when I see another figure, and I startle.

It's one of the nekkers, still half out of the water, farther down. As it comes my way, the horse shifts, as if in warning, but it doesn't move. The figure keeps coming, and my throat seizes as I make out the form of my aunt.

"Gail," I whisper.

I leave Ben and walk toward her. She comes until the water is up to her knees, and then she stands there, swaying as she watches me. I force myself closer, taking in the whole of her, the gray and bloated skin, the ragged holes in her flesh that I now know are bites from the nekkers claiming her as their own.

Her one remaining eye is growing, turning dark and liquid like a seal's. It fixes on me, but loosely, not fully focused. She continues to sway, her expression placid and empty, with only the slightest hint of confusion. As if she's seeing someone she vaguely remembers but feels no inclination to identify. Just the vaguest sense of "I know you, don't I?"

Smits said the nekkers lose their consciousness, and I think he *was* right in this. Austin had targeted me, but it seemed like vestigial hate, something animal and instinctive. That first time, Gail had called for me, asked for help, her faculties already fading and terror taking over. Looking at her now is like seeing my mother during her worst episodes, when I glimpse a future where my mother will no longer even mistake me for Gail, where she'll only have the faintest sense that she knew me, once upon a time, but that it's not important anymore.

"I'm sorry," I whisper as my eyes fill. "I should have made you stay behind." A harsh and humorless bubble of a laugh. "Yes, I have no idea how I'd have done that, but I should have found a way. I shouldn't have come myself, and then you'd have—" My throat constricts. "If I had any idea . . ."

Tears fall, hot on my cold skin.

"I wish I could set you free," I say. "I wish I knew how to do that. All I can do is leave. I think that will help. If I'm gone, you can rest. You can all rest."

She watches me vaguely for another moment, and then turns and trudges back into the lake, and the water rises higher and higher, until it closes over her head.

Thirty-Five

I'm on the shore with Ben. He's alive but obviously drugged, and I can't rouse him. I have my phone. I should call for help. But he's breathing evenly and his heart beats strong, and I do not dare summon anyone out here. Not at night. I can't take the chance that they will innocently incur the horseman's wrath.

So I pull Ben as far as I can onto the shore, and I sit with him, keeping him warm, while ten feet away, the horseman stands watch, a silent sentinel at the lake's edge.

It's long past midnight when Ben finally stirs. He's groggy for the next couple of hours, but whenever I suggest getting him to the hospital, he only mumbles that he's fine, just let him sleep, and I do.

Even when he's awake enough to stay conscious, he doesn't want to go until I tell him what happened. I do that, under the horseman's watchful eye, Ben glancing that way every now and then, as if checking that he's really seeing what he's seeing.

Telling him about Josie is the hardest part. He asks me to go through it twice, and he asks if there's any way I could be wrong and she's not . . .

Yes, she is, and we're both silent after that, lost in quiet grief and rage at the senselessness of it.

When I'm done explaining, Ben comes up with a story for the police. I haven't thought of that. Couldn't think of it even after he mentioned it, and I can only shudder to imagine what I could have said if I'd actually called them before he woke.

Our story is as close to the truth as possible. Ben and Smits were in the forest. Smits injected Ben with something, and Ben lost consciousness without any hint of Smits's motive. Then Smits took me looking for Ben and sent Josie away.

Suspicious, Josie hung around, and when she was sure she had reason for her misgivings, she confronted him. Smits threatened me, and she pulled out her gun. They fought. She died. Smits ran off into the forest, and I found Ben, and we hid along the shoreline all night, too terrified of Smits to call for help.

When dawn does come, it's time for me to make that call, but Ben stops me.

"You can't leave the property," he says.

"Why? Because I need money for the mother who caused all this? Who woke the nekkers, bound me to them, and ordered Smits to murder my father? Branded my father a child killer?" I snort, bitterness raw. "I don't need the money now, do I?"

"Just don't leave—"

My voice sharpens. "I am not staying here. Not risking anyone else dying for what my mother did."

"I don't mean that, Sam. The police will insist you go to the station for a statement. Let them be the ones who make you leave." He meets my eyes. "Trust me. I'm a lawyer."

That makes me laugh, and I shake my head, but I agree and place the call.

Ben was right. The state police don't arrest me, but they do need me to go with them, both to make a statement and to have my hands and clothing tested for gunpowder residue. They take Ben to the hospital and perform the same tests. Both of us are clean.

They find the gun near Josie's body, where Smits left it. Only her prints and his are on it, and footprints in the dirt confirm my story of a struggle that turned tragic. After realizing he'd killed his daughter, Smits ran. Now he's the subject of a manhunt.

As for why he drugged Ben, no one knows, but they find the injection mark, the tox screen shows he was sedated, and a crime-scene team locates the abandoned syringe where Ben said Smits attacked him.

As soon as I can, I contact Ms. Jimenez and explain using the version we gave the police. I tell her I was taken in for questioning, and I'm not allowed back on the property—it's the scene of a crime and a manhunt.

She tells me I must obey the police, and that no one can hold that against me. Moreover, with Smits last seen on the property, she is personally advising me to stay off it. My life is in danger, which fulfills the exception.

Do I imagine relief in her voice as she says that? I remind myself that the lawyer was never my enemy here. She was doing her job, as uncomfortable as it was.

I'm struggling with the fact that my grandfather was right about my dad. He knew about the affair between my mom and Smits, but if he thought Smits killed Dad, he'd have said so. No, in the end, I need to accept that Douglas Payne had no secret knowledge. That I didn't fail my father by *not* believing in him.

What was it Ben said? *He's allowed to be right. Doesn't make him less of an asshole.*

My grandfather didn't send me to Paynes Hollow to "remember." Not really. He sent me there to torment me under the guise of helping me remember, and in the end, I had nothing *to* remember. But my grandfather still got his wish, in a way that I can only hope would horrify him. I will forever be haunted by what happened this summer at Paynes Hollow. By the terrible death of Gail, my aunt, his daughter.

Ben and I have spent the last two nights in a motel between Paynes Hollow and Syracuse. I have no place to return to and, as he says, he's "sure as hell" not going back to his apartment over his parents' garage.

Wherever we go, there will be questions, so we are holed up, recovering. We started with separate rooms, but after I woke up screaming—

dreams of Josie being dragged into the lake by her father—we opted for one room and two beds. After what we've been through, I don't want to be alone, and I don't think Ben does either.

On the third day, I return from grabbing lunch to find him dressed in jeans and a button-down shirt, showered, his beard and hair trimmed. My gut clenches, seeing it as a sign he's leaving.

"Eat up and clean up," he says. "We're going to see Ms. Jimenez. Sign some papers to get you that inheritance."

I stand there, holding the takeout bags. "But they still need me to go back and finish the month. Which I won't do."

"You don't need to," he says. "I've combed through all the paperwork, talked to Ms. Jimenez, and showed her the interpretation she needed to let you skip it. Permanently."

I blink at him. "You showed *her*?"

He exhales, as if I'm making this very difficult, as he lowers himself onto the end of his bed. "I said I took a few law courses. That may have been . . . an understatement. I went to law school. Undergrad and then law, passed the bar a few years ago. Partly online but—" He shrugs. "My caretaking job takes a few hours a week and no one gives a shit if I vanish for a half day here and there."

"So you're . . . actually a lawyer? You weren't kidding about that?"

He blows out a long breath. "No, I wasn't kidding. I just . . . I don't practice. I mostly got it to prove I could. Just me being a contrary son of a bitch. Only thing I used it for was helping locals who got in trouble with Smits and couldn't afford counsel."

"So Smits knew you were a lawyer? Who only used his degree to thwart him?" My lips twitch. "No wonder he hated you."

"One of many reasons, but since I wasn't open about having done more than 'take a few courses,' Smits sure as hell wasn't telling anyone the truth. Would have made it hard to call me a lazy good-for-nothing if others knew I was a lawyer. But *he* knew. Which was enough for me."

"So what are you going to do now? Practice for real?"

"Dunno. You gonna go to med school?"

"Dunno."

"Then we make a fine pair. Now, like I said, eat up and clean up.

You're about to inherit a helluva lot of money, and I'm looking for my share. A hundred grand, remember?"

I smile. "I think you deserve more than that."

He shakes a finger at me. "Don't go reneging on my deal. Your grandfather pays for my dad's pension, and I get a hundred grand from you. Now pass me my burger."

Thirty-Six

Ben wasn't exaggerating his legal expertise. The property is mine, and my grandfather included a poison pill that keeps my uncle and cousin from challenging it—if they do, their own inheritance is tied up until the case is over, and it's forfeit if they lose.

So I have the property, which I will never set foot on again. I am also the sole beneficiary of my aunt's will and life insurance, and I'll receive it whenever she's declared legally dead. I won't think about that. I can't.

As for the property, I'm not selling it for ten million. I don't know what I want to see done with the land our cottages sit on, but even if I'm convinced no one is in danger by being there, I don't want it developed into million-dollar vacation properties.

I have sold part to a developer, though. I've severed and sold fifty inland acres near to Paynes Hollow. I'll clear nearly two million after taxes. The town approved of the decision and granted me speedy severance approval, and they're looking forward to the new subdivision, mixing affordable housing with modest vacation homes. That gave me the money to pay Ben, quietly slip another hundred grand to Liz Smits, settle my debts, and do pretty much anything I want, med school included.

Now I just need to get through this one thing.

Inside the doors to the care facility, Nurse Vickie meets me, and she's beaming. "Your mother is having an excellent day. The best she's had in months."

Which is what I've been waiting for, but I only smile and say, "Good. So she's lucid?"

"Very lucid. It happens sometimes. A ray of sunshine in the dark." She casts a worried glance my way. "It doesn't mean she's recovering..."

"I know."

"But it's lovely to see, and I'm so glad you're here for it."

"So am I." I look at her. "Is it okay if Mom and I speak in private? Maybe on the side deck? It's a lovely day, and if she's in a good place mentally, I want her all to myself."

"Of course. I know she's hoping to go out, but you can start in there."

"Thank you."

I head to the side deck. It's smaller than the main one, without the gorgeous view of the river. I lean on the railing, looking out and thinking.

"There you are." Mom's voice comes as the sliding door whooshes open and then shuts again. "I've been waiting for you all morning, Sam."

A month ago, I'd have flinched with guilt. Mom woke up lucid and asked for me, and I didn't get here until... I check my watch. 9:20. Yep, I didn't exactly leave her dangling all morning.

She walks over and air-hugs me, just the lightest touch. I always told myself there was nothing wrong with that. Lots of people aren't huggers. Yet I'd always felt rejection in it, especially as a child, when my dad would scoop me up and hold me close and pull my mother into the embrace, and she'd give that moue of distaste.

Mom continues, "I know you wanted to talk, Sam, but I really do need to go out. My good spell won't last, and I want to take full advantage. Get my hair done. Buy some new clothing. We can talk in the car, yes?"

Again, a month ago, guilt would have washed over me. Of course Mom would want to use her limited lucid time to full advantage. Sure, the home had an excellent hairstylist who visited monthly and my mom's closet held three times as much clothing as my own, but what sort of monstrous daughter would deny her ailing mother these small pleasures? Maybe the same daughter who always hoped her mother would want to spend her lucid time with *her*, and not simply treat her as a credit-card-bearing chauffeur.

"Sit down, Mom."

She sighs. "Sam, darling, I can sit anytime. I want—"

"We need to talk about the nekkers."

She goes still, and when her gaze slowly moves my way, there's something like panic in it before she erases it with a wave. "This is something to do with your job, I presume? Some medical terminology."

"The nekkers in the lake. At the Paynes Hollow property. The drowned dead and the headless horseman."

Her laugh comes high and tight. "Ah, the horseman. You have been traipsing down memory lane. Those old stories with your grandfather. I never heard the ones about . . . what did you call them? The drowned dead."

"Cut the shit, Mom."

Her head whips my way, eyes narrowing. "I beg your pardon?"

"I spent the last week at the lake. Had a nice chat with your old boyfriend, Craig Smits."

She stiffens. "If you mean that sheriff, the man is a boor. I felt sorry for his wife and befriended her—"

"He's dead now. Killed by the nekkers. Gail is dead, too. Killed by the horseman, because no one bothered to warn her what might happen if she struck me, even unintentionally."

My mother goes still, and I want to say the look creeping into her eyes is horror for Gail's death, but I know better. It's horror on realizing I might actually know what I'm talking about.

"I've found the journal," I say. "I've seen the drowned dead. I've seen the horseman. Spent a night with him standing guard. Bram. That was his name in life. But you know that, from the journal Smits gave you. You bonded me to the horseman, resurrecting the old legends, using the magic to fend off your disease. It worked, too, until

Austin died and you told Smits to shoot Dad and blame him for Austin, and then my grandfather booted you off the property. You snuck back for one more sacrifice with Smits, only it wasn't enough. Without me staying there the whole summer, the magic faded, and soon you were in no shape to renew it . . . and the disease took hold."

I meet her gaze. "You killed innocent people, including my father. And for what? You still ended up here, losing your mind."

"I don't know what—"

"You *killed* my father," I say, struggling to whisper-hiss the words when I want to shout them, struggling against the tears I've been shedding for days now. "You had Smits murder him and even that wasn't enough. You wrote his suicide note, having Dad take the blame for killing Austin so there'd be no doubt. You murdered him and then shredded and burned his memory. You stole my father from me in every way possible, and then you didn't even bother to replace him. Always only half there, always with better things to do than take care of your grieving daughter."

Her head tilts, mouth moueing in a calm way that sends shivers through me. "Are you well, Sam? You've been under a great deal of pressure. I know it was such a disappointment, not getting into medical school."

I blink at her. "Not—not getting in? I got in. You needed the money for your care."

"Now, Sam, you know that was just what we said when you didn't get in. That you graciously let me use your tuition money, which was mine after all."

I sputter. "Yours? Dad's the one who started the fund, and the only one who contributed to it. As for not getting in, I still have the offers of admission."

She sighs. "Sam, there's no shame—"

"Here," I snarl, fingers trembling as I hit my phone screen. "I have them right here. Two offers, which I have kept on my phone and every now and then, when things get really bad, when I'm working at midnight to make extra money or eating fucking ramen again, I open them up to remind myself that I could have done it, that maybe someday I will do it. And then I'd open a photo of you to remind me why I'm *not* doing it now."

"Sam, you're getting all worked up—"

I shove the phone at her. "This is the photo of you I pull up. This one, where you're smiling and looking at me like you love me. It's the only one I have like that. It was taken the day I said I wouldn't go to fucking med school so you could have the fucking money."

"Watch your language, young—"

"You aren't even listening to me. Not hearing me. You never did. This photo"—I wag the phone—"is a lie that I clung to. The lie of a mother who never was. You ordered your lover to murder my father. You framed him for a child's death. You told me Dad was a monster, and you wouldn't let me talk about him. When I begged for us to move away, you said no, some bullshit about your dad and his dementia, despite the fact you barely visited him. You had friends, a good job, a support network, why would you leave Syracuse? You forced me to stay in the same goddamned *school*, where everyone knew my father was a murderer, where I was the child of a killer."

"You loved that school. That's what I remember, and if—"

"You made me stay with my grandfather that week, and it was hell, and I *hated* you for it. Then I got older and I felt so guilty for the hate. You were only trying to help, right? Trying to repair the relationship? No, you threw me to him in hopes I'd soften his heart and he'd give you the money you needed."

"Oh, that's nonsense. You're rewriting history, Sam—"

"Do you like it here, Mom?" I wave at the home. "Best place money could buy, even if it meant I lived in the tiniest, shittiest apartment I could find, working endless hours, letting my cat die because I couldn't afford her care."

"Are you really comparing *my* care to your cat's?"

"But it's fine now. I came into a shitload of money from my grandfather. Enough to buy a swanky condo, go to med school, get *all* the cats."

Her lips tighten. "Good for you."

"It is. I deserve it. I mean, Gail deserved it. So did Dad. But I'm finally accepting that I do, too. Still, this place . . ." I look at the building and wrinkle my nose. "Do *you* deserve it, Mom? That's the real question."

Her eyes narrow. "Samantha Jane—"

"Do you know what I think you deserve? A jail cell. But since you won't get that, I'm giving you the next best thing. I'm giving you . . ." I lean toward her and smile. "Nothing."

She blinks.

I back up. "You're paid up here for the next three months. After that? Whoops, seems my phone number no longer works. I'm no longer living where I was. No longer working where I was. No one can find me to pay for your stay. No one can find me to pay for that trial medication. Such a damned shame."

"You're angry. I understand that."

I sputter a laugh. "Angry? No, Mom. I'm fucking furious. I'm a broken fucking mess, thanks to you, and the only satisfaction I'm going to get is imagining you wasting away in whatever shitty care facility your insurance will cover."

"You can't do this," she says, her voice low with warning. "I'm your mother. Someone will make you—"

"Pay for your care? Uh, no. You aren't a child. I don't owe you shit. But if you want to try, you can sue me for it. Tell the nurses I'm leaving. Send someone to force me to pay. It won't work—I've consulted with two lawyers—but if you want to try, go for it. Just know that if you do, I'll be forced to retaliate."

"With what?"

I smile at her. "Oh, I have a few cards, and they're all aces. Just remember this—whatever place they put you, it'll be better than what will happen if I play those cards and show the world what kind of person you really are."

I'm bluffing, but the rising fury in her eyes tells me I've pulled it off. I head for the door.

"Samantha Jane, don't you dare—"

"Bye, Mom. Remember that I loved you. That Dad loved you. And for his sake, I hope you get everything you deserve."

That evening, as the sun sets, I make one last stop. I've left my aunt's car at her condo, with the keys in it, and Ben and I drove here in his pickup. It's a piece of junk, but we'll replace it soon enough. We'll need something better for the next part of our plan. For now, we've done everything we needed to do, settled our affairs, and stuffed our bank accounts full of cash.

Ben parks the pickup and gets out, but he stays behind as I walk, my arms full of flowers, to kneel at the headstone beside my grandfather's.

At my father's grave.

I lay the flowers down and touch my fingers to the marble. I've never visited before. If there was a service, we weren't invited. My grandfather handled all that.

"Hey, Dad," I say, as my eyes fill. "Sorry it took me so long."

My voice catches, and I let the tears fall.

After a moment, I continue, "I want to apologize for all the rest, too. For not believing you. For telling Mom what I saw. For listening to the lies. But if you were here, you'd say none of that was my fault. I'm going to try—really try—to lay the blame where it belongs. On Mom and on Craig Smits. I can still wish . . ."

My throat clogs, more tears falling. "I'll try not to do that either. Wishing won't fix anything, and you'd want me to move on. That's what I'm going to try to do."

I shift, getting comfortable. "I'm going on a road trip. Remember how you and I always talked about that? When I graduated from high school, we'd drive around the country all summer. Just the two of us. Well, that's what I'm doing, and I'm sorry it's not with you, but I won't be alone. Remember Ben Vandergriff? He'll be with me."

I laugh softly, as if hearing my dad's reply. "No, not like that. We're just friends. I don't know if it'll ever be more, but for now, what we both need is a friend. We're . . ." I swallow. "We're broken, Dad. Both of us. We've spent years pretending we aren't, and we need to stop pretending and deal with it. Deal with what happened fourteen years ago. Deal with what happened this summer. We're going to do that together, because no one should do it alone."

I swallow and force a smile. "We're going to adopt a dog, too. Remember how you always wanted to do that, but Mom hated pets? Ben and I are hitting the shelter later. Adding another stray to our little pack."

I press my fingers to the gravestone, tears running down my face. "I'm sorry you faced those last moments alone. I'm sorry you faced your own fears and worries alone. You tried to protect us, and you died for it, and I am so, *so* sorry. I love you. Love you so damn much."

I lean forward until my forehead touches the cool marble, and I just sit like that for a few minutes, thinking and regretting and promising. Then I say my goodbyes, rise, and walk to the pickup. Ben silently opens the passenger door for me, and I climb in, and as we drive away, I watch my father's grave until it disappears behind us.

About the Author

Kathryn Hollinrake

Kelley Armstrong believes experience is the best teacher, though she's been told this shouldn't apply to writing her murder scenes. To craft her books, she has studied aikido, archery, and fencing. She sucks at all of them. She has also crawled through very shallow cave systems and climbed half a mountain before chickening out. She is, however, an expert coffee drinker and a true connoisseur of chocolate-chip cookies.